During the entire time we were married, he never reached for my breasts. Instead, he perfected a "no hands" style of riding me. He could stay on board for

**Finally I've found you—
But let me tell you what
I've been through . . .**

Clasping her dream lover to her breast, Alice Berry whispers the sweet nothings that are the story of her search for The One—of The Tooter, a trumpet player "more careful than Dracula to leave before sunup," of the aging artist who makes love with "partial passion," and of her great love, the brilliant novelist gripped by the nausea of creativity. SWEET NOTHINGS: the most hilarious blue-streak spritz ever delivered by one woman . . . in one night.

"A fun read-in-one-sitting romp. Laura Cunningham is a talent mining the same gold as Lisa Alther. I'm not worried about her heroine—this funny, gritty lay-dee is a survivor."
Barbara Goldsmith, author of THE STRAW MAN

"As wittily devastating as Dorothy Parker and a tighter writer than Anita Loos, Laura Cunningham makes sexual passion the funniest thing to hit the mattress."
Memphis Press-Scimitar

"A skillful parody . . . trenchantly amusing."
Cosmopolitan

Sweet Nothings

LAURA CUNNINGHAM

 AVON
PUBLISHERS OF BARD, CAMELOT AND DISCUS BOOKS

For Barry

Photograph of the author by Ken Mori.

A portion of this book originally appeared in slightly
different form, in the *Atlantic Monthly,* under
the title "Grounds."

AVON BOOKS
A division of
The Hearst Corporation
959 Eighth Avenue
New York, New York 10019

Copyright © 1977 by Laura Cunningham
Published by arrangement with Doubleday and Company,
Inc.
Library of Congress Catalog Card Number: 76-48602
ISBN: 0-380-38562-7

First Avon Printing, August, 1978

AVON TRADEMARK REG. U.S. PAT. OFF. AND IN
OTHER COUNTRIES, MARCA REGISTRADA, HECHO
EN U.S.A.

Printed in the U.S.A.

Acknowledgments

I wish to thank—

My Uncles, Ben and Abe, for all the years of love and encouragement

Suzanne Watson, for her friendship

Owen Laster, for being so considerate, and working so hard

Betty Prashker and Hugh O'Neill, for all their work and enthusiasm

$\mathcal{N}$ow, how are we going to do this? My head on your chest, or the other way?

Ah, you're right about this. Your head on my breast. Oh, no head has ever felt like your head. I can feel your breath on my skin.

That's a sign, isn't it? When something ordinary, like breathing, becomes so special. I know what it means: *This is it.*

The second you touched me—that beautiful moment over by the refrigerator—I knew: *You're the One.*

All the others were mistakes.

That's why I always held back until now. I stayed a spectator, because I knew that one night I would have to report it all to you.

And now you're here.

I'll bet you've saved up a secret or two, yourself. Come on, you can tell me.

Me first? Well, that's a switch. Any other man would . . . well, of course, you're different.

Okay, I'll start. You won't get jealous, will you? You shouldn't. Because if all my nights with men add up to anything, it's that the shocks and disappointments make me more able to appreciate you.

In a funny way, it seemed you were always with me— sitting up there in a sort of mezzanine. Whenever I was with a man, I felt another presence hovering above us. . . .

This feeling was especially strong during my marriage.

Yes, I was married. Once. For six years. But, Darling, it wasn't a serious marriage. I knew, the whole time, I had to get a divorce. I said so, every day: "Let's just end this. Let's get a divorce."

And Robert would come back at me with, "Cut this crap about divorce. We're happy."

7

～

Let me speak without rancor of him, whose name I still bear. "Berry" is his. I hung onto Berry, not because I prefer it to Smilgiewicz, or think it's prettier, but because I've become identified as Berry in my work. Believe me, I'd love to be Alice Smilgiewicz again. Maybe I could still go back? No, there are too many little statues around signed "Berry." A switch back to Smilgiewicz can only cause confusion. And I'm afraid to lose even a small following.

That Robert has filed an action to force me to relinquish his name is a sad issue that I shall not take up here. Suffice to say, it reveals that he is still tugging at his end of the rope. There are bonds that even the serrated blade of divorce cannot sever. This must be one.

My lawyer, by the way, says Robert doesn't stand a chance. I can be a Berry for as long as I want. There's no way he can prove that my sexual "shenanigans" are damaging his business, a sports complex in Cheesequake, New Jersey (Christ, I'm almost fifty miles away). But no, Robert has hired a team of lawyers.

We met two weeks ago to talk over his so-called "defamation." I hadn't seen Robert in over a year, and I was surprised—he's gotten shorter. Oh, he's handsome as ever—protected by his blondness, but definitely an inch or two shorter. Time has punctuated his face: His mouth, all of a sudden, is in parentheses. The mean little lines at the corners of his eyes are, I suppose, the result of my sleeping with other men.

Which I was *never* supposed to do. Our bedtime litany: "You'll never ever sleep with anyone else."

"Never. Ever."

"And you never slept with anyone before me?"

"Never. Ever."

Robert was obsessed with the fear (unrealistic) that another man would invade our Dutch Colonial renovated barn and steal me away. "I'll kill him. I'll kill him," Robert would promise. "I'll kill him."

8

And I, on the other side of the bed, would mentally cry: "Where is he? Where are *you?*" Even, "Hurry up!"

Robert planned to kill the other man, and I prayed for him to come. The only direct bearing this had on our lives was that Robert forced me to wear small sweaters over my more revealing dresses. This custom harkened back to my prenuptial nights, when my father forced me to wear small sweaters and threatened to kill Robert.

Someday, I'd think, listening to Robert mouth-breathe in his sleep (he dreamed of driving a firetruck), I'd like to sleep with someone without talk of killing or little sweaters. And I'd better hurry, because as you can see, there's nothing exceptional under the little sweater. And it can't get better.

So now it's all come to pass. I sleep with other men, and he has lines around his eyes. But at least when we met at my lawyer's office, Belkin, Mensch, and Feingold, Robert did not bite his lower lip. That was how he held me for six years—by biting his lip.

And by saying, "Come on, let's forget all this nonsense and go to bed." Other version: "Have some coffee."

That still doesn't sound bad. I'm afraid if he did say "Come on, let's . . ." I'd say:

"Okay," because that's what I said six thousand times. As often as I said, "That's it! I've had it." If only I *had* had it. But I kept on having it.

∽

All through the marriage, whenever I'd hear Robert braying his political beliefs to a bunch of his buddies, I'd marvel: *No one forced me to marry him.*

I had gone willingly—even gladly, down the aisle.

Now, I have to ask myself why?

I think it had something to do with the custom, in those days, of "saving yourself."

The idea was to deliver your body, as untouched as possible, to the man you would marry. I was very intent on saving myself so that when, one night, everything was stolen out from under me, I may have overreacted. I went into a deep shock that didn't lift until I was married.

∽

I'd been such a great little saver. I'd saved my breasts for years. All through high school, no one got my breasts.

Then—one afternoon—I was helping a boy named Steve with equations, and he slid across the couch and ducked his head under my sweater.

He bit them, Darling. I cried out (not out loud— why bother—it was too late) to the ceiling, and apologized to the one for whom I'd been saving my breasts: "I'm sorry—I couldn't help this—You see what happened!"

My mouth had gone a few years earlier. You don't care about the mouth, do you? That went early: I could only have been thirteen. Jimmy Halpern, my best friend's brother, just jammed his tongue in there. He'd asked me if I wanted to "soul kiss." I was saying "no" and that created the opening.

Say "no" and see what happens.

There. But you and I have the good tongues. Jimmy Halpern didn't have a good tongue. He had the cold mackerel type. He just *rested* the tongue in my mouth for a while, but after that, my mouth was occupied territory. I couldn't hold the line there again. Any one who kissed me could also slip a tongue in. . . . The other boundaries went the same way. My breasts, lower sections of my body, and then, finally, the big boundary.

∽

Robert took that. But I don't blame him. It was an accident. He was only testing my virginity—"just to feel the resistance." I had agreed, as a measure to prevent further inroads. We were well into this "testing" when the car radio came on without warning and Robert, startled, plunged into me.

Once there was this "slippage," I saw the uselessness of continuing to save myself. *So this is sex,* I thought, feeling the stab far into my interior, *this total lack of pleasure.*

But I'd been raised to make the best of a bad situation. While my heart screamed to my unknown true love: "This should have been yours!" I threw my body into a series of hula rolls so that at least Robert could be thrilled beyond his wildest dreams.

We went on this way for one year, and then got married. Often, during the "courtship," I looked over Robert's bare shoulder at a motel wall and vaguely saw someone (you?) standing off to one side, shaking his head, warning me: *Mistake. Mistake.*

I knew I was making a mistake. Even as I eased the gold wedding band over Robert's knuckle, I thought: *This isn't the real marriage.* And one year later, when I ran into the living room to find him lolling on the bearings of his widening rear, his eyes fixed on a Giants game and his hand outstretched for a Coke, I knew for sure:

That's not my real husband.

My real husband, you see, was out there somewhere. His collar turned to the wind. His eyes narrowed in a search—for himself, for Truth, and for Alice Smilgiewicz, his perfect mate.

∽

When I was twelve, my friends and I would sit on beds crowded with stuffed animals and play a game: "What is your future husband doing now?"

"This second," I'd suggest, "squeeze your eyes shut. Picture him. What's he doing?"

We pictured our future husbands involved in introspective tasks at windy outposts. What *were* they doing? If later accounts can be trusted, our future husbands were pulling each other's penises and competing with one another at their various bodily functions. Well, we were close at the "windy outposts" part.

The problem with "picture your future husband" is that I continued to do that, even after I was married. I never stopped looking. I looked in the woods behind our house. I looked on the Interstate. I looked in movie theaters, I looked on city streets and on suburban *cul de sacs*.

I even looked in my living room. While Robert watched the interminable Game, I looked around, half expecting another fellow, a more scholarly type, to turn up in the corner of the couch. My fellow would be reading, nursing a Cognac, perhaps, and occasionally exchanging a meaningful look with me.

༄

Ah, well. Picture my actual husband (although never my soulmate) as I first saw him, on the playing fields of the State University of New York at Stony Brook.

He was nineteen and trying out for the pole vaulting team. He was young. Only a sporadic shaver. You think I can't cry remembering this? He shaved just around the jawbone and above the lip.

Later I would know the fuzzed feel of his kisses. I'd watch, naked and giggling, while he did his partial shaving before the bathroom mirror at a five-dollar motel. Yuzzo's. Oh, Yuzzo's . . . I haven't thought of Yuzzo's for years. The chenille bedspread. The TV you had to feed a quarter.

Well, that was later—although, not much. First there was that squint-bright afternoon when I watched my Intended fly over his rebounding rod to vault high into the blue sky.

If I shut my eyes, I can still see his hips, narrower then, swivel, and his hair whip over his eyes. I can see him perfectly in focus, because I snapped a mental Polaroid, something I do at key moments in my life. I check the shot a few minutes later to see if it's taken. If not, I shut my eyes and snap another.

When Robert thrust that pole, and it stuck, quivering in moist sod, I knew that was a key moment. Deep within me, I felt the shiver of recognition that has always been mine: *That's him.*

Oh, why did I have to cross that field? Why stop and watch him? Why stay with him? Why stick with a decision made in the wisdom of my teens . . . a decision made while holding a loose-leaf binder . . . a decision made in sneakers?

That shiver on the SUNY field was a mistake. But like all my shivers, it did foretell that something was afoot. And I've learned from that mistaken shiver: I've never looked for love among pole vaulters again.

The warnings are always there, in those first seconds. If I hadn't been pawing the earth in desire, I'd have paid closer heed when my Intended sprang to his feet, spit on the sand, cried "shit!," and kicked his still-trembling pole.

He hadn't cleared, you see. Some technicality over an ankle. "Goddamn, I'm going to get this damn thing," he was saying, as I tiptoed closer. Then his eyes met mine, held, and he said:

"Grab the other end of this bar."

∽

So you see—one minisecond—the whole story could be told. A punishing energy. A wild rush. Impatience. Kicking. A command.

Six years later, I stood in our Delft blue-tiled kitchen dialing Legal Aid.

∽

The good parts? He raced home every night to encircle my waist as I bent over the Crusetware. "How's my cutie-pie?"

He had a special position to hold me while we watched "The Late Show": I rested between his raised knees.

When I felt sad, he said, "Yer all right." Not a complex form of therapy, but maybe "Yer all right" was the insight I needed. If "Yer all right" didn't snap me around, Robert would cook up my childhood favorites: "Have a hamburgie and some chockie pudding." He had other effective means at the dinner table: "Pass the ketchoopi."

He also, and this counted strongly in his favor, found me irresistible in what he called "the sack." "Whatta body!" he said, every time I undressed. Every time. Then: "Let me see you do your little dance."

And—oh, I wince to remember this—I would undulate around our bed, clicking imaginary cymbals. For years, his ardor kept the bedsprings squealing, the pictures rattling on the wall. Often he didn't wait for dark, but seized me in dusty beams of sunlight. I couldn't bend over to pick up a piece of lint without feeling his sudden entrance from behind. I spent many an afternoon crouched on the living room floor, where I learned by heart the intricate maroon-and-green pattern of our Omar Khan.

It was risky to stir-fry. Or dust with any gusto. He said it set things in motion.

At night, I fell asleep after the second round, to be prodded awake for a third. I'd have to surface in stages, from subterranean depths. He may not have been awake either—I could feel him knocking where there was no door. My hand would reach back and steer that warm, blind being into its burrow.

～

What could separate us? What sort of tensions could build that would eventually make my lawyer, Abe Belkin, afraid to leave us alone in his office, for just the three minutes it would take Abe Belkin to run across the hall to the men's room? "Can I leave you alone?" His eyes would travel from Robert's blue gaze to my brown one. What did Abe Belkin think we would do—start clawing each other or wildly copulate?

If you like stories of sex and violence, stick with us.

Our marital differences eventually became a matter for the Shawnagunk Lake Police Department. But I'm getting ahead of myself.

◦ᢖ

Were the rocks in the bed? I didn't feel them. Sure, the ride was bumpy, but with the jaunty-bumpiness of a Jeep on rustic terrain. I jounced along, enjoying the ride, for one or two years. Then I began to lag. One time . . . fine. Twice? That's nice. But three or four times a night?

◦ᢖ

Although, reminiscing, the sting seems to have gone out of this.

Maybe it's that I'm coming out of a sexual Sahara (the past few months, Darling, have been awful), but I can't quite recapture what was so wearing. Let me try and think. Oh, yes. It's coming back.

◦ᢖ

I remember one night: He woke me at some dark and dire hour. The longest hour—the one that lasts three hours. No cars could be heard outside. The bedroom window glared a Stygian black. There was no silver edge to remember twilight or to promise dawn. Our beagle, Buffo, snored at the foot of the bed. Drafts attacked, infiltrating the window frame. The radiator gave off weak hisses.

Sparks flew as Robert pulled the crackling covers off me. Naked, blue, pebble-skinned, I cried, trying to maintain the suggestion of desire in my voice: "Can't we keep the covers over us?"

"I'll warm you up." He mounted side-saddle and rode me hard. Buffo awoke, his eyes showing sad disbelief, his ears flapping in time.

As the subzero sex continued, I became determined

to know what hour it was, just so that I'd make a point of never being awake for it again. Disguising my motions as a coquettish crawl, I undulated on my belly to our bedside table, where I read the radial numbers on our digital alarm: 4:45 A.M.

Old Oak Tree . . ." My foot tapped the accelerator. I made, bigger, tighter turns than I'd ever made in my life. I was on my way, on my way.

Mornings were no picnic, either. Is there any light starker than a 7:00 A.M. sun streaming over one's naked face? Say what you will about red lights in dark bordellos, the true pornographic mood comes before breakfast. Bodies are paler than, more blotched. Hairs sprout where there were none the night before.

No question: The mornings were rough.

∾

Especially if you feel you must put in an ecstatic performance. And don't ask for whose benefit. No one was watching. Except Buffo. Yet I felt I should end with a flourish. Call me a ham.

As the Maria Callas of the marriage bed, I would sometimes be caught up in midwriting to notice that something internal was actually happening. Although, I hasten to add, that while there may be no such thing as an unsatisfying climax, I had them.

Weak twitches. A poor connection. Nothing I could mistake for the soul shudders that would reverberate when I was joined to my true love (you) whom I was still looking for. . . .

I assure you, I looked up at the ceiling and apologized: "These are just reflexes . . . something to hold me over."

I hardly ever had them anyway—those nonsched shaky flights. And then, only in one position, one in which I sat at Robert's level and we eyed each other, rocking to and fro.

∾

What Robert didn't know: Under the mattress upon which we rocked rested the slim blue bankbook given by Marine Midland Savings and Loan to their depositors. The bankbook recorded, in purple, the sum total of my disillusionment with Robert. The most frequent deposit, $25.25, represented the proceeds, plus tax, from the sale of a statuette of a Naiad.

The thought that sustained me through the last four years was: *When I have a thousand dollars, I'm leaving.*

The first entry marked the date Robert showed his true nature outside Wee Willie Winkie's gift shop, where I had been marketing my Naiads. He appeared, as if from nowhere, and yelled, "I've been honking at you for an hour! Get your head out of the clouds."

We drove home at ninety miles an hour. Robert's zippier turns left me bunched against my window. Red-faced at the wheel, he went on shouting: "Shape up! Wise up!" and several "Get with it!"'s.

(He was right, he was right.)

Was this the way I wanted to travel through life? In answer, I tucked my Wee Willie Winkie mint-green check into a hidden compartment of my purse. From that day forth, I was a secret saver.

I'm not proud of myself. I would admire the woman who could walk off with only a few dollars in her pocket. But I am not her. I do not come from money, and so will always want more of it.

Let's not forget that I continued to kick in on Saturday budget nights. I gave Robert everything I earned by day. What I worked on at night, I figured was extra. And everytime Robert threw a fit, I threw a Naiad. Toward the end, I stayed up all night, turning them out in a frenzy: hundreds of Naiads who, I hoped, would lead me to freedom.

Still, there were mellow periods: The bankbook reflects these as gaps between deposits. Although, at the end, the sums mounted up again, purple smears filling the pages. Marine Midland had to give me a new book. But that was later.

～

For the middle years, my sauces were the glue that held the marriage together. Each night I cooked a new treat. Enlisted in the Time-Life series of international cookbooks, I started in *Provincial France*, worked my way through *Vienna's Empire*, and was deep in *Pacific and Southeast Asian Cooking* when the marriage blew up. Specifically: I was rubber-gloved and at work on Javanese *gado-gado*, a salad in a complex peanut and coconut milk sauce, highly seasoned with chilies and ginger.

Still, I can remember Robert spearing a beef chunk from my *carbonnades à la flammande* and declaring, "I've made myself the happiest man in the world."

～

The happiest man in the world began to throw small household objects during the second year of nuptial bliss. At first he threw unbreakable items—a pillow, a sponge—and aimed them only at invulnerable targets— the wall, the floor.

Later he picked up fragile pieces, admittedly not our favorites. An ugly set of Nipponware was the first to go. At the end of four years, Robert had reduced a service for twelve to a service for two, plus a few serving pieces. In the end, there was only a gravy boat.

While I didn't love sweeping up broken china, I came to look back upon those occasions as "the good old days."

～

Yet, he was happy. He'd bound home from Sporto-rama famished, excited, eager to relate the day's adventure to "cutie-pie." "Where is she?" he'd call, thumping through "Dream House." "Where is she? Where's my girl?"

~

The end was unexpected, although there were warnings. A rainy season had trapped him at home. He wore a warmup suit and jogged through the house. Hour after hour, he jogged, staring out the window at an iron sky. And I—unmindful of the storm within—sat in the kitchen, preparing the fateful *gado-gado*.

And that's the day it happened: the event so awful that even I could see the necessity of leaving home. Quickly. With only $786.87.

~

But before that day, and the savage act that ended the marriage, there were times when I held Robert, bounced with him. Nights when, encapsulated in the dark, I could inquire as to the reasons behind his rage.

"I've always been a hothead," was his explanation. "Shoot, it doesn't mean anything."

Shoot, it did too. To me. Yet even now, when I can no longer give Robert my unlisted phone number, I do not blame him for his outbursts. Was the anger his fault, or something that was forged into him from birth?

You're not from Texas, are you? I didn't think so. I watch out for that. Well, even if you were from Texas too . . . I didn't mean to disparage the whole crowd. I'm sure there are many tender Texans. But I sensed, after my first trip there, that the state most known for the Alamo and the foot-long corndog could not also spawn the man of my dreams. My mysterious one, the Loner—wandering through the Astrodome?

Robert sprang from west of Houston: Lake Conroe, Texas—only it wasn't "Lake" Conroe then; the lake came later. "Look," Robert pointed out the VW window on that first trip. "There she is, twenty-two thousand acres of manmade lake, the biggest artificial body of water in the U.S.A."

And thar she was—an inland ocean where but a few

short years ago there'd been prickly plain. The change so sudden, trees still stretched their branches out of the water, the dead limbs thrown skyward in shock and indignation.

"I used to ride my horse, Buddy, there . . . I think over there we had the silo, the barn. . . ." Robert looked out: now, he saw only ripples and traumatized treetops. Nature displaced. Robert displaced?

After the "change," Mom and Dad Berry had moved farther west, to a barren land that the government paid Dad Berry not to farm. The first years I visited them, the Berrys were enjoying new prosperity: They were paid not to farm more land than ever before.

The drive to Texas was a long one in those days. Now there is a highway that whips you right down there. But then the trip took three days.

Robert and I took turns driving. We stopped and bought peaches from roadside stands. For three days, we drove, ate peaches, and wiped at each other's chins with Kleenex.

We had been married for one week.

Throughout the drive, we kept up a repartee on two themes. I cried out, every time I saw one: "Look, a cow." And Robert would correct me:

"Steer."

Almost as often, I'd asked about his parents: "Will they like me?"

"They'll *love* you."

When, at last, we pulled into a driveway that right-angled the highway, I asked for the last time: "You're sure they'll like me?"

In answer, Robert wiggled his finger under my skirt, and inside me. "They'll *love* you." Then, his voice changed and he withdrew his hand. "It doesn't matter anyway . . . if they like you or not. Because I don't care what they think. I hate everything they stand for. . . ."

What did they stand for? This land, famous for its dust and drear? This house—a red split-level which

20

had grown a silver trailer on its right flank? This plaster deer that looked so sincerely worried?

On the lawn, a sprinkler head turned in hysterical circles. I paused, feeling the mist on my bare arms and legs. When I looked up, a door had slammed and Robert had disappeared.

I never found him again, in the sense that I'd known him until that moment. Alone, I walked up the cement path. An aluminum door opened, and I greeted the tall, broad-shouldered woman who had given Robert life.

Cecelia Berry, called Cece (pronunced "Cease"), took one look at me and proclaimed: "You're the daughter I never had. I always wanted a girl. I love you as much as my own flesh and blood. If you were killed in an accident, or died of a disease, I'd be as heartbroken as if I'd lost one of my own."

That was quick.

Her blanched eyes, so like my new husband's, searched mine. "And that's the truth. God strike me down right here as I stand if it's not." She reached behind her and brought forth a black cast-iron hush puppy fryer. "I've been saving this for Robert's bride."

～

Later I learned the whole story. Cece had tried desperately to have a daughter. Having five sons was only proof that she had failed five times. For years she had been reduced to watching other women bathe their baby girls. When she hit menopause, Cece had gone on a ruffling rampage of the house, stapling pink ruffles to anything that might support them.

For herself, she had abandoned all frills. Although family albums document the fact that she once held an untenable blond flip and wore shirtwaists, now, she kept her hair cropped, and dressed in golf jackets, jeans, and Frye boots.

When I took a bath that night, she sat on the toilet

seat and watched, like a foreman, to see that I did the job right. I understood that it had been hard on Cece—living with six males, in scrub country, and wearing golf jackets, but, frankly, I felt uneasy with her there. Yet it was on that occasion that she shared with me her insight into her son's mood changes: "He always throws things when it rains, don't he?" She went on, with more nuance. . . .

❧

I caught up with Robert in the family room, where he had rejoined Dad and his two kid brothers, Ken and Mike. The four tow-headed males occupied different levels, as the big cats do in cages. Two sat up on chairs, the others stretched out on the chintz couches. All four heads cocked toward a rabbit-eared Zenith on which the University of Texas battled Indiana State for the football championship.

Two other brothers, George and John, were "in the service," stationed unblinkingly at Communist borders near Cambodia. They sent back scarves and clever lanterns, which hung on the walls among sad-eyed trophy heads. I avoided the hurt gaze of a moose.

The boys had been talking: a slow exchange of game scores. The "nyah" of indifference resounded in their voices, perhaps the result of saying "Indiana" all afternoon. As I entered, I heard: "nyah . . . nyee . . . nyaaah."

Ken and Mike greeted me with shy "Hey"s. Dad, although upright in a chair, turned out to be asleep. Robert himself raised an eyebrow, as if wondering: "Who's she? How'd she get in here?" He recognized me, but was not certain "from where."

He turned back to the game, remarking to Ken and Mike: "Nyah, he fumbled the ball . . . nyah . . . they're nyat going to make it." Cece appeared in the doorway and demanded the score. "What hyappened?"

"Nyathing," Ken told her.

"Nyap," Mike agreed.

Cece and I retired to her pine kitchen and slapped together ham and cheese heroes for "Dad and the boys." *This isn't me*, I thought as I handed out the loaves and offered "More mayo?"

I peeked at Robert, although for an instant I had trouble singling him out of the blond tribe. Then I did catch his eye, and appealed:

Send me a signal. That I'm here with you. That you touched me in the car. That you love me.

"Hey there," he said.

Stumbling back for corn relish, I thought: *I don't fit in here.*

~

I didn't fit in there. Not when they gathered around a Hammond organ to sing: "There's power, power, power . . . in the blood, in the blood, in the blood . . . of the lamb," or when, minutes later, they sat down to dinner.

The dining table had been set with an extra chair, unlike the others, angled onto a corner of the oval table. This chair, a metal folding one, was for me.

A draft at my back, I hunched into place for a long, gelatinous meal. The first three dishes contained mystery green Jell-Os.

Midway through a green star-shaped Jell-O, I heard a high-pitched yipping and the thunder of fat feet. Cece staggered in, listing forward with the weight of a twenty-pound glazed ham. "Ooooowweeeeyeeee . . . here it comes. . . . *Watch out!*" She crash-landed the ham on the table.

When the men sampled the pink meat, all proclaimed it "decent." Then conversation turned to major crackups on Interstate 66. "Two semis weekend before last," announced Dad.

"You missed the big one, though," Ken told Robert. "Four trailers and a microbus."

They reminisced about the time 88 iced up and nine

cars "turned to bubble gum." More anecdotes centered on local teen drivers, who, crazed by their endless horizons, raced head-on into opposing lanes.

I wanted to join in the dinner conversation, and finally thought of an appropriate story; how I'd once seen an ambulance run over a pedestrian. "They stopped the ambulance and threw the new guy in the back with the original patient, then kept on going."

After I finished, Dad nodded, "That's something." He looked over at Robert, who was forking up a pineapple ring. "You got yourself quite a gal. I bet you wouldn't take nothing for her."

My sense of belonging disappeared at bedtime. Once again, I did not fit in. Cece produced a metal folding bed and stretched it out for me at the foot of the steps. Robert had opted for his "own" bed, a bunk above Ken's.

"G'nite, Baba," Dad said to my new husband, as Robert stepped over me to reach the upstairs bedrooms.

"G'nite, Big Baba," he replied.

"G'nite, Baba Mike."

"G'nite, Baba Ken."

And "G'nite, Mama Baba."

A Berry family ritual, which exhausted all the combinations. I'd hoped to get in on it, but I never did.

❧

Robert reintroduced himself to me—and into me— on the return drive. The visit to his family evaporated, as the mist off manmade Lake Conroe.

A few hours on the road, and Robert seemed to undergo a mysterious physical change. In Texas, his face had foreshortened, crowding his eyes and turning his nose up at a porcine angle. A few miles over the border, his face lengthened. By the time we reached Florida, a reddish cast that had seeped into his cheeks began to fade.

❧

We drove across Florida, ending in what had once been Everglades swamp but was now a seniors retirement community called Seminole Village. And there, among the lush palmetto groves, we found Sophie and Max Smilgiewicz, my parents.

They waited outside their cedar-shake "condo." A handsome couple with historic "statue" faces and sturdily constructed bodies, they look, as Sophie herself would tell you, "Just like brother and sister. People can't believe we're married."

Max and Sophie do, in fact, share the same curly black-turning-to-silver hair, and identical sets of espresso-bean eyes. They walk and stand absolutely abreast—ready to face anything. Coming upon them in midpalmetto grove, I felt that I'd caught them in the middle of a decades-long trek that might take them across continents, through war and social change.

"You had trouble finding us?" they said in unison.

Max stooped to pick up our suitcases.

"Max, Max, be careful, you'll strain yourself." Sophie looked at us. "He forgets he's a guy with two hernias." With a quick gesture, she seized the cases.

"Oh, that's what you needed." Max grabbed them back. "With your heart."

I tugged the suitcases, got them, and winked at Robert as my parents urged: "Come in and relax."

Outside, the Smilgiewicz "condo" looked like the eighty-odd other "villas"—a simple cedar-shake A-frame, with fake thatching to recall the Seminole huts. Inside, the condo was an exact duplication of 5C, our Junior Four, in the Luxor Towers high-rise in Queens. That Junior Four had, in turn, been a reproduction of some cramped atelier in the Warsaw ghetto, which Max and Sophie had hated to leave, and to which they returned on vacation, in 1937.

"So we got a little homesick and picked the wrong time to go back." Fortunately, a shrewd uncle in the fur trade convinced Max and Sophie to high-tail it back to Bensonhurst. The uncle and the other Warsaw Smilgiewiczes had followed—albeit reluctantly.

Back among the Warsaw antimacassars, sitting on a claw-footed horsehair settee and staring at a portrait-on-black-velvet (a rabbi doubled over in prayer), I could imagine myself in Apt. 5C, Luxor Towers, Queens. The menorah still sat on the television. The carpet still bore the stain of spilled *kreplach* soup, a memento of the Passover of '56, when Max tripped, carrying a steaming bowl to the table. The family pet, a parakeet named Izzie, still squawked from its corner cage, the only words we'd taught him: "Vus maks-doo?"

Yet my parents can't get over the difference in their "lifestyle." "This is some place," Max extolled, settling himself in a stuffed easy chair. "I don't care, you can look all over Florida, and you won't see anything like Seminole Village."

"Gertie and Frank were here for Easter," my mother called from the kitchen. "They loved it so much, I wouldn't be surprised if they never came back. Some people can't stand to see other people in paradise." The Lipshitzes had also come. "They went out of their minds when they saw what we had." Now the Lipshitzes live in the thatched villa next door. On tropical nights they all gather on the patios and there play mah-jongg, surrounded by swamp and interconnecting snake-infested waterways.

Max and Sophie still sleep together in a double bed, with secret dividing line, at which the bed splits apart during "forbidden times." As a child I used to amuse myself by lying on their bed and pressing the headboard button so that I could watch my legs splay apart, each leg going off on a separate bed.

I've never been able to imagine what Max and Sophie do when it's not a "forbidden time." It's easier knowing that most times are forbidden, anyway. "Twelve days before, and twelve days after, and nothing in between" was the way Max, of all people, broke it down for me. Sophie, although still sensual-looking, cannot yet bring herself to discuss "the details."

She will say only, "I love your father. And when

you're in love, it's not bestiality." Especially since it makes him happy, she might add. And Sophie and Max are nothing if not concerned that each should be happy. They would each tell you, out of earshot of the other, "I don't care anything for myself. Do I need this condo? It's not for me, it's for Max." Likewise: "This isn't for me. It's for Sophie."

"Our marriage is perfect," Sophie would sum it up. "We were childhood sweethearts, never knew anyone else was even alive. Your father hasn't said a harsh word to me in forty years. Never even a mean look. It's been almost a half century of complete paradise."

"I don't deserve your mother," is Max's epilogue to this speech. "She's got everything: beauty, intelligence. . . ."

"No, Max," she'd interrupt, "I don't deserve you."

They can argue over "who deserves who" for hours, days, perhaps centuries. They have another running debate over who will "go" first.

"If you go first, I'll never forgive you, Max."

"No, I'm going first. I don't want to be there after you go."

"Well, if you go, I'm going with you."

They discuss this "going," which is the final one, as often and as casually as they discussed going to the family business establishment, "Max-So's Delicatrestaurant." Max and Sophie owned and operated "Max-So's" for forty years, until their sudden retirement.

∽

Six years ago, Sophie was at home, hanging a kitchen curtain. As she reached for the rod, she felt a pain "like a waffle iron" squash down on her chest. Recognizing a coronary, she leaned out the window and hollered, "I'm fading out!"

Neighbors rushed her to the hospital. Gus, the super, shuffled over to Max-So's deli to tell Max, in person, what had happened. Gus didn't walk two steps past the pickle barrel when Max read the news on his face:

"Don't say a word. It's Sophie!" Then, pulling on his herringbone topcoat, he added, inevitably, "Why wasn't it me?"

It *was* him. With his left arm in the coat, Max buckled over, gasping for breath. A pain that he described as "a hot cleaver" clopped him on the solar plexus. Recognizing a coronary, he hollered:

"I'm fading out!"

He was rushed to the hospital and placed in the intensive care ward with Sophie. Their beds faced one another. On electronic screens they could read each other's vital signs, something they had always wanted to do. They could also listen for a danger *beep*, which would signal that one of them was *going*.

They called back and forth to one another, in weak cricket voices. But they were both so anxious, they could never exchange any information.

"How're you doing, Sophie?"

"Never mind me. What's with you?"

"I don't care about me. How do you feel?"

"Forget about me. I don't like the way your needle is jumping. Does that mean you're upset?"

"That doesn't matter. You should see your needle. What's that, your blood pressure? You're not supposed to worry!"

"How can I not worry . . . your respiration rate's not right."

"Take it easy."

"How can I take it easy when you're not taking it easy?"

And so on, until both were fitted with heart pacemakers. The pacemakers, inserted under the skin, create small rectangular bulges, which are visible even under the acrylic knit sport clothes Max and Sophie wear for "the easy life in Seminole Village."

"Good as new," Sophie says, speaking for them both, rapping her pacemaker, now definitely showing under her décolletage. "We can do anything. Just have to be careful. We can't use microwave ovens. Heat up a hot dog, and we're through. We also have to watch out for radar, or something."

Microwaves and radar notwithstanding, Sophie and Max are having "a ball" in Seminole Village. "There are countless activities," Sophie will recite: "Sailing, snorkeling, tennis, waterskiing . . ."

To my knowledge, they participate in none of these activities. Yet it makes their day to know they're available. "We can go sailing anytime we want."

Robert took them at their word, and before Max or Sophie could cry "Be careful!" they were teetering on board an orange Fiberglas catamaran, *The Pelican*. (May I still like Robert for helping them onto a boat "for the very first time"?)

∾

A mental Polaroid has captured the way they looked that day: Sophie, her hair tucked under a flowery hat, wearing the low-cut yellow sweater, golf skirt, and spectator pumps; Max in plaid sport shirt, pleated trousers, and shined Thom McAns.

As we skidded across the turquoise water, up an inland swamp canal, even Max and Sophie suspected their incongruity in such a scene: "Bet you never thought you'd see your old folks sailing by crocodiles and ducking under banyan trees, huh?" Max cried out. Sophie's comment:

"This isn't Queens."

Back at the thatched condo, Sophie regaled us with quotes from "Laughter Is the Best Medicine" in the current *Reader's Digest*. Max and Sophie still read a lot: He loves Irwin Shaw: "solid." And she enjoys magazine stories of international romance and intrigue.

They also spend some time, it appears, creating what can only be called a shrine consecrated to their only child. One wall is papered with photographs documenting the childhood and adolescence of "Little Alice." Cardboard banners proclaim, purportedly in my voice,

"Look at me, now—all grown up!" and "Don't I look pretty?"

❦

A crayon headline announces: "I'm the greatest, smartest, most beautiful girl in the world." I have asked them to take that down, but they won't. And to tell the truth, I rather like seeing it. Do me something. Anyway, they "waited so long for a baby," as Sophie puts it, "why shouldn't we show a little enthusiasm?"

The flip side of their praise is that they must downplay the achievements of other women. Not only my girl cousins, whom God should "take pity on," but also:

"Simone de Beauvoir? She's nothing. That's a book?"

I've told them that it would be okay if they liked another woman, but they feel they must go on with the list: "Liz Taylor? She's nothing. Jackie Onassis? Where'd she be without money? Barbra Streisand, why'd she get rid of the *a?*"

The rationale behind these disparagements is, I believe, their wish to egg me on to greater accomplishments. When a woman breaks a record—the last was a swimmer who circled Manhattan—Sophie will call and say, "You could do that."

❦

Robert could not believe such parents, and Max and Sophie adored him, embraced him as their own: "We don't care what you are. To us, you're a person." (Sweetheart, they'll love you, too.)

His big appetite and interest in discussing travel plans (Robert and Max started mapping out our departure route the minute we arrived) won them over. They especially loved him for marrying me, when, as Sophie put it, "He could have violated you and left your body for the wolves."

After the apocalyptic events that precipitated our divorce, my parents' enthusiasm for Robert diminished, although their only remark on record was, "We're not saying anything."

We left after the visit's highlight: a Max-and-Sophie rendition of "Hernando's Hideaway," an act that had netted them second prize (a pressure cooker) at a Grossinger's "Talent Night." Also, they claimed, the attention of a "talent scout: You'd know his name, we can't remember it, Sophie lost the matchbook cover on which he wrote it out for us. . . ."

Too soon after enjoying the sight of Max and Sophie tip-toeing, and singing "we know a secret place," my new husband and I were on the road home—and onto a six-year trek toward divorce. My family had prepared me to be half a song-and-dance team. And Robert's? Well, we were to see what his childhood could lead to. . . .

❧

$\mathcal{B}$lood is blood," I was to tell Abe Belkin six years later. "Nobody stays in a marriage after bloodshed. I draw the line at blood. There is no question, now, of reconciliation."

"I agree with you 100 per cent."

～

In marriage, we must all play peek-a-boo with the unconscious motives of our "partners." When Robert lost all control, in our last year, I was forced to remember my first conversation with Cece, and the telling vignettes she had related as she overseered my bath.

She had started at the very beginning:

"I had a hard time borning that one. Was in labor for three days. He was in me ass-first. The doc had to tie my legs to the bed. They tried to get him turned around, but he wouldn't budge. And that's how he come out: ass first. They had to use scissors, knives, and what you call forceps."

At the actual moment of birth, Cece's bones had "spread apart." She had leaned forward, "like to die," and seen Robert make his entrance—red-faced, screaming, much as I would know him twenty years later.

"From then on, he was a bad baby. Contrary. Hated to be held. His little back would stiff up when I reached to burp him." The other boys had been angels—"come out real easy, and never gave me two minutes a' trouble."

His brothers were weaned without incident, but "Robert was still hanging onto my teat when his shoes could hit the floor. I couldn't wean that baby until he was almost in school. Then, you know how I did it?"

"How?"

Cece laughed, remembering. "Everytime he reached

for my breast, I gave him a good whack with the spatula I used to flip pancakes. He learned to use his bottle then, the little monkey."

❧

During the entire time we were married, he never reached for my breasts. Instead, he perfected a "no hands" style of riding me. He could stay on board for an hour, without ever touching me.

There came a night when Robert had galloped me to the edge of our bed. The redundant jounce gradually moved me backward, until my head and shoulders hung over the edge of the mattress. Another bounce sent my head actually to the floor and twisted my neck at an unnatural angle.

I feared, for a second, that my neck might snap. Imagine the local headline: "Horizon Homes Woman Dies in Household Accident."

As I looked, upside down, around my bedroom and came in eye contact with Robert's sweat sock and a drained beer can, I had to ask the inevitable question: "Is this all there is?"

Perhaps the extra blood, rushing to my brain, brought the answer, straight from my pounded pudenda: "There must be more."

❧

I dreamed of another style: a liquid, horizontal ballet. Slow, and with expression.

❧

Later, after several other men, I came to reassess Robert's strong points. Stamina. Energy. Crowbar hardness.

But upside down in a renovated barn in Dutchess County, I took those attributes for granted. I thought even his athleticism was standard.

"Feel this," he'd instruct, drawing in his abdomen until I could see the delineation of his classic muscles. Then, with the same concentration he applied to lifting new and heavier weights, he'd *wag* his own stout pole within me. Left. Right. Right. Left. One. Two. Hold for five seconds. Left. Right . . .

Ahem; I'm getting off the track. . . . What I was going to say was: I was searching for his eyes. But except in our one seesaw routine, I could never find them. Robert stared off to a flat horizon.

∽

He didn't caress. His hands stayed either up in the air, or planted in push-up position on the mattress. If I tried to run my hands over the musclescape of his young, fuzzed body, he'd stop me with:

"Don't tickle."

Yet his mouth found mine. And his lips would cover my complete terrain. He'd kiss what he wouldn't touch, a contradiction that, I admit, had its interesting and even juicy moments.

Still, the mood, if there was one, was sporty. Most of our activities seemed so harmlessly gymnastic that even a spectator gallery would not have been shocked. Such an exhibition might have merited applause, for after an awkward training season, Robert and I had perfected our bounces and flips.

So for an aeon of nights and daylight sessions, we rode a trampoline of sex: It was good exercise, sometimes enjoyable. (Am I allowed to say that?) But it was not what I was searching for.

Then, one night, as I lay in a rear hold, I pretended that the steady pumping was not Robert, but someone more like Yves Montand.

It's not Robert, I told myself, shifting my hip so that he could gain easier access.

Amazing. You would not believe the difference. The minute I thought "Yves," Robert swerved into narrower, more Gallic turns. His moves became more subtle, with a gentler, rolling gait.

He was so foreign, so exciting, my breath quickened. I found a swivel I thought I had lost. With the unheard plaint of Edith Piaf driving us on, I thought, *This is it. The answer.*

Then: disaster. Two hands reached down and flattened my thighs against the mattress: He spread me out like a frog dissection.

Yves, I felt, would not have done that.

My mistake, of course, had been to open my eyes. The next night, I was not so careless. As Yves cupped me to his warm belly (softer, more curved than my husband's), I rotated in small circles, as a clay bowl fashions itself on the potter's wheel.

Oh, yes, we were creating art . . . here. . . .

Until, at climax, Yves Montand bellowed:

"Hot damn!"

❧

During the next years, I occasionally introduced another lover into the marriage bed. Most of my efforts failed, for lapses in continuity. Would Nureyev bang my head against the bedposts? I didn't think so.

The only one who had credibility was Burt Lancaster. I believed, every second, he was Burt. Not a false move. But did I want Burt?

He just was not the One.

❧

"Sweetheart," I said one night, after a run with Jean-Paul Belmondo, "what would you say to a nice, amicable separation?"

"I'd say," came his strong voice in the dark, "there ain't no such animal. You're my wife, and I love you. If you're not my wife, you can drop dead."

(He had a point.)

～

There is an etiquette to violence: Rage is private, like sex. I never told anyone until the actual bloodshed, but Robert's anger had been threatening to explode for some time.

After a stage of liquid throwing, he advanced to hurling the actual container.

"Look," I told him one morning, "I can't take this anymore—the shouting, the throwing things." I pointed to the soda bottle that still rolled on the kitchen tiles.

"You threw a bottle," I said. (Count on me for obvious commentary. Why I'm not narrating "Wide World of Sports," I don't know.) "It could have shattered in my face." *And I'm concerned about that.*

"Never!" Robert bent, picked up the Tab, and began one of our highly technical discussions. "This is plastic, not glass."

"It's glass."

"Look. It's one of those clever synthetics, covered with styrofoam."

"It looks like glass."

"Tap it."

"It does sound a little flat."

"These things can withstand pressure. . . . I don't see what you're so upset about. . . ."

We moved on to an affectionate wrap-up: "Donch you look cute today . . . pigtails." Kiss. "Sorry I barked at you and threw a bottle . . . a *plastic* bottle. If only you'd cooperate . . . not provoke. I love you, you know that. You're my cutie-pie."

(If you're thinking, "Why was I still there?" I'm right behind you.)

I spoke the dark word that had been percolating through my brain: *"Divorce. Divorce. Divorce!"*

"We can't get a divorce. . . ."

"Why not?" *Because we love each other?*

"Because the Renchmans are coming to dinner."

～

I cried "Divorce!" sporadically for the last year. At last, I ended before Abe Belkin. "I draw the line at blood. Shouting, okay. Throwing stuff, not great. But *blood* . . ."

I showed him my wound. "This I can't overlook."

"I agree with you 100 percent."

❧

On an August afternoon, only hours after the big fight, I sat, trembling with relief (at last, no doubts) before Abe Belkin. And Abe Belkin, Old World Munchkin, doubled over though he was by his suspenders, promised to come to my aid. "Don't worry, Dollink. I'll take care of it."

He opened a wax sandwich bag and brought forth a tuna salad on rye. "Do you mind?"

"Go ahead," I encouraged. "I appreciate your seeing me on such short notice." I looked down at my ripped stockings, the least of my problems. "It's an emergency, as you can see."

"Adultery used to be the only grounds."

"That's not part of this. . . ."

"What then?"

And so I had to confide in him that Robert Berry had come at me with a kitchen utensil.

"A knife?"

"What difference does it make? It was a weapon!"

"Metal or plastic?"

Abe Belkin drew me into the same kind of technical discussion I'd been having with Robert.

"Metal."

"Sharp or dull?"

"In between. Serrated."

"A serrated blade!"

"Not a blade, exactly . . . it was more of a . . . it was . . . a peeler."

"A peeler?"

"The rotary kind. For peeling apples, carrots."

"How did this come about?" asked Abe Belkin. "Did something happen to provoke his anger?"

"Nothing! I was in the kitchen. Fixing dinner. I had sensed some tension, and thought, 'Perhaps a special dinner would ease things.' To tell you the truth, I'd felt trouble brewing for a few weeks. I don't know how I knew. But I knew. You remember the bad rains? All through the last two weeks of July?"

"That was some rain."

Yes. It rained and rained. No sun came out to ripen my tomatoes. The clothes I washed never dried. There was mildew, and my husband—Robert—he couldn't go out. He had to stay in the house. It was his vacation. He started to jog.

He jogged up the stairs. He jogged in the bedroom. He jogged through the living room. He jogged so hard, the wine glasses shook in the breakfront. I don't remember exactly when, but one day he picked up his tennis racket and started whacking balls against the dining room wall. Bam. Bam. Bam. A picture fell. It hit a ceramic jug. The jug broke. Even the dog got scared. He crawled under the couch and made sounds under there.

Then, today . . . just before . . . I've lost my sense of time. Was it only two hours ago? The pounding stopped. Robert walked into the kitchen. He said, nicely enough, "I can't find my *Tennis* magazine. Have you seen it?"

I told him I hadn't seen it. He accused me of lying. Or throwing the magazine out to spite him. I was sitting in the breakfast nook, peeling decorative stripes on a cucumber. I'd planned to serve a nice fresh salad. The main course was spicy, and I'd thought that the cool crispness of the cucumber would be . . . oh, well, it doesn't matter now. I told him softly that I hadn't seen the magazine.

"You have an attitude," he said. Then he grabbed my wrist. "And I don't like it!"

His motion made me open my palm. The peeler fell to the table. He picked up the peeler and pointed it at me. Perhaps my remark, "Take it easy, nutso!" was not the correct thing to say. Maybe I was being insensitive. Still, he was the one pointing a peeler. I could almost feel its pointy little teeth.

"You think I'm crazy, don't you?" he asked. "Well, I'll give you something to think I'm crazy about. . . ."

"Oh, c'mon," I couldn't resist saying, "you must be joking." For truly, I'd never seen anything like this except in B movies.

His arm wrapped around my throat, and the peeler aimed at my nose. "Am I right or wrong?" he almost sang. "Am I right or wrong?"

He kept insisting: I should say it. Say he was right.

Should I have said, "You're right, dear," and let it go at that? Maybe, if I'd said that, I could have averted tragedy. "It's not a question of right or wrong," I started to say, but a pressure around my neck made me stop, I looked up at Robert: His right eyeball had lit up in the most frightening way. His whole face pulled to the right. His lip was high, and I could see his right canines.

What was he going to do?

With his free hand, he reached for a measuring cup filled with heavy cream—the cream I'd planned for a lovely frozen soufflé. . . . But no matter; he poured the cream over my head.

"Now, look. Just look at yourself—hysterical bitch!"

In an armlock, he escorted me to my wall oven, and the shield inside that is like a mirror. We looked in and could see a reflection. I looked very much like someone with cream running down her face, in the grip of a peeler-wielding husband. "Now, say it; say it: 'Robert is right.' "

I know. I know. I should have said it—just for the sake of peace in the house. But I didn't. I turned around and spit in his face: "Coward. Big fat coward. Look at you."

Then, ducking my head, which was all wet, under his arm, I broke his hold, and tore through the dutch door to our patio. I could feel him right behind me.

I ran as I have never run in my life—across the patio, through the garden, over our newly landscaped Japanese goldfish sanctuary.

Maybe I could have made it to the car, if I hadn't tripped on a seedling. But I did trip: I landed next to one of my markers, "Summer Savory." As a cool drizzle fell, I looked up and saw framed against a gray sky— Robert, all teeth and eyes, his hand held high with the peeler.

What was he going to do? Peel me?

~

"Excuse me—I hate to interrupt," said Abe Belkin. "But you will need three examples."

"Three examples?"

"In New York State, on grounds of physical cruelty, you need three examples. I just wanted to stop you, in case you have only this one."

"Don't worry," I assured him, "I have others."

Off the top of my head, I came up with an arm twisting and a kick in the shins.

"He said he was kicking a chair . . . and there was a chair, hanging on his leg. But anyone could see the chair was just a prop, to cover what he was really doing. People don't walk around with chairs hanging on their legs."

"They'll get away with all they can," was Belkin's remark. He folded his empty wax wrapper and placed it in an airline bag under his desk. He took out a legal pad and began to write. "A kicking and an arm twisting . . ." He scratched something out. "I don't know about the arm twisting; that doesn't sound bad enough."

"He threw me out of a car!" I cried. "Just now, on my way to see you."

"How fast were you going?"

"Not fast. The car was parked. I'd just gotten in. I was trying to start the car. Before I could pull out, Robert got in on the passenger side. I thought, 'Oh, he's coming with me.' But no, he reached across my chest and pulled the handle on my door. Then he shoved my shoulder: I fell out. Onto gravel. My stockings ripped."

"Pushed from a *parked* car," Belkin repeated. "That's a different story."

"No good?"

"It would have been better if it was moving. You're sure there's no adultery? We only need one example."

"No adultery."

I told him about the soda bottle. "Robert threw a soda bottle. It could have hit me in the face, but it hit the refrigerator. It was a giant soda bottle. The keg size."

"Glass or plastic?"

"Plastic. One of those synthetics; they use heavy styrofoam labels."

Belkin shook his head. I could see he didn't give much weight to my plastic soda bottles and parked cars. "How about a separation agreement? No grounds— you just stay apart, legal, for one year. Then it's a divorce."

"I have to have the divorce right away."

"Well, maybe we can go with alienation of affection. Did he withhold his body from you at any time?"

"Never."

"Then there's no alienation of affection."

"Not in that sense, no."

"And you said he is in what profession?"

"Part owner of a sports complex."

Belkin turned to a fresh page and began to write. "Income?"

"I'm not sure. All I know is, I've had it with him. Blood!"

"More than fifty thousand?"

"No."

"Twenty-five thousand dollars?"

"Around there. It's been shooting up every year."

Belkin smiled. "That's not bad. We'll get him."

"Get him?"

"Children?"

"No, with the marriage so bad, I thought, better not; I mean, the father of your children should be . . ."

"You're sure?" He held his pen, a fountain pen, high in the air. "There'll be no children?" He leaned slightly forward, as if checking my body.

"How could there be children? I've had it! I'm through, finished."

"With children, you would get more. You own your own home?"

"Yes."

"And you work or stay at home?"

"Both. I'm a potter and a sculptor. I do little clay figures from mythology."

"My daughter is good in art," Belkin confided. "Your income?"

"Well, it varies. One year, I made almost nine thousand dollars. . . ."

"This year?"

"I've been upset."

"How much?"

"Three thousand, five hundred and twenty-five dollars."

"Good. That's low enough. I can get you something."

"I don't want anything."

"Come on, what's wrong with a settlement? Or a regular little alimony? You worked hard. How long? Five years. Worked five years for this guy . . . helped him build up a sports empire . . . washed his socks . . . cooked his meals. . . . Who took care of him when he had even a little sniffle? And how does he repay all this love and devotion? This man, who promised before God, to love and to cherish: *How does he repay this little angel who devoted her life to him?*"

Belkin rose and stood behind his desk. He wore his trousers high—around his armpits.

"How?" I asked.

He boomed out, to an imaginary jury: "What does this man do? This man, who is made of the food you cooked for him? What does he do?" Belkin took a deep breath, then shouted: *"He attacks you with a metal kitchen utensil! He throws you from a parked car! He twists your little arm*—the arm that worked for him"—his voice softened—"the arm that held him."

Belkin scratched something on his notepad. "Forget the arm," he said to himself. "Stick with the peeler, the kick, and the push from the parked car."

His speech had moved me. He handed me a Kleenex, which he kept in a box on his desk.

"So," said Belkin, when I'd wiped at my eyes, "tell me the rest. How did he draw the blood?"

It was hard to speak with my lower lip out of control. "Look—I'll tell you, but no alimony, okay?"

Belkin nodded and waved his white hand. "For now, just tell me what happened, Dollink, so we can see what's what."

∽

And so I had to tell him how Robert had chased me, at peeler point, through our oriental garden until I tripped on the seedling. Lying there, looking up at him, that glint of the maniac shining off his right eyeball, I had to scream. Out of sheer animal instinct, I yelled, "Help! Somebody, help!"

My screams attracted the attention of Vito Vingiello and Angelo Bologna, two handymen who had been repairing our leaking leaders and gutters and whose presence we had forgotten.

I looked up; I could see them: two gargoyles, straddling our peaked, slate roof. They flanked the weathervane. Vito Vingiello and Angelo Bologna sat perfectly still. One of them held a hammer.

"And you know something? You'd think they'd help me, wouldn't you? Well, they never made a sound or a motion."

"We have their names, just in case."

"Robert didn't even see Vito Vingiello or Angelo Bologna. He was oblivious to everything but what he was going to do to me. He was a demon. His eyes, slits, and I knew then that while, ordinarily, he could be a terrific guy, he could, at that moment, kill me."

"Some nice people go crazy," Belkin agreed. "It's no reflection."

"Yes, and I want to stress that while I've brought out the difficult side of the marriage, there was also a wonderful side. We actually got along very well most of the time. We had wonderful dinners in our garden. And you know, we never sat down to eat, unless by candlelight. And we both enjoyed going to the movies."

"I've got the picture."

"It's just this crazy thing. His temper. He's from Texas. They sang about lamb blood. . . ."

"I'm not surprised."

"His mother hit him with a spatula when she nursed him."

"That makes sense too."

"They ate a very tasteless Jell-O mold every night."

"Different cultures, different religions. It's hard."

"We didn't fight about religion, but maybe that was underneath."

"You think genes don't remember?"

"This fight wasn't about a *Tennis* magazine, was it?"

"There's more to it," Belkin nodded.

"Well, he would get violent, for no reason. But he had never used a weapon before. That was new. So I got really scared, and started screaming."

"You said there was blood?" Belkin reminded me.

"Well, he did it. He really did it. He attacked. He jumped from a small compost mound. Oh, it was horrible: the flash of the peeler; his enormous body diving on top of me. . . ."

"He hurt you?"

I lifted my sweater, and showed, as discreetly as I could manage, the crescent gouge on my left breast. With my right hand, I covered my nipple. He could still see the gouge, just below.

A small gouge: perhaps the diameter of a dime. The peeler had not been large, or, thank God, sharp; I had dulled it coring crab apples for my famous sour apple pies.

Abe Belkin muttered something I didn't understand, except in my blood and in my bone:

"Feenstermeeesh."

The instant after he gouged my breast, Robert collapsed and held me in his arms. Bang. It was over. And he was, once more, the man who had loved me, held me while I slept, the man whose chest had been my pillow for five years. Six if you count the year we just lived together.

"He says it was an accident. He wasn't aiming for me. 'I tripped. My foot slipped on the mulch. You know how slippery it gets. I would never hurt you, my little doll.'

"But," as I repeated to Belkin, "I've had it with technicalities: the distinctions between plastic and metal, the difference between standing on dry ground or wet mulch. Blood is blood."

True, Robert had broken down, and explained what was "behind" his attack. "It's not you, you're a cutie-pie. It's me. I have problems. . . ."

As I lay on the moist earth, Robert explained that Sportorama had invested heavily in flab-removing machines—vibrating belts and so on—and that club members seemed reluctant to use them. The machines had not, as hoped, attracted new members. "And it was my decision, so if the money goes down the drain, it's all my fault. It's the damn responsibility. And Ned Campbell would just love to see me fall flat on my face." Ned Campbell is a partner in Sportorama, too. Robert went on, almost crying—and I've never seen him cry!—to say that the suction device, called a galvanatron, which works on thighs and paunches, cost twenty thousand dollars. "And it's just sitting there."

I understood all that, and conveyed my support, but when I saw my chance, I jumped up and ran for my car.

"Now get me out," I begged Abe Belkin.

"First, I need a picture of Robert."

I flipped through my wallet and pulled out a color Instamatic of Robert, tanned, holding up the big-mouth bass he'd caught, on a lure, at Lake Mohonk last summer.

"Very nice," said Belkin. "I give this to the process server so he can recognize Robert. Then he slaps him."

"Slaps him?"

"With a subpoena."

"We have to slap him?"

"He can come in, himself, if you tell him and he's calmed down. That's how we do it in the civilized ones."

I pictured the possibilities: the subpoena man slapping Robert at Sportorama. What would Robert be doing? Sitting in the cedar sauna? Or smashing a forehand "down the line"?

Much as these visions disturbed me, I also knew that "Honey, could you go into town and pick up a subpoena?" was a line that would stick to the roof of my mouth.

Belkin was moving faster than I'd anticipated. "You have a joint checking account? It's yours. Clean it out first thing in the morning. We slap him tomorrow afternoon. . . ."

I raised my hand. "Hold on a minute."

Belkin's mouth pulled downward. "What's this? I thought you were sure. Ordinarily, I make a nice little plea for reconciliation." He faced his imaginary jury once more.

"Why can't these two kids get back together? What problem in life is so insurmountable that two healthy young people who once loved each other . . . *who may still love each other* . . . for does love ever die? *Can't they find those feelings* that first brought them together, *that they made sacred*"—his voice dropped—"before God?"

I whimpered. "Maybe I was a little hasty?"

"Look. It's up to you. I thought I could skip the reconciliation plea in your case."

"Mine is one of the worst?"

46

"Eh. I could tell you stories. But *blood is blood.*"

"You think I'd be stupid to stay?"

"That's up to you."

"I wish someone would just tell me that it's out of the question."

"It's out of the question."

Belkin convinced me. That did it. Blood *was* blood. Nobody stayed in a marriage after blood. "But no slapping. No subpoena, I'll do it the other way. I'll tell Robert he has to come here. That's the adult way. The straight way. I'm going home, and I'm going to tell him right now."

"I agree with you 100 per cent."

༄

Don't tell me that the accident was not an accident, that I caused it in some way. I will grant you, that may happen in some cases, and that the circumstances— driving home from a divorce lawyer—might stir up some subconscious tension that could make me step too leadenly on the gas, or not notice a red light. But that's not what happened.

"Gus n' Eddie's Sunoco" report, an automotive autopsy (for the poor baby was totaled), revealed a congenital defect in the steering apparatus. The rod that joins the steering wheel to the tires had this hairline fissure. The fissure had been there for two years, a secret metal grin, which cracked open forty minutes after my decision to get a divorce, and as I approached the tricky intersection of routes 4 and 17.

My car, a peppy Italian compact, went wild. We zigzagged across four lanes, hopped a divider, sideswiped a VW minibus, and then arrived at our final destination.

So I repeat: *It was not my fault in any way. I was not to blame.* It was this rod. This fissure. If you must blame someone, blame that not-so-peppy assembly line worker in Milano who fused my steering rod while under the influence of too much Frascati.

I'd begun to feel so much stronger that afternoon. The half hour before the accident was my strongest, my toughest, half hour. I could take on anything.

A sunset reddened the western sky. A song played on the AM-FM radio: "Tie a Yellow Ribbon 'Round the Old Oak Tree. . . ." My foot tapped the accelerator. I made nippier, tighter turns than I'd ever made in my life. I was on my way, on my way.

A few peeks into the rear-view mirror confirmed: I even looked stronger. There was a tough, independent woman if I've ever seen one: snug in a French designer shirt (soon to be scissored off in the emergency room) and a lovely blue silk scarf (returned to me later, as a driftwood of dried black blood).

Paused for a red light, I enjoyed a soft breeze through the vent window (splinters of which are still working their way through my elbow, even now, two years later).

My last thought was, "Maybe I'll stop for a Dairy Queen." My throat felt the effects of my long verbal exchanges with Robert and Abe Belkin. A Dairy Queen would be just the thing.

I teased forward, eager for the light to change. At the green, I stepped on the gas, led traffic. Up ahead, I spotted a cluster of roadside franchises. And ah, yes, there was the cottage-style roof of Dairy Queen. I twisted the wheel to make a right.

And that's when it happened.

The wheel kept turning.

∽

Tell me the truth: Does my smile look crooked to you? It shows in photos. And in the mirror. A definite droop to the left. I'm askew.

You don't see it? Oh, you're just being kind.

∽

Imagine: You turn the wheel to the right, and it spins completely around. A roulette wheel all of a sudden.

Okay, I think. *It's a little loose.* Take a left. I turn the wheel. Around she goes. Where she stops, nobody knows.

Next, the car bucks, rising on its rear wheels. We part traffic, cross the highway. I yank up: The wheel rises on its shaft. I stuff it back down.

We are hopping over the divider.

This all takes two seconds, which feel like two centuries. And I'm thinking, *"This is it. Oh, terrific."*

And right on the macadem, I can read, *"You're dying."*

White script on black asphalt. No kidding. Talk about writing on the wall. This was writing on the road.

There were other special effects. Oh, yes, my life did flash before my eyes, just like a slide show. But flashbacks are nothing new for me. I have to go over a few key scenes every day anyway.

This slide collection included some oldies. What struck me, even at the time, was how *mundane* some of the shots were. Okay, see special events, trauma, even. But I saw a perfectly ordinary nonevent: me, age four, plus panda bear, looking into a bakery window at sprinkle cookies. I'd forgotten that, but so what? Why see it now?

Better to see sprinkle cookies than what's really coming at me: the wide-lipped rump of a sanitation truck. Elephantine. Gray.

In the traditional slow motion, I have time to check my speed—fifty—and hear the last line of "Tie a Yellow Ribbon 'Round the Old Oak Tree. . . ." I was aware, almost pleasantly, of the sun's warmth on my windshield.

My clever Italian seat belt snapped open. I fell forward: My forehead rapped glass, and rebounded. Something happened to my elbow in the vent window. But that was a side order.

As I started to scream, my face smacked against glass, and I bit through the windshield.

I hope you never know the sensation. Of swallowing glass and teeth, together. *Stay alive,* I ordered myself. *Don't fade out!*

Pain? Not really—more of an *effort,* an effort not to swallow more glass and teeth, which made me gag. This nausea—not of the stomach, but in my head—kept my brain rolling over and over within my skull.

Later, in the ambulance, after I'd had a whacking injection of Demerol, and nursed on oxygen, I reassessed my life. *How simple things are now. What was a divorce? Nothing to me.* I cried out, "This is the happiest day of my life."

❧

Check my smile again. It doesn't strike you as uneven? My own front teeth were different. Smaller. More shy. These are bold ones. You really wouldn't have known?

❧

There was talk of retrieving some teeth and encouraging them to set down roots on the old locale. Someone was even dispatched to the intersection of routes 4 and 17 to look around for a couple of shy little teeth.

But it was no go. There was hope for the future—corrective surgery, implants, miracle dentistry—but "in the meantime" I had to be fitted with something I'd never wanted to hear about: a "prosthesis."

It wasn't just a question of teeth. Only four, by the way. And you'd never know if I hadn't told you, right? There aren't any movable things or plates in my mouth. Now.

But then hunks of my gums were missing. I guess they were on the car hood or the highway. Inside, the roof of my mouth had collapsed. Bone lay on top of my tongue.

Surgery helped the roof and gum situation. But as soon as I was ambulatory, I was sent to Fenschman's, a dental lab in mid-Manhattan near the leather district, to get what would later be called "my temporary teeth."

Want to hear about a terrific afternoon? Imagine, without several teeth in your head—but dressed to the nines—strolling down Fifth Avenue to a dentist who once did Kirk Douglas's teeth in a special way for *Spartacus*.

If you can handle that, you should have no trouble leaving the "miracle dentist" to go to Fenschman's dental lab, even though you are holding a paper bag that contains a mold of your mouth.

I won't tell you about Fenschman's, or their lab posters that show people munching ribs, gnawing corn on the cob, or sinking their new ones into a McIntosh. Or the "happy face" sign that promised "Smile-U-Wait." And the lab assistant's joke, "Kiss the wrong fella, sweetheart?"

～

There are catalogues of tooth color. You flip through, as if selecting a wallpaper. From Ultra White to Putrid Black, with a hefty swatch of "Yellows" and a slim packet in "Green."

I was pleased to be close to Ultra White, only two flips away. The assistant noted my shade—"Young Ivory No. 2"—and within hours called me into an inner office and showed me my new smile, which was lying on a table. A click-on jobbie, which came in three sections.

Two Chiclet-white front teeth. Two somewhat more yellow "side" teeth. And a plastic wedge of "gum."

The assistant, teasing me with his own grin, demonstrated how to click and hinge my sections into one major device, which I could then snap into my mouth.

I wondered, aloud, why, if the three sections clicked together, why they could not have been prejoined? Why . . . ?

"Just show me if you can do it," was the assistant's reply.

I bent over the table and fooled with the little sections. Why the extras? To make me feel more in pieces? To humble me?

To whom? That power on high who had thrown me through the windshield as I made my first drive toward freedom? Or to Fenschman's and the "miracle dentist," his emissaries on earth?

I set down the little Chiclet teeth and gum section. "Look, I'll be able to do this when I get it home." What I didn't need was someone watching me struggle to fit my "prosthesis."

"I have to see you do it."

Bitter— I don't like to entertain people—I bent again and refashioned my smile, suddenly propelled fifty years ahead: a sneak preview into geriatrics. For the first time, I addressed that as yet unknown person, my true love, with some doubt. "Can you love me with these?" I asked the dental table.

As I clicked in, for the first time, I suspected that I would not be pursuing my life course as recently charted by Abe Belkin. Perhaps, a stronger woman could go, without her teeth, to a divorce lawyer and say, even though she sounded like Gabby Hayes, "Pro-theed!" And then, toothless, take New York by the tail.

I could not. Not just with gums.

In one year, the miracle dentist had promised, I could be fixed up "permanent." It would take that long, he explained, for my gums to "settle."

~

Waiting for my mouth to shrink, I went back home, lay on the couch, and disconsolately spooned purées. The "Smile-U-Wait" job, you see, wasn't functional: If I bit into a McIntosh, my teeth would stay there. The temporary business was supposed to be "cosmetic."

Some cosmetic. The two front ones were cute, but the side teeth seemed too small and yellow—corn kernel teeth. I hated to click them in. The gum section, I admit, was lifelike. But its very detail—transparency at the tooth border, an authentic "ripple" surface, especially the pink-traced "capillaries"—depressed the hell out of me.

"Yer all right," said Robert. "Yer all right."

❧

The year passed. My mouth shrank. I returned to the miracle dentist, world famous in dental circles for his finesse and, also, a literary work: *Analgesic Drilling: It Doesn't Have to Hurt.*

Informed of his sophisticated methods, I was surprised when he came at me with large implements: a hammer and pliers.

"You won't feel this," he said each time he inserted clamps, then forced a rubber frame into my mouth. Since I knew any complaint from me would hurt his feelings, possibly damage his reputation, I tried not to scream.

A brilliant monologuist, the miracle dentist spoke non-stop as I gaped, silent, beneath him. Every week, as he entered parts of my mouth with successively larger instruments, he reported that he had addressed another convention of oral surgeons and out-of-town dentists. Sometimes he would have journeyed to far-flung cities or even a Soviet bloc nation to explain his progressive technique. Once he recited for me his entire lecture, "Pain Is a Four-letter Word."

One afternoon, while snow turned the city as white as our dental cubicle, the miracle dentist did something with pliers that made tears run off my cheeks and into my ears. He motioned to his assistant, a heavy menopause blonde, who moved in on rubber soles. They pulled out straps and buckled them around my arms.

"Now you're getting it. The permanent. This is it." He added a warning: "You may have a little sensitivity."

A lever pressed. My head lowered backward. My feet raised. Dr. Margolis (for that was his name) crawled on top of me. In one hand, he held a hammer. In the other, my new, permanent smile.

He eyed his assistant, who, sturdy as a refrigerator, braced herself beside my head. Then, he cupped my nose with a rubber mask. Breathing in the sweet coolness of nitrous oxide, I told myself, *"I can stand it. It'll just be another minute. Then my life can begin again. Then I can find you...."* I was talking to my true love again, the person I always knew I had to seek out, that special man I now know is you....

Sex, however, was not on my mind. In fact, as Dr. Margolis made some witticism in reference to our compromising pose (I could feel him against my pubic bone), my only response was the gaseous, chilly nausea. *Ugh. Sex. Who would ever feel well enough to want it?*

Then the first spoke of pain was driven into my brain, finishing not only Sex, for me, but also Change. Hastily, I withdrew my plan for a divorce, telling God that if he would pull the spoke, my part would be never to commit any adulterous act, even kissing. *I'd be happy with what I have....*

And what kind of marriage did I have? In the past year, a time of limbo, waiting for teeth, I'd found a new, albeit toothless contentment with Robert. What I had thought dull now seemed solid. His resistance to divorce ("Divorce? Forget it. We're happy.") now struck me as reassuring. The rotary peeling? Well, maybe he *had* tripped on moist mulch.

∽

"I'll never let anything bad happen to my cutie-pie," he'd said as I lay prone at Good Samaritan Hospital, attended by nun nurses. Could any man have been more devoted after the accident?

He slept on the hospital floor, beside my bed. He used his shoes for a pillow. If I stirred or cried, he jumped up to hold my hand, and whisper, "Yer all right. Yer all right."

His hand on mine, something I'd never dreamed was

54

possible. Maybe it took a near-fatal crash, a mouth smashing, to make it happen.

Why let go of that hand for a life of aimless searching? Of standing alone and unasked to dance in discotheques. Or presenting my now uncertain mouth to strangers for closer scrutiny?

No question. The loss of teeth had cemented the bond between me and Robert. I felt a new easiness with him around dream house. I stopped wearing makeup all the time. He'd seen me without incisors; why not without lipstick?

As I slapped around on backless slippers, I had to congratulate myself. I could relax for the rest of my life, wearing this very same safety-pinned chenille robe, if I wanted. More time to paint, sculpt. Enjoy the cozy drowsiness that seemed to overtake me every few hours.

Yet, at the base of my skull, one disturbing message still tingled: *You stayed after blood. Stayed with a man who peeled you. Where is your spunk?*

And spunk was what I was supposed to have. Men had courage. Women had spunk.

So where was my spunk?

There, with me, on the couch, where I could most often be found reclining, staring drowsily into a crackling fire. Or, more likely, bathed in the blue light of the television set, which stayed on even as I fluttered back and forth from some nether world to my own living room.

One afternoon I watched a drama of a woman with a severed breast who wondered if her husband would still love her. He did in a way, but not the way she wanted. He was shown fingering an empty brassiere cup.

～

My husband, Robert, kissed me. Kissed me without teeth. Amazing. Why hadn't he left me?

Wasn't this love?

～

Then came the day Robert tore through the house. "Where are my hockey shoes?" and inadvertently stepped on my temporary teeth, knocking them into a snaggled grin.

Toothless again, I begged him to drive me to Dr. Margolis, wonderful Dr. Margolis, and then to Fenschman's lab.

"I have to play hockey," said Robert. "Take the bus."

"Without teeth?" I cried softly.

"Keep your mouth closed," he replied.

∽

Oh, you don't realize how you need those teeth until they're gone. Forget the McIntosh, the spareribs. Just to say, "A round-trip ticket to New York, please."

I developed a style of speaking through sealed lips. But it was not a success. All through that long, mumbling day, as I paced, again, with a paper bag of mouth molds, I felt new resolve harden within me.

This is it. I've had it. Sent me into the city without teeth. My lips puckered around the word "divorth." I traded in my old theme, *when I have a thousand dollars, I'm leaving!* for the less ambitious, but more crucial, *When I have teeth . . .*

∽

After the accident, the time between my crash and the arrival of the ambulance had provided an intermission. It seemed a long intermission to me—stretched as I was on the yellow hood, facing a metal statuette of a racing hound and the questions of my own mortality; for I knew for sure that this could well be the end of the little person known as Alice Smilgiewicz Berry.

Why do I have to die this way? What does it mean? My thoughts took a philosophical, nauseous turn. I loved life. I had been looking forward to a frozen custard. *Why me? Why now?*

The first person to reach me with any answers was Fred, the ambulance attendant.

"You're going to be okay," he said, loading me into a comfy stretcher. Then, he'd gone on to tell a little inspirational story that involved his dog, Trixie. "You're going to come through just like Trixie come through."

Trixie had made an ill-timed crossing of the Taconic Parkway—"God knows why, weren't anything on the other side better than what she got at home." Fred slipped me into the rear of the ambulance and pulled up a chair near my head. "We all thought she'd die. But she come through. Don't even limp."

His words encouraged me, but I still felt in danger of fading out. Death was sitting on my chest, squashing the air out of me. I used all my concentration to raise and lower my rib cage. But inside me, things were not going well.

"Think you might retch?" Fred asked, gently.

I whispered that I might.

"Then turn your head the other way."

Fred's words would haunt me through the next year. I guess that was the start of my "dark thoughts."

෨

It's not true that human beings can't remember pain. I can.

I remember the weight of Death on my chest. . . . Death straddling me, laughing, squeezing the breath out of me. And I remember Dr. Margolis, in the same position, hammering the new teeth into some raw sockets prepared to receive them. Pain was fluorescent; it winced on and off. When I looked up, Dr. Margolis and his attendant appeared as in a 3-D comic: red, blue, and overly outlined.

Then it was over. And I was snapping my new teeth in anticipation. Dr. Margolis held up a mirror.

He was a genius. What teeth he'd given me! Bold white beauties, with a slightly impudent overbite.

I rushed home and went, without taking off my coat, to the refrigerator. I crunched into a red, crisp McIntosh, gnawed into some fibrous pale celery. I boiled some corn on the cob, and ate it—did everything I'd dreamed of doing for a year.

❧

At night, I dreamed of ravenous kisses in wet caves. By day I often slid deep down into an easy chair and invoked my night phantoms: a man, an underground river, an aquamarine cave. As my mind wandered down ceramic channels, my hand dropped into my lap, there to find my underwear too binding.

I was building up to something.

*A*s soon as I had teeth, I sank them into Robert: We waged our last war, over whether or not we could have an amicable divorce.

We separated. I moved to a love seat in the sewing room. He stayed in the master bedroom.

There followed a cold and raw season as drafts of hatred whipped through dream house. Doors and cabinets slammed.

In the process of becoming strangers, Robert and I instituted formalities. We were as careful as house guests not to be caught naked. We dressed for sleep (we who had been naked together for six years). Now, if he walked into a room as I was slipping into my clothes, he jumped backward into the hall: "Excuse me!" We dressed even for bed. I wore ski underwear, and he (on the occasions that I glimpsed him) seemed to favor his warmup suit.

All our habits changed. For the first time in six years, we locked the bathroom door. I did less housework, and he did more. I would still do laundry, but I would not fold it. In Robert's bureau, where once he'd found stacks of Fruit of the Loom and black sock balls, he now faced a wrinkled confusion.

I rose at dawn, earlier than my married custom, so that I could appear, coiffed and dressed in a suit and high heels, at the breakfast table. In our heyday, I'd have worn only one of Robert's X-large T-shirts and served up steaming platters of bacon, eggs, and his favorite butter-crunchy toasted English muffins. Now, uncommitted to his well-being, I left small, unopened boxes of nonnutritive breakfast cereal in his empty bowl. Sometimes I threw in an unopened can of synthetic juice, one with dyes.

Yet I joined him for this repast. Sitting in my formal attire, I'd sip a bitter cup of coffee and gnaw a Ry-Krisp. The silence that is supposed to hang between the hostile pair of departing mates did not haunt our breakfast nook. There was no loud clink of silver or studied chewing.

We talked like passengers in a dining car, as if we lacked a common reference but were headed in the same direction. "And where will you be going?" Robert asked one morning as he knifed open his box of oversweetened corn puffs.

"I'm thinking of New York. Where will you be going?"

"Well, I've been looking at A-frames. Down in Jersey. I could have a horse down there. . . ."

"That sounds nice," we would compliment each other.

∽

Yet no one left. We seemed to be in cold storage. We had not made love for a month, not since my last "final" decision.

One night, at the blackest hour, I woke up in the sewing room, on the converted love seat upon which I slept. *What was I doing here? Where was I?*

Then I sorted out forms—my dress dummy, the floor lamp—and remembered. I was in the sewing room, getting a divorce.

Outside, wind blew, shrieking and howling at obeisant bushes. Although I was indoors, under two blankets, and wearing ski underwear, I felt the wind as though I stood naked out in the backyard. A breakfront, heavy and black, loomed over my improvised divorce bed. The room felt empty, but too busy—with shadows and phantoms—and, at once, I had to get out of there. . . .

I tiptoed out into the hall, toward the old bedroom.

If we could only hold each other one more night, I thought, *then we could leave, on a high note, in the morning*.

The bedroom door opened with a gothic creak. A lump—Robert, his arms around our beagle, Buffo—stirred. Robert must have been awake, for, as I crawled across the mattress to my estranged husband, I heard the instant zip of what turned out to be his Wrangler jeans.

Buffo sat up, yawned, and shuffled off the bed. I heard his nails clacking on the parquet floor. He would not be voyeur to our last rites.

Robert had dressed heavily. In the interest of divorce, he'd worn the Wranglers, his warmup jacket, and, I now noticed, his SUNY track sweatshirt.

Then he was naked, but for Fruit of the Loom jockey shorts and an Ace bandage wrapped around a thigh injury that I'd not even known he'd incurred. *How far apart we'd drifted*.

Moved to see him thus, I lay motionless as he pulled off my thermal long-sleeved ski shirt. I expected he would pull off my long bottoms, but he surprised me.

Not ready for too much intimacy, he simply unsnapped my drop seat, and, flipping me around, then reasserted the marital bond through the small square trapdoor. I felt a buffered warmth, and looked back over my shoulder to see that he hadn't entirely disrobed either: He poked forth from the mystery slit of his Fruit of the Looms, the slit I liked to slip my finger through, when I had, on occasion, worn these briefs myself.

So this is how we end, I thought, moving to the old tempo, *in our underwear*.

This cottony farewell continued for some time. At first, we were accompanied only by the hysterical November wind and Robert's measured breathing. Then a new sound effect:

In the same loud voice he used in his work, instructing novice tennis players, Robert began to issue orders.

"Move back. Farther. Now, faster. That's it. Okay. Now, wider. Open!"

"Open!" tripped off some alarm within me. I found, to my surprise, that instead of my usual moves, I'd turned around to hammer my fists against Robert's chest. And I was hissing, in a new voice, "No! No! No! No!"

We grappled, never breaking the vital connection, but shoving and pushing each other, as if we were not there of our own volition, but had been roped together by some outside villain. As we struggled on the island of our bed, it was clear that all we wanted was to get free of one another.

Who broke the groinlock? I couldn't tell. Maybe I did. Maybe Robert. We flew, in our underwear bottoms, off to different rooms: He to the kitchen, I to the bath.

From behind the bathroom door, I heard the distant crash of china. Later, I would find the last of our Nipponware service, the gravy boat, severed in the sink. When I heard the crispy tinkle of falling crystal, I pressed the lock button on the doorknob and went to sit on the edge of the bathtub.

Each smash outside was accompanied by a shout. Lamps keeled over. Chairs fell backward. As I'd feared, the stampede of feet was headed for my bolted bathroom door.

I saw the brass knob jiggle. I held my breath and gripped the bathtub rim. *Oh, why hadn't I left him already? Why did I have to stay for this?*

While I pondered these questions, and the bathroom door heaved on its hinges, I was also looking about the narrow room. Was there a way to escape?

I jumped up, ran to the small frosted window, opened it, and peered down a steep embankment that Robert and I had terraced with boulders and dwarf Japanese trees. Could I survive the twenty-foot fall? Hope to catch a dwarf branch on my descent?

Probably not. Too late to try . . .

The door shook. I heard splinters rip through the wood. I turned to see Robert enter, the door on his shoulder.

Our guest towels fell.

Some instinct sent me diving into the empty bathtub, to curl into its deepest corner. I'd seen cringing in movies, and tried to do some now. My back and shoulders hunched, and I kept my face down, not looking up.

Robert hurled bath brushes into the tub, along with insults. Everything somehow missed: "Wake up, baby. You're living in a dream world. Well, okay, Sleeping Beauty, you want a divorce, *you got it!*"

I peeked over the crook of my elbow and caught sight of what I at first took to be a wooden club but later recognized as a toilet plunger. *My husband, brandishing a plunger.* What was he going to do? Plunge me? Well, that left no doubt in my mind. *I'd had it with him.*

"No . . . no . . . ," I whispered. "Don't . . ."

He froze in place, his arm high with the plunger. A minute passed, then he threw the plunger to the floor and turned and walked swiftly through the ravaged doorway.

Crouched in the tub, I heard the thud of suitcases fall from an upper closet shelf. Then his steps. Within minutes, a door slam, then the rev of his Gremlin, the roar of his exhaust, and he was off—to a divorce dude ranch in Reno, it turned out.

For quite a few minutes, I rested in the bathtub. My heart thumped. I drew my knees up against my chest. Only my fingers were busy, indenting the bubbles on the fleshy rubber bathmat. I may not have looked like a winner at that second, but I knew I was one.

It's over. It's over. Hurrah.

lood is, blood," I was to tell Abe Belkin six years

*W*hat a relief. Robert: off galloping for six weeks to obtain our Nevada divorce. No need to go into court with my rolling soda bottles, peelers, or parked cars. He was divorcing me, on grounds of mental cruelty.

Fine. Fine. I had only to pack my outfits, artwork, memorabilia, and strike out for a new life in the Big Apple, where, I suspected, my true love, the Loner, was hanging out.

I was going to do all that, but I was a little drowsy. During the day, I sank down on sun-warmed sofas, or even floorboards, and drifted off. At night, I twitched with alertness.

During this phase, I took nocturnal drives and wanderings. I meant to drive all the way to New York, but somehow I usually stopped at the halfway mark, Suffern.

Suffern. Even the name. Why I wandered through Suffern, I don't know. The town offered neither the leafy charms of a rural hamlet nor the neon excitement of the big city. Suffern was, is, still sunk in the Depression, the original Depression. The town's economic status dipped so low in the thirties, that it never rose to be buffeted by the recessions of the fifties or the seventies. Suffern just shlumped along, its buildings painted green, its streets and stores named for Lafayette.

This small cluster of old but not picturesque structures rotted in the crotch of the Ramapo Mountains, bordered by dead-end railroads, a smoking Avon factory, and the clogged Ramapo River. In stormy weather, the Ramapo could be encouraged to flow. Really record rains might force the gray little river to slop over its banks and dampen more of the area. This ambience, plus a pizzeria, the Lafayette movie theater, and a laundromat were the delights of Suffern by night.

An unlikely place to fall in love? I did not expect to find the Loner in Suffern. I did not even keep an eye peeled for him while I wandered, my hands jammed down in the pockets of Robert's old pea coat, along a broken stretch of rail.

If someone had told me I was going to fall in love (mistakenly) that night, in that pea coat, in that town, I would have said they were nuts. But that's just what happened: I fell in love with a person I shall call "the tooter."

Of course, that love was not true love, only a vengeful lust to purge me of marriage. But who knew that then, as I walked, without a plan, into a section of Suffern that never recovered from heavy rains?

Small estuaries of the Ramapo trickled in the gutters. Every crater in the pavement held a small lake and a trembling moon. Sidestepping the puddles, I walked the high onyx belly at the center of the road.

I tried to think: Had I spoken to anyone today? Yesterday? I could not remember.

～

The sound came so naturally, so gradually that at first I thought I heard my own soul: beginning low and hesitantly, then keening toward the heavens, soaring from galaxy to galaxy, then taking a scorched fall to earth. High and hopeless, a call no one could answer.

Transfixed, I slowly realized that what I heard was not in my own mind, but was coming from outside: music. Music, so new and fearless in its lost way that I instantly gave my heart to it. The notes climbed my vertebrae, one by one, then, at climax, exploded in crystalline fire inside my skull. My first aural shiver.

Walking, I followed the music over a rushing gutter, across listing cement, and through the swinging door of a little-known jazz club, Blackie's.

Who could issue those ecstatic, mournful toots?

He would have to be ugly, cursed in every way but this. Most likely handicapped. At least blind in one eye.

65

Inside, through a smoked ultraviolet dawn, I saw him. My mental camera clicked.

The tooter arched his back in a final paroxysm of man and horn. He held the last toot for an eternity; then, slowly, slowly, he lowered the trumpet, and I saw his face.

Not ugly. Handsome. A starved medieval prince: black-banged, and all-white protruding cheekbones. I felt the next shiver in my thighs, which knocked together: *That's him.*

I was wrong. My ears, eyes, and thighs tricked me. But many a sweated night would pass before I would realize that he was not The One.

When the tooter surrendered himself to those piercing notes, I'd felt his music fill that vacuum that had been inside me all through my marriage. The problem had not been Robert, or his rage, but the dead air space around him.

Finished, the tooter switched open the valves on his shining horn; saliva dribbled to the floor in rainbow bubbles. Next, he reached down the throat of his instrument and withdrew the rubber suction cup, the "mute" that had gentled his wild cry.

He looked sad, drained. His adolescent-thin shoulders hunched.

Thank God we've found each other, I thought.

He walked past me. I saw his face in close-up: The black shining bangs and slanted cheekbones kept his eyes dark secret. His mouth, I noted, was wet and parted.

Kiss me, I mentally begged.

The warnings are always there, and they were there in Blackie's. "Excuse me," he said, "I'm trying to get out the door."

I stepped aside, but returned the next night, and the next, and the next. I went to Blackie's every night for two weeks. Eventually I adjusted my blusher to the unflattering purple light. Each time I listened to the tooter, I felt more certain that my throbs were true throbs, and less sure of how to let the tooter know I was throbbing.

I drank sloe gin fizzes.

At last, one night, a crowd of heavy-necked men occupied the front table at Blackie's. Usually, when the tooter played, you couldn't hear ice rattle. But these crudies kept up a high guffaw.

The tooter turned his back. He played to the wall. I saw his shoulder blades flinch under his blue denim cowboy shirt. He continued, and so did the guffaws.

I overheard, "That was somethin' when you got that spare. I thought Marve would piss himself. . . ."

Unable to bear it, I shushed the rowdies. When that went unnoticed, I threw a straw. In the ensuing disturbance, the tooter spun around, lowering the trumpet to below his silver Mexican belt buckle. His dark eyes met mine.

Later he joined me, although we did not speak for several moments. He sat down, as if by random choice, at my table. I watched, covertly, as he stretched his long legs on a chair beside the damp, rippling wall. Inside me, the shivers came at regular intervals.

Oh, do something! I ordered him.

Lighting matches from a book, he quietly bent them and watched them die out in an ashtray. Finally, in a low mumble, he began to talk. He told me he appreciated my hushing the loud men, but warned me that he was not worth the trouble. He only brought unhappiness.

"Stay away from me," he invited.

Oh, why didn't I?

∽

An hour later, in my king-sized marriage bed, he blotted his glans head with a Kleenex and explained: "It's nothing personal. I just never stay with a girl for long. I don't want to hurt you."

Twenty minutes before, he'd slid into me as if he

67

were on a greased track. *"Ooh wee*, this is a dream,"
he'd complimented as he rested within me. "You're a
luscious piece of ass."

Now something stuck to his lip: He pulled forth an
auburn curlicue, my own. I flushed. In the dark, he did
not notice.

"Really lady, you are . . ." he pasted the tight little
spit-curl to my pillowcase ". . . a beautiful, wonderful
girl."

Whom you don't want, I finished for him.

The tooter explained that though he loved women—
"God, how I love 'em"—he never loved 'em for long.
He ended with the words that were to become his
theme: "I got to keep movin' on."

Between my legs, I felt the chafed burn where his lip,
toughened by tooting, had produced a series of violent,
electric sensations. I remembered the old saying
"There's a thin line between pain and pleasure" and
felt that I might be straddling it.

(Does that hurt you, my love? Hearing about the
tooter lip? Oh, no. It mustn't. Believe me, he was nothing like you. And, when you hear what happened, you'll
understand why I stopped throbbing for him.)

We ran through our act again, but I was a little un-
nerved. I could not concentrate on the trumpet-lip
sensation, for the tooter kept moaning, "Lay-dee, Lay-
dee . . . I'm going to stay in you forever," which seemed
a direct contradiction of his "movin' on" speech. Which
was it? And why was he calling me "Lay-dee"?

"Well," he said, after he had collapsed on top of me,
"I'm goin' to have to be movin' on."

Did he mean in ten minutes, or ten days? Would
there be time to cook up some bacon and eggs, for
instance? Or should I dish out some of Robert's old
cold cereal? Maybe just hand him a candy bar on his
way out the door?

I was to learn the answer, to these and other questions, during my time with the tooter.

Why do I call him the tooter? Well, why did he call
me "Lay-dee"? I shall never call that man by his real

name, because he never let any of his women have their own names.

Oh, boy, did I hear about those women, and in what detail. He described them intimately, in gynecological terms, but referred to them in the manner of song titles: "the lil' gal I left behind in Jonesburg," "the doctor's wife," "the college girl," and "the widow from Chicago."

The college girl had been "tight and dry." The "gal in Jonesburg" was slack as old inner tube. The doctor's wife was "bigger than Howe Cavern." (He "got lost poking around in there.")

The key person in the tooter's past was "the widow from Chicago." The widow had soft breasts that swung around her waist, puckers on her belly, and a wild, grief-stricken style of oral loving. At the tooter told me in our postcoital damp, "The widow would call me by her old man's name, then suck me so hard I thought it'd break off. . . ."

This combo—use of a dead man's name and intense thirst for life—had held the tooter "in her thrall." He stayed with her longer than he had with any other woman. Then, without warning, he had "moved on."

A tough act to follow, I thought.

He still loved the widow the most. But soon, he said, "Lay-dee, you run a close second." Yet, in his postcoital sadness, he'd stand silhouetted by my window—his hips sapling thin, his back curved, and smoke unfiltered Gauloises and look to the northwest. And I, sitting up in bed, would know he was yearning toward Chicago and the widow's insistent lips.

Perhaps all this added something, as bitters do to a beer. All I knew was that a centuries' old pressure was upon me, which involved the serving up of enormous pies. Each time the tooter said "movin' on," I threw a chuck steak into the pressure cooker, and pulled a Ma Smith's frozen deep-dish pie out of the freezer. Every time I did this, I added at least three hours to our future.

Looking back, I know I didn't want him. Then: my tender parts burned, and my mind whirled with involved recipes. I bought a vaginal cream and *The Chilean Secrets of Slow Terra-cotta Cookery*.

Weeks passed. As Robert galloped toward divorce, the tooter led me on a fast canter through dream house. His obsession: to "take" me on locations where I had not been taken by Robert.

"How about here? Did he give it to you here?" he'd ask on the living room rug.

Staring down at the familiar Omar Khan, I would have to nod: He had.

"Here?" in the shower.

"Here?" on top of the oval Chippendale dining table, which seated six but opened for eight.

"Here too?" on the marbled sink of the guest bath.

I had to confess that my estranged had enjoyed me in all those locales. The tooter, his lip maroon with hurt, carted me up to the attic, pausing at an odd corner of our random stairwell. At last, he set me down beside the grunting furnace in the cellar. There he thrust away, satisfied that "He never had you here."

What he didn't know: Robert *had* taken me there, right on the very same sisal mat. I lied. The only place Robert had never taken me was a crawlspace under the kitchen, and frankly, I wasn't anxious to go there.

By the orange glow of the furnace, the tooter slumped over me in exhaustion. We lay there, listening to the oil burner roar and belch. The sisal scratched my back, but otherwise I was content.

"How about on the coffee table?" the tooter said, after a bit.

I admitted Robert had overlooked the coffee table. Within minutes, I lay prone on that old table, improvised from a Colonial barn door and upon which I had so often spread out my cheese dips and crackers. Oh, what had my life come to?

As I experienced my first doubts, Buffo the beagle, inflamed perhaps by the new mood of decadence, slyly attached himself to the tooter's foot and rode his heel with lascivious delight.

Not only my marriage, but my whole lifestyle, I

realized, had fallen apart. Where was I headed? Where would it end?

As I wondered, the phone on the coffee table rang. Distracted, I picked up and heard a nasal twang:

"What hyappened?"

I wriggled away from the tooter. My mother-in-law was on the phone: "You and Robert have a fight? He said he broke down the bathroom door, and you got mad."

"Wrong." My throat tightened. "I'm divorcing Robert because he thinks I'm mad about the door. It's everything. It's him."

The tooter buzzed my thigh with his leathered lip. I motioned him to hold on: This was important. At first, Cece was sympathetic. She saw my side.

"He always was fulla beans. I had trouble bornin' him. He came out ass first. Spread my bones apart."

"Then you understand."

"The Berrys don't ever get divorced," she said in a stern tone. "We believe 'till death do us part.'" That interpretation was literal, for, as Cece explained, her Uncle Earl had choked his wife, Connie, in an argument over lawn food. "They'd had a good marriage till then."

When I said my marriage had passed beyond her help, Cece's voice quickened, playing on too high a speed. She berated me for not using the hush puppy fryer. "I gave you a beautiful fryer, and you never used it. I saw it there, collecting dust." She went on to accuse me of hiding a set of Ardsley "Indian Tree" china that had been in her family for three generations.

Her accusations made my heart hammer. I went wild with excitement, hearing these things for the first time. "No, no . . ." I denied, but deep down, I knew it was all true.

"I was wise to you the first time I laid eyes on you— wearing a skirt up to your navel."

Why didn't I hang up? I stayed, spellbound, as if in transatlantic conversation with Simone de Beauvoir. At last, Cece wrapped it up: "Good riddance to bad rubbish. Lie down with dogs and you rise up with fleas.

My boy may be a hothead, but he's decent. He was a good boy at home. If he's gone loco, it's your spicy cooking that's done it. I had to take Alka Seltzer every time I visited you. And don't think I don't have your number. I spotted you for a Jezebel. I hope a car hits you, and you rot in hell."

She hung up.

Sweat beads, as big as tears, rolled down my naked sides. I turned to the tooter, who sat naked, hands clasped around his knees, his dark bunch of fruit hanging right on my coffee table.

"Look," I said, slowly, "I've been holding out on you. There's a crawlspace . . . under the kitchen." I took one hand from his knees. "Let's get down there."

～

We met only at night, in the wee hours, after his "gig" at Blackie's. Then we would go to dream house, take another carnal tour, and fall asleep.

The tooter took care never to stay the whole night. "I don't want you to get too used to me," he'd say, un-gluing himself before dawn. "Remember: I got to be movin' on."

He was more careful than Dracula to leave before daybreak: I didn't see sunlight on his face until the very end. His whereabouts were mysterious: I didn't know exactly where he lived, only that it was a transient place, just a room to hang up his horn.

To stress the fact that ours was a fleeting love, the tooter took me only to fast-food franchises.

I noticed contradictions early on: Yes, we went to fast-food franchises, but he wanted to linger there, over his Big Mac, for hours and hours. Comfortable in the blue light of the microwave oven, he'd go over his repertoire of other "gal" stories. I heard more about the "widow in Chicago," and the "college girl." Also: his first woman, a teen hooker, of flame-colored hair and "snatch," of whom he said: "Reminds me just of you.

You could be sisters. Only you're better than she ever was. . . . You're worth a hundred a night."

"Well . . . thank you." I bit down on a fish fry sandwich and a sour new idea.

Although I still felt pressure to keep the tooter from "movin' on," I was also aware of a growing unease. I hated the fish fry night at McDonald's. I wasn't sure about the tooter's brand of compliments, and I was repelled by the small gifts he brought me.

I didn't mind that they were cheap (and the best of the gifts could only have cost a buck and a half), but I did resent the thoughtlessness with which they had been selected.

Did he really believe I would love the severed foot of a rabbit, on a chain? Or the nylon undergarments known as "Answer-Pants," which featured "Yes!" on the front and "No!" on the back?

I forced myself to gush and make much of these offerings. But the minute the tooter left, I shoved his presents to the back of my drawer.

Meanwhile, he had his strong points. It was a pleasure to watch him eat my cooking. While Robert had been a gobbler, the tooter took his time: He'd roll the food over in his mouth and chew thoughtfully, with appreciative pauses.

∾

This phrasing carried over into bed.

He held himself high above me, pausing every few beats. He would solo for several minutes, then sit back, and invite me to perform. I would take a few turns, then he'd return to his theme. Was this a carry-over from his work with the band at Blackie's? Were we "trading fours"?

If so, it was all right with me, as was his finale: a long, improvisational solo. Used to a more gymnastic style, I sometimes found myself rushing in too soon, and he'd give me the same annoyed look he gave his sax player: "Not yet."

To accompany our physical union, the tooter played records with themes of "departure." I suppose this was another reminder that he was leaving. "By the Time I Get to Phoenix" was a standard. Often his selections needed no vocalist: saxophone instrumentals of such cauterizing despair I expected the tooter to keel over in midthrust. I wanted to say: "I can't enjoy myself to these dirges. Can't we have something peppier?" But, still afraid he would "move on," I kept my mouth shut.

His trumpet lip worked strongly in his favor. I had never felt lip like it: tough as razor strap. He also employed a breathing method that was interesting. No question: He had talent.

Yet, was he the one I was searching for?

Of course not.

I knew, because I continued to hold back.

One night, as we lay on a bathmat, he sensed this reserve in me.

"I'm going to get you," he announced. Then, in the same tone in which he had declared his intention of "having" me on new locations in dream house, he said, "I'm going to lick you where he never licked you."

If you can find a spot, be my guest.

I had saved one small space—perhaps only a half centimeter in diameter, in an unlikely nook of my body —but some instinct made me refuse to reveal the exact location to the tooter.

(Hey, you know, I'd forgotten about that unlicked spot. Till now. I still have it. You want to know where it is? You devil. I'll tell you, but let's save that for later. . . .)

*M*y instinct to hold back, not to give everything to the tooter, was a wise one. After his vengeful penetration of dream house, and my own body, the tooter's mood changed.

He slipped into Robert's Barcolounger and a deep depression. Never really talkative, he soon stopped talking for hours at a stretch.

I'd beg him: "What's the matter, honey?"

But all he'd say was, "I've been here a long time, Lay-dee."

My attempts to dig into his past produced only a few nuggets. He told me he had left a coal town in Pennsylvania. "My Dad sells insurance for miners. At inflated rates."

His early family life had been unhappy, perhaps because the town he lived in was most famous for its air pollution. "We drove with our lights on in the morning," was all he would say.

Why didn't the family move out of the area, known in Pennsylvania as "Black Valley"?

"They like it there. They'll never leave. Don't know any better." Then the tooter would glare at my RCA color TV, which he claimed he hated, but had turned on to a Steeler's game, and said: "Most people just live and die where they've got their appliances. I got to keep movin' on."

In the interim, he'd been hard on my furniture. His fornicator's journey had broken several chairs and worn the nap from the arms of my sofa. I took this to mean he was not only venting himself on me, but also my comfy way of life. I assured him that dream house no longer meant anything to me, that I was ready to step off my Omar-Khan carpet forever.

He did not respond. He lay prone, his feet high on the recliner rest. His hand dragged inside a pretzel box. He sighed, and he grunted.

One night I wandered in with an offer of more salade niçoise, and he did not even look up.

"Robert!" I snapped: a serious slipup. But the tooter was too far gone to notice.

Several nights later, when he lay in the same pose—his hand, this time, in a box of Cheeze-its—I heard myself squawk: "Yer all right. Snap out of it!"

Robert's very words. I choked them back. What was this—a catechism I had to pass on?

I lay down on top of the torpid tooter. "I'm sorry, Angel," I whispered. "Please just tell me what's wrong?"

"I got to be free." He caught me in his thin arms. "It's time to be movin' on. . . ."

Yet, his penis wasn't movin' on—it was movin' in. Although as a rehearsal for his real departure, he withdrew before I could climax. Yet he seemed in no hurry to actually leave me.

We went on this way until I looked at a calendar and caught my breath. The weeks had passed quickly. In only one more week, Robert would have galloped through his divorce residence requirement at San Pedro's Dude Ranch, Reno, Nevada.

I had done none of the things I'd planned for my new life. One night, I called the tooter at Blackie's and told him I had to stay in and pack. "Where will you be going?" His voice idled. He couldn't really care.

"New York."

"Well . . . look . . . come to my place after work. . . . We have to talk."

Okay, the big farewell. I braced myself and took down his address: a transient hotel in Suffern.

At four in the morning, I drove once more to the section of Suffern that never recovered from heavy rains.

I waded up to the old green frame hotel. Inside, I held my breath against the lavatory sting.

Poor baby . . . having to stay even a night in this dump.

As I climbed a listing stair, I berated myself for detaining the tooter this long. I should have let him go: *He wants to leave me now, and I'll say it's okay.*

No question which door was his: I heard Billie Holiday wailing "Why was I born?" from behind a green door marked "29."

I knocked: the door fell open, and I stepped into that place the tooter called home. Backing up Billie Holiday, sleet began to needle the room's one windowpane. A miasma—decomposed sock, old Gauloises—assailed me, as did the apparition of the tooter himself.

He lay diagonally across a narrow bed. His torso followed the sag of the mattress. He wore only a black nylon panty, which I had never seen before.

Piled around him: the flotsam and jetsam of a thousand chain smokes and take-out dinners. I noted an old cantaloupe rind doing duty as an ashtray. A small tower of empty pizza boxes, and the trapezoidal containers used by Chinese restaurants leaned against one corner. Beer and wine bottles lined the windowsill. The only furnishings other than the bed were a scarred bureau and a boudoir chair, in a listless floral skirt. On the chair, swaddled in socks and underwear, sat the tooter's trumpet and instrument case.

I had known the tooter did not live well—material things did not matter to him—but this? To hide my shock, I emptied ashtrays into an already full trash basket.

"Come here, Luscious." The tooter opened his pale arms.

Sensing what he needed, I dumped another ashtray, then pulled off my raincoat and dress. I stepped out of my panties and walked to the bed.

We fell into our usual routine, heightened perhaps by Billie Holiday, now moaning, "You don't love me no more. . . ."

"Oh, Lay-dee, Lay-dee, I'm going to keep it in you forever."

His words stopped me in midswivel. *Now, which was it? Was he staying or "movin' on"?*

"All right . . ." He sighed, as if I'd been engaged in a persuasive speech. "You win. I give in. We'll do it."

I felt him move—metronomically inside me.

"What?"

"Stay together," he explained. His lip curled. "Get married, if you insist. Hell, we'll even have a kid—everything you want."

"But I never said I wanted that. I thought you were 'movin' on.' "

His hands moved to my hips and clapsed the extra flesh I have there. "Well, I may just hang on to the 'Lay-dee from Horizon Homes.' "

As he thrust his pelvis up at me, he went on. "You're the one. Better'n any woman I've ever known . . . even the widow in Chicago. . . ."

I liked that part, and asked for more details.

"Well, you're special, that's all."

"How, in what way?"

I expected him to list my sterling qualities: charm, generosity, compassion, whatever. . . .

"Well." His lips paused. "You know what I think it was, that was so special it won me over?"

"What?"

"The way your puss always wet up."

"That was it?"

"Well . . . that's not all of course. . . ."

Oh, now the real praise: my pleasing character traits.

"Not only does it wet up—every time—and you don't know how rare that is, but—it never stinks like most women's."

～

You may have noticed that all his compliments have had this ring. In the past, I'd tried to overlook his wording. A compliment is a compliment, right? If this adulation did not make me glow, I held my own counsel.

Through the dishwater light before dawn, the tooter whispered more of these endearments. His search, he swore, had ended. He would give up this freedom, this room, *which he had lived in for seven years*.

Seven years. Who had he been kidding about "movin' on"? Me? Or himself?

I lay stiffly between him and the buckling green wall as he murmured that we would never part, we could live together, perhaps purchase a townhouse out on Route 59.

Numb, I nodded until he sank down in slumber. Slowly, the night faded: Sunlight spilled into the room. For the first time, I took a hard, brightly lit look at my lover:

The man I saw was young. But he had been young for a long time. The hoarfrost was on his cheek, even on his chest.

Meaning to soothe, I stroked his face and hair. To my horror, his bangs moved with my hand—exposing premonitories of shined scalp. Not a toupee, I noted, tugging gently, but a clever comb forward. Quickly, I patted the hair back in place. He would never know anything had been disturbed.

"Never love a balding man," my mother had warned. "All his emotion will go into watching his hair die. He will have nothing left for you." She had gone on to say that totally bald men were fine: "They can feel for someone else, once it's over." (Darling! *You're* not bald.)

Well, if I'd really loved the tooter, it would not have mattered that he was not adolescent, shaggy-haired, or a wanderer—that he was, in fact, a balding, aging guy who wanted to get married and keep his contempt for the idea at the same time. At his stage in life, "freedom" had an inflated value; I held his head for another hour, then eased off the bed. Careful not to wake him, I set about dressing, then performed a ritual house-cleaning.

Why did I do it? Take his socks and underwear, stuff them in a bag, and carry them down to the Lafayette Laundromat? I don't know. I know only that I did, and that I carefully gave him a full "sock and jock" job —rolling the socks, stacking the shorts before I left, for the last time, his fouled abode.

For it was I who was "movin' on."

*N*ever have I accomplished so much so fast. In one week, I packed all my belongings—no mean feat, since these included a hunk of quarry stone that weighed two hundred pounds. Why take the stone? Well, it was no ordinary rock. This rock had attracted me by its suggestive shape. I took one look and knew that my masterpiece lay trapped within it. I would have to wait for inspiration, but, no question, the rock was my most important possession.

The movers, the trip to the city, the rental agent—all these passed in a blur. I awoke a new woman, in this very apartment, just one year ago.

Why Hell's Kitchen? A good question. A lot of people ask. Well, all my life I had more or less orbited the big city—living within sight of it but never at its center. And what could be more central than Hell's Kitchen?

Actually, I had ridden in on the bus, and the Port Authority is right across the street.

I took the first place I came to. The super showed it to me by flashlight. He said everything would be fixed before I moved in—and it's still in the same crumble in which I found it.

Look, I'm not kidding myself. I know it's a dump. But don't you think I've fixed it up nicely? The plants help.

Anyway, it's a steal. No one wants to live here, because the produce trucks roll in before dawn. You'll be hearing them later. But I love that—and I can get the best lettuce and tomatoes in town. There's also a meat market.

The rest of the building is all Italian. Very friendly people. But I'm not close to anyone in the building. I don't need people knowing my business.

There's a married couple next door. I don't know

them, but I can hear them fight: She calls him "The Grand Duke" and he calls her "Her Royal Highness." As in:

"Where's my good shirt?"

"I don't know. The Grand Duke can find it himself."

"Well, thank you. I don't want to disturb Her Royal Highness."

Once in a while he wants to make love to her, and she says, "If the Grand Duke can be so kind as to bring Her Royal Highness her diaphragm?"

Is that enough to keep you single?

Well, anyway, when I have more money, I'll find a bigger place. But this is okay for now. This is what I always wanted—to be totally on my own.

The funny part was that the first week I was here, all I did was sleep. Right here. Every time I woke up, I congratulated myself. "This is what I wanted to be free for, this is why I got divorced . . . to lie here."

Finally, I looked up at the ceiling and asked the light fixture: "Where's your spunk?"

"Here," I said. And I got up.

"Where's your spunk?" I had to ask myself that so many times in that first month. "Where?"

"Here," I'd say, filling out my application at Career Blazers employment agency. I wrote:

"I'm interested in creative work in the art field. Will consider career in advertising, media, or publishing. Want to work with exciting, talented people."

&

I got a job collating for IBM. I couldn't collate that well.

&

That ended: On my own, I went to work at Manny's Delicatessen on Broadway and Forty-ninth Street. Something I knew.

82

Working at the deli was a break of sorts: At least I could eat in comfort, back among the familiar vats of potato salad and coleslaw. I had found that I was unhappy eating alone in restaurants. Restaurants—who could afford them? I was unhappy eating alone in coffee shops and souvlaki stands.

I had always been part of a team. There had always been a face across the table. Alone, I became conscious of my chewing.

Eating alone at home was better and worse. Better, because I had a great appetite. I stuffed myself. But worse, because I could see my manners deteriorate.

At first, I ordered myself to maintain the high culinary standard of my marriage. *You're worth cooking for*, I said the first night I unpacked my whisk and copper pans.

And so I sat down, alone, to a candlelit coq au vin, with fried eggplant and saffron rice. Cherries jubilee for dessert. I enjoyed it, but thought, *maybe, next time, something less elaborate.* It doesn't have to be time-consuming to be good. I don't have to "jubilee."

The next night I whipped up an omelette. Perfect. Delicious, civilized, yet easy to prepare. (I'll fix one for you later, if you like. Wait'll you see me flip it.)

There, I told myself, finishing the omelette, *no need to let things slide.* Then I saw my reflection on the plate, and realized that unconsciously, I had been licking it. I set the plate down with a smack, and went back to a souvlaki stand where I ate, standing up, facing a wall.

My contacts with men?

Glances on the street. A look on the subway. Sometimes more than a look: the pressure of a hard, foreign penis against my behind.

The Pervert seemed to be everywhere. He could not

have been, but he seemed to be the same fellow. Small, wiry, with a tropical complexion, shaded by pork-pie hat. He followed me. I could feel him just over my shoulder. He made sounds, and he whispered humid intentions: "I know how to do eet. I do eeet with my tongue. I do eet so good. Sexy."

Sometimes he spelled it out. Other times he left off with sucking noises.

The Pervert took my subway. He lurked around street corners. He popped out of doorways. Always, always: "I want to suck you. . . . I suck you so gooood. . . ."

Did he really think he could convince me? That I'd turn around and say, "It's okay."

If I went to the movies, he appeared in the next seat. He did things with newspapers, popcorn boxes, raincoats, umbrellas. Something always rustled in his lap. I'd change my seat. Then, I'd hear him behind me—breathing.

∼

There was also the Construction Worker. Yellow hard hat. No eyes. A big studded strawberry nose. He worked rafters across the street.

Every morning, I had to pass him and listen to his critique of my grooming. I never won his complete approval: "Hey, your slip's showing."

Or, "Your skirt and blouse don't go."

And, "What kind a crazy shoes are those?"

Finally, "What'ya wearin' a hat for? You in disguise?"

Another rafter man was more encouraging: "Lookin' good, baby. Lookin' fine."

I liked him.

"Ummmmummm . . . struttin' fine. Ummmm, I'd like to marry you! Will you marry me?"

Give me one more month.

I was looking for you. I looked on the streets, at the lines outside Cinema I. . . . The world was a parade of couples. Lexington Avenue on Saturday could have been the ramp up to Noah's Ark. Two by two. Two by two.

How I hated to go to the cashier and whisper, "One, please."

A crazy little thing. I often forgot my purse. Robert. I was used to his being there. There—in that vacuum of space at my right side.

At night, I bunched three pillows into human form. That's only natural, isn't it, after six years of sleeping with someone? It's nothing personal—about Robert, I mean. Just body heat.

It was at night; I noticed the guy across the courtyard. (If I opened the blinds, you could see him, but I don't want to encourage him. He has nothing better to do than look in here.)

What bothered me about him was how aimless he was. He walked around in his underwear. Not doing anything, although sometimes he held a chicken leg. He just sort of wandered around his little room. And scratched himself. Maybe once in a while, he'd move a little to music. I think that's what he was doing, anyway. But most of the time he just walked around, or sat in front of the TV.

He kept one hand on his crotch almost all the time.

Afraid that I would get like that, I signed up for art classes at the Art Students' League.

Considering how empty my life was, I'm sure you'll understand how I mistook my respect for Paul Whiting for something else. When I think how I rushed into that situation, with a man older than my own dad. Well, it was an obvious mistake . . . but I've been slow to correct it.

∾

During that first class, I never dreamed, even as I experienced one of my mistaken shivers, that I would actually be joined to his venerable body. And as he addressed Painting: Photo-realism I, Paul Whiting showed no special interest in me.

"What is reality?" he asked. "What do we see with *these?*" He gestured to his own flecked hazel eyes. "Do we see things as they actually are, or as a mirage?"

What I saw: a handsome, silvery-haired older man, tall but listing to the left, and dressed in a blue work shirt, jeans, and steerhorn belt.

He held a sixty-watt electric bulb in one hand. In his other hand, he held a small painting of the identical bulb. The bulb had been reproduced with eerie authenticity: the filaments glowed, the glass gave off the same frosted halo. Yet there was a difference between the real light bulb and Paul Whiting's "portrait of a light bulb"—

"Emotion. My emotion. And an essence—of something else. A mystery . . . is in the air around us." He maintained, "All reality eludes us." Therefore, "Why attempt to be surreal? The most ordinary object, as faithfully represented as possible, is still surreal."

He delivered his punch line. "In this class, you will be as faithful to these"—again, his eyes—"as you can be. Add nothing. Because the forces around you will appear on canvas, anyway. When you have finished, you will look at your work and be able to separate the subject from what has infiltrated—mood, mystery, yourself."

His words plucked a chord in my spine. *Ah, ha,* I thought. *This is it.* And deep within me, as I sat upon the art stool, I felt another shiver—although, looking back, I can see that my shiver for Paul Whiting was only a partial shiver.

The warnings were there, as they always are. In Paul Whiting's case, the first warning was that mention of "reality versus illusion." The second I heard that, I should have run for cover. True, reality does elude us, but it doesn't have to elude us that much. . . . Another warning was his body, which turned out to be in deep trouble.

But I get ahead of myself. I really didn't think that anything would happen between us. As he wandered among the easels during my twice-weekly classes, he passed me with the barest nods. He did not praise my work—a shattered picture tube—as he did the pen-and-ink sketches of severed garden hoses done by twin middle-aged sisters in the front row. "Look at that," he'd cry over their easels. "If this isn't grief, I don't know what is. . . ."

All he said to me was: "You have energy."

I expected no more. Paul Whiting had world fame. His work was hung in the Louvre—an outer wing. He had known Picasso and Matisse. He had lived most of his life (which had to be nearly over) in France (although it turned out he was born in Newark).

He figured in several nonfiction accounts of the "movable feast" period in Paris. A famous woman painter had written a scalding memoir, which included descriptions of his "fervent lovemaking . . . his attention to detail, his touch, his fire!"

I should write to her and demand a retraction. She got me into that mess. With a man twice my age. Twice! Almost thrice! *What was my hurry?* I'd have to ask myself, later, in his aged embrace. *I could have waited a few years to get to these liver spots.*

Well, maybe I'm not being fair. Maybe he was in better shape when the famous lady painter knew him. Okay. It was my own doing. But I blame my subconscious, because if it hadn't been for the Dream, I wouldn't have ended up in bed with him.

The Dream:

He's sitting in an armchair. I sit on his lap. We are both dressed. I wear a short skirt. He wears paint-splattered jeans, the jeans he always wears to class. And his male parts are all bunched over to one side. He opens his pants and unbunches his male parts.

I realize this is ridiculous, but he starts to unravel himself—white and distended beyond all belief. With a mysterious smile, he inserts this long white hose into me, under my skirt.

We begin a slow, circular motion. . . .

What actually happened could not have been more different, except for the paint-splattered jeans, which were in there, all right.

But I get ahead of myself. I was weeks away from the actual act with Paul Whiting. For the present, I was content with my studies, and the Dream.

Was it possible? Did I really wake in the night, moaning, "Paul . . . Paul . . . Oh, fill, fill me."

My days were less satisfactory: As "slicer" at Manny's Delicatessen, I worked in an aislelike kitchen. There, I sawed off the rotted parts of vegetables and peeled mold from salamis.

Every afternoon, salami smell on my hands, I dialed the employment agency I had visited. "Please . . . please . . . get me something more interesting. Anything."

❧

I had almost given up when Career Blazers called back. Something in publishing, they said. I wrote down a name, address, and prepared for my interview.

I wore my best suit—a black wool—with my best white silk shirt, and a new slouch hat. I even wore pantyhose, for the first time in God-knew-how-long. After all—a career in publishing.

Fox-MacKneill occupied a Tudor fortress in a wind-swept area otherwise devoted to parking lots and demolition. A stiff river wind at my back, I almost flew into the building, which, I noted, wore a brass script name-tag: "The Juggernaut."

I knew little of Fox-MacKneill: only that their enterprise was vast. In a glassed-in reception area on the twentieth floor, I studied the walls, papered with Fox-MacKneill book and magazine covers. Tomes on the economy and math textbooks dominated one wall. I was more interested in the other wall: a display of their best-selling novels. A few of the book jackets blazed with graphic designs. Perhaps . . . did I dare hope? I would be designing the next Fox-MacKneill dust jacket, over their famed imprint, the horned eland?

As I perused the fiction section, I remember being struck by a startling black-and-white dust jacket: a novel, *Naked Faces*, by one J. D. Sarkoff—*the* J. D. Sarkoff who, within a few months, would wreck my emotional health and contribute to a gynecological problem.

Thus is the present seeded with hints to our future. But who knew that then as I chewed Trident and waited to be summoned inside.

A tall girl, in horn rims, led me back to an inner sanctum: the office of my prospective employer. The tag on his door read: J. Marrone, Periodicals.

J. Marrone himself sat at his desk. He turned the pages of a book. As he read, his moustache twitched.

Thinking him unaware of my presence, I stood poised in the doorway.

So this is publishing. These shelves striped with colored book bindings. This avocado plant leaning toward the window. These fluorescent lights. This green carpet. This raft-sized desk covered with scrolls of paper.

This man who looked like Don Ameche.

Publishing. Could I fit in here?

"I don't care what anyone says," J. Marrone, whom I would come to call Mr. Marrone, said suddenly. "There's no one like Thurber." He looked up at me. "Is there?"

"No one," I agreed at once.

He gestured: "Look at this," and I rushed over, laughing and nodding already. For the next few minutes, we agreed that "Thurber has been unsurpassed. Although Feiffer is good, too." Mr. Marrone shook his head, closed the book, patted it. Then he reached for his pipe and started the interview in earnest.

"Career Blazers sent you?"

I nodded, and held up my portfolio.

He took the portfolio and motioned for me to sit down. I did.

I watched him read my résumé and frown: "You haven't much background in English at all."

"Just the required courses. But my art background is solid."

He flipped through my portfolio and paused at one of my better life studies, the photorealistic "Shattered Picture Tube." Would he see the emotion in that shattered tube? Or had I failed?

"I'm primarily a sculptor, but, of course, I realize that's no use here in publishing. But I do love to work in all mediums. . . ."

Mr. Marrone closed my portfolio.

"There are some contour drawings at the back," I spoke quickly. "I'm told I have some skill with caricature."

Maybe he needed someone to sketch in profiles of literary greats? Mr. Marrone reopened my portfolio. "Robert Redford," he laughed. "Not bad."

He looked at me again. "You're talented and diverse in your interests."

I smiled.

"What we're looking for is a sort of renaissance person, someone with both literary and artistic gifts. I have a feeling about you, in spite of your weak English background. You're bright, curious, and can learn fast."

How did Mr. Marrone know all that? Was it true?

"Publishing jobs cannot pay as much as other types of work, but the rewards are far greater. Intellectually. Of course. We take that for granted. And the work does bring you in contact with exciting, creative people."

He wants me, I realized.

We skirted around the subject of my salary. A man of great sensibility, Mr. Marrone didn't speak the actual figures aloud, but scribbled them on his leatherbound notepad, then turned the pad so that I could read: "$125?"

One hundred twenty-five dollars? That's all? Still, this was publishing. I nodded.

Mr. Marrone held up a cautionary hand: "I have to

warn you. There's been some turnover on this particular job. You will be assistant art director of a nationally circulated magazine. The work requires a special brand of talent, and a certain aesthetic discipline. I just had to let a woman go. She couldn't handle the workload. Three other people, all highly trained, by the way, have had the job so far this year—and frankly, none of them were even adequate." He drew on his pipe. "If you're looking for an easy relaxing job . . ." He waved the pipe, and did not finish the sentence, for I rushed in:

"No. I want *this* job."

"Well. It's official then." He checked his handsome gold watch. "I was about to call it a day. Shall we drink to our new association?"

Giddy, I followed Mr. Marrone, now in a tweed overcoat. We passed the rows of secretaries in a blur of introductions, and moved on down the gleaming, endless corridors of Fox-MacKneill. Near the elevator, we passed a thin-lipped man, as gray-faced as his suit.

I didn't think much of The Gray Man at the time, but I learned later that he was Gordon Fox, the scion who owned Fox-MacKneill. Within weeks he would become my love slave. But who knew that then?

Outside, on Forty-third Street, Mr. Marrone raised his arm for a taxi, but as a Checker cab coasted over, Marrone lowered his hand: "The hell with it; it's such a lovely day, let's walk."

I wondered why he said that—it wasn't a lovely day. A fifty-mile-an-hour wind whipped off the Hudson and stung the backs of my legs. My hair flew before my face. I supposed he meant that, *in every other sense, it was a lovely day: our new association, and so forth.* So I walked briskly, at his side, uptown until we finally ducked into the paneled lobby of the Algonquin Hotel.

There, on a green leather settee, Mr. Marrone celebrated my appointment as assistant art director of *Actual Slayings.*

&

Known in the trade as a "Dick" book, *Actual Slayings* appeared monthly, featuring twelve true stories of murder, rape, arson, and other felonies. Its sister publication, *Official Slayings*, offered much the same fare, but, I was told later, to "lower income" readership.

The stories were absolutely factual—drawn from newspapers all over the United States, Canada, and (in dry spells) Western Europe. "We go no further abroad, because readers cannot identify with killings in Asia, Africa, or behind the Iron Curtain," explained Mr. Marrone later in our relationship.

My work on *AS* (the in-house abbreviation for *Actual Slayings*) involved the usual assistant art director's duties: paste-up, layout. For each *AS* "Exclusive" I arranged a composition of photographs, type, and other art. Most often, I worked with police photos of manacled suspects, victims, and other relevant material.

On a standard layout, I would paste up two photos of the victim. The first—a "Before"—showed the victim alive, usually in her official yearbook or wedding portrait. The "After" photos were supplied by the police labs: a morgue shot, body bag, or something dark and gushy, labeled "unidentifiable remains."

Once the "victims" were set on the layout, I would line up portraits of the police "sleuths" who had "cracked" the case. Also, pictures of any clues, such as a tire iron, or ski mask. Last came a full-page shot of the killer, being led, in cuffs, by the "police probers."

"Miscellaneous art" might include "slay scenes," or "architecture" shots of the courthouse, prison, or related buildings. If "art" was in short supply, I might glue in a cast of "witnesses" or "weeping relatives."

My fine arts background came in handy. Another function of my job was to circle bloodstains and draw arrows to severed limbs, so that readers would be sure not to miss them. In "sniper" cases, I had the added responsibility of drawing the trajectory lines.

So much for the creative part. As I soon learned,

publishing is business. Big business. Advertisements were the bread and butter of *AS* and *OS*.

Our major advertisers were the self-improvement schools: "Meat Cutting Offers You Success and Security," "Learn Upholstery at Home." I usually placed the most expensive ad, a full-page layout of apprentice butchers hacking away at chuck roasts, on the inside cover. The second-best spot was the back cover, which usually went to a pen-and-ink illustration of a married couple slashing apart their sofa. Back-of-the-book ads were postage-stamp sized, and proposed less of a challenge: I simply lined them up at the borders.

∽

My office measured six feet by eight feet, coincidentally the size of a regulation prison cell. I shared this space with the art director, Denny Goldman. The sign on our door read: "Art Department: *AS, OS,* and *SS.*"

∽

"Here you are," Mr. Marrone had announced that first day as he ushered me into the Art Department. "This is where you'll be working, and this is the man who knows all the answers: Denny?"

Denny, asleep on top of a layout, "WAS THE SHY GREASER BOLD ENOUGH TO KILL TWO WACS? *Indiana Police Probers say he was!*" opened one eye, then jumped to his feet. A pear-shaped young man, his girth seemed to fill the small room. Mr. Marrone gave him a look. "You'll show Alice the ropes?"

Denny nodded, wiping his palms on his jeans. Quickly, he pulled a matte knife and began to slash at the oak tag portrait of a pocked goon. "This will be mounted on a separate page," he explained.

Mr. Marrone said: "Well, I'll leave you to your own

93

recognizance" and bowed back out the *AS, OS,* and *SS* door.

The instant Mr. Marrone left, Denny sprang to the door and pressed the lock button. Then he leaned against the door, as if blocking an ambush, and turned to me. His voice went hoarse.

"What's he paying you?"

"One twenty-five."

Denny spun round, kicking the door. "Shit." He went on: "Cheap bastards. They cut the salary for fuckin' assistant—it's supposed to be one-fifty. . . . I was supposed to get the difference, and it's not reflected on the fuckin' check. *Shit!*"

He picked up a discarded stat of a bloodied pipe and crumpled it. "*Pricks!*"

Then the anger went out of his fat frame and he sighed and heaved himself back onto the drafting stool. After another minute, Denny looked up from the pocked goon and said, in a defeated tone, "You know we're goners, don't you?"

"Goners?" For a second I thought he meant we must die there, in the Art Department.

Denny explained: "*Actual Slayings* is on its last legs. Circulation is half what it used to be. The ads are dropping off. *OS* is doing a little better, but it's going to die too."

"And *SS?*" I wanted to know. "How about *SS?* And what *is SS?*"

"Oh *SS* . . ." Denny looked at the initials on the door. "I guess I should scratch that off. *SS* was *Startling Slayings* . . . aimed at a younger readership." His lip twisted. "There was no younger readership." Denny fished something out of a desk drawer. "Look at this. . . . Isn't this a shame? *SS* had the prettiest logo."

I sat down on the second stool and rested my head on my new art table. At PS 53, when I was a kid, you were allowed to do that when things weren't going well. You just folded your arms around your head and cried a little. No one acknowledged that you were doing this.

When it was over, you rejoined the group efforts at multiplication tables, or whatever had caused your distress.

It was the same here at *AS*. Denny ignored me while I sniffled against an oak tag. After a few minutes I looked up, played with my paste jar, and asked Denny, how long he thought we would have.

"Oh, you can relax; *AS* and *SS* will die, but not tomorrow. Marrone may squeeze out a few more years. *Startling* hung on by its fingernails for five years—and that was without ads. Well, we had ads, but no one had paid to put them in. They were just there to save face. We had almost zero circulation. Marrone kept it alive because he's such a cheap bastard, he can put these rags out on a shoestring."

Denny looked around his domain, which was papered with old *AS*, *OS*, and *SS* covers, all depicting young girls in varying states of terror or actual rigor mortis. "He should have five people in here. What kind of Art Department is this? Shit, I've got to put out *AS* and *OS*, plus shoot the covers, and work up our own house ads. Plus I put out a special year-end bonus edition, *The Best of OS and AS*, and a nostalgia issue, *Great Slayings of Yesteryears*.

I assured Denny that I meant to help him to the best of my abilities.

"Yeah, yeah." He returned to work with his matte knife. "But I could use four more of you. And I heard him con you into writing. You're not supposed to do that. That's another job. He must have cut back in Editorial too."

I didn't mind. What had Marrone said—a renaissance person? Well, I could try. Whatever I am, I'm not a quitter.

Denny gave me my first assignment: a layout with the headline, and blurb: "CALIFORNIA'S CASE OF THE MISSING REDHEAD—*with only a tooth to lead them, West Coast sleuthers followed a cold trail up the San Fernando Valley, in pursuit of two sex fiends who had just started their four-state sex spree.*"

My publishing education began. I immediately learned two key principles: "First, you gotta name the state—you know, California, Florida, wherever she was bumped off. People want a killing in their own state. Especially in the Southwest. If we can get a Texas or West Virginia slaying on the cover, our sales really go through the roof.

"Next," Denny proceeded, "you got to make the victim sound attractive. Our readers don't want to know if some dog gets axed." He pointed to a spread of graduation pictures of slain coeds. "These girls weren't bad-looking, so I call 'em 'dead beauties.' If the girl's just average, describe her as 'pert' or 'vivacious.' 'Shapely' is a good all-purpose word. If the girl was a real beast, sometimes I won't even use her picture. I'll stick with a body bag shot and caption it, 'Inside this bag rest the shapely remains of Vicki Mason, the vivacious coed.' "

Denny went on to say we could "go heavy on stewardesses, models, actresses, go-go girls. Anything with pizazz. Show biz. If she was just a housewife, call her a lovely bride. Oh, and dead married couples can go as 'slain honeymooners.' "

Next, we turned our attention to the task at hand: "CALIFORNIA'S CASE OF THE MISSING REDHEAD." Denny opened the folder and pulled out a Fact Sheet, and an envelope marked "Art." "Now, this one will be a toughie"—he showed me a blowup of a molar—"because this is the only picture we've got of the victim. And you've got to get across, from this molar, that she was a sexy, vivacious broad, someone the *AS* reader can give a fuck about. . . ."

He emptied the "Art" envelope. "Jesus, what's Marrone trying to pull? Nothing but a molar, a picture of a road intersection, and a Taco Bell. How the hell are you supposed to do a good job with this crap?"

This is a test, I realized. For the next hour, I poured over the fact sheet:

"Sue Ellen Bott, twenty-two, was abducted from

Sepulveda Boulevard by two brothers in a pink-and-white '59 Rambler sedan. One man stuffed his T-shirt in Sue Ellen's mouth and forced her to lie on the floor of the back seat. Taking money from her purse, the brothers drove to a Taco Bell, where they loaded up with Cokes, burritos, and cheese empanadas, also a dessert chip known as 'sugar crustos.' Sue Ellen might have made a break for freedom at Taco Bell, but she did not try, apparently believing her abductors would free her if she co-operated."

Reading this, I vowed: *If I'm ever lying on the floor of a car, with an undershirt stuffed in my mouth, I'll make a break for it.*

Sue Ellen, as her molar indicated, did not. She was taken to a deserted lot and raped for five hours. The brothers took turns, until, in ennui, the older brother picked up a rock and bashed in Sue Ellen's head.

The men lazily dug a two-inch grave and covered Sue Ellen with old Jai Alai posters and sand. When the vultures and coyotes had finished, all that was left was the gold-inlay molar. An astute "LAPD homicide prober" following a "hunch" led to a positive ID. The ID in turn led to the Taco Bell, which led to a description of the two men. The LAPD homiciders, as we called them, "drew a bead" on the brothers. The "nicer" brother quickly turned state's evidence to convict his sibling.

I went over the story from all angles, and remembered the principles Denny had taught me. At last, I slipped a specially lined paper into my old Underwood and I tapped out, in the alloted space: "This gold inlay was all that remained of luscious Sue Ellen Bott. She smiles no more, raped and bludgeoned before she could finish stewardess training."

When Denny returned from his lunch break, he looked at my work and gave a low whistle.

"I'm impressed."

∾

My specialty turned out to be "no art" layouts, such as Sue Ellen's. The less photographic evidence I was given, the more challenged I felt—

How to describe the Ohio Torso Victim, when the only "art" is a garbage pail? "This pail carried the severed pretty head of gorgeous, blond-tressed Lulu Jenks."

On the same case, we had a photo of a dirt road. Nothing special about the road: no bloodstains, or even tire treads. What to say about it? "Lulu never knew, as she pedaled along this lonely road, that her long, flashing legs had excited the passion of the escaped Torso Killer, hiding in the bushes (*far right*)."

On another assignment I opened the Art folder and found nothing but a photo of an Esso station, to accompany "BLUDGEON DEATH AT BLACK ROCK, ARKANSAS, HAD LAWMEN WONDERING: *Could the mild CPA be a Satanist?*" A note from *AS* stringer Bill Folsom apologized for the lack of art: He had arrived late, and a rival publication, *Real Detective*, had grabbed the good photos of the corpse and all that was left was the Esso station, which, Folsom admitted, had no relation to the crime.

After several hours (I skipped lunch) of pondering the Esso station, I wrote, "If pretty Polly Johnson had seen this gas station (*above*) and asked for a road map, she might not have detoured to Black Rock, where a devil-worshiping CPA waited, holding a studded baseball bat."

"How the hell do you do it?" Denny asked. "None of the other assistants could handle the toughies."

I didn't explain my secret to Denny—that I could actually visualize every crime I had to caption. The objects, scenery, and characters became real to me: I actually *saw* Polly pass that Esso station, *saw* Lulu pedal by the bushes. This "imagining" was an old pastime of mine.

~

I had started "imagining" as a child, to fill the long hours after school, while I waited for Max and Sophie to come home from the deli. Some nights they worked quite late and I was home alone. I spent the time sitting by the window.

My mother kept a ceramic "dish garden" on the windowsill. In the dish garden were an oriental woman, a man with a bundle, and a curved bridge. I liked to look into the garden and imagine stories . . . sometimes romances. Most often, the woman was about to fall off the bridge and drown unless the man saved her.

As they worked out their situation, I rubbed the little figures. I rubbed so long, and so hard, that eventually the color wore off the bas-relief: the woman's high hairdo, and her breasts, and the man's bulky bundle. The ceramic glaze dulled and showed a coarse white. Funny, after all these years, I can still feel that cool ceramic, every bump and ridge on those two little people.

My parents would find me, glassy-eyed in the twilight of the windowsill. I'd blink: Complicated bubbles appeared in the air. The bubbles were linked—like paramecia. It always took a minute or two for the air to clear, and for me to re-enter the spirit of our living room.

Now, this old habit of transporting myself, with few props, served to further my career in publishing.

∽

At night class at the Art Students League, I had to work to suppress this same tendency. "Do not create a mood!" Paul Whiting would warn. "The mood will be there of its own."

As he spoke, I moistened between my legs. Oh, why did I moisten? Why couldn't I simply have turned to this man for guidance, for friendship, for anything but what I did turn to him for?—the gratification of my twenty-six years of pent-up passion.

~

"I'm too old for you," he said himself on our first after-class coffee break at the Fifty-eighth Street and Lexington Avenue Zum Zum.

"No," I protested.

His hazel eyes kindled. "You remind me of my greatest love . . . years ago . . . in Paris . . . Par*ee*." His hand fluttered: "Oh, where is my French going?" He snatched air, as if hoping to grab back the language he had spoken so fluently while part of the movable feast.

Does he want me? I wondered.

"You know," he said slowly, "sometimes it is a good thing—a young woman and a man of experience."

Although we sat at a counter, under a display of plastic bratwurst, and people on both sides of us were eating heavily onioned Zumburgers, suddenly Paul Whiting and I were the only two people in the world.

That was the moment I first realized that the Dream might come true. I remembered the last night's: how he'd unraveled that tapeworm of his, and it had, of its own intelligence, tunneled into me.

I blushed, and looked down at my *apfelkuchen*. My thighs shook with mistaken notions.

~

At Fox-MacKneill, the wishes expressed on my application came true: At last, I was among creative, artistic people.

Mr. Marrone expanded my horizons to include a literary world. One afternoon, after he had approved my layout on "*South Dakota Kill Spree Leaves Two Go-go Girls Dead, and One Crying: 'Get the Tattooed Man with the Wall Eye!'*" Marrone gestured to his framed magazine covers: "*Liberty. Collier's. The Saturday Evening Post.* Where are they today?"

"They're dead," I said sadly.

"Well, it's not going to happen here. We're going to

keep our little magazines alive. We are not going to give up. We are not going to let down our readers."

❧

Next door to my office were the "confessions" magazines. Maggie Johnson, a birdlike woman, presided over *Uncensored Romances, Exciting Confessions,* and *Thrilling Confessions*.

Maggie was nicknamed "Maggie One Time" Johnson, because she loved to use "One Time" on her covers. "One Time Before I'm Married . . . I Must Make Love to My Doctor!," "Will My Husband Know If I Cheat One Time?," and "One Time for Money Doesn't Make Me Bad, Does It?"

Maggie's assistant editor, Shirley Zucker, fresh from NYU, had her own specialty: "Half Times." She was obsessed with halves, as in "Half Raped: Will the Police Believe My Story?" "Half a Woman—Am I Married to Half a Man?" Everyone agreed Shirley peaked with a sellout issue that featured: "Any Man Can Have Half of Me for Half the Night."

Not everyone was as happy at Fox-MacKneill as I was. The austere Pam Richards, a society deb with an M.A. from Radcliffe, often expressed her resentment at being "Rape Editor" at *Thrilling Confessions*. I overheard her complain on the coffee line:

"I've been raped by my stepfather, raped by my doctor, by the preacher . . . by gangs of boys, on beaches, in schools, in drive-ins. I was 'Raped for Two Years—And No One Believed Me!'

"I am goddamn sick and tired of being raped. Why won't Maggie assign me a 'One Time' story? Or one of Shirley's 'Half' things? My God, I'd even prefer *Uncensored's* 'Meatball Recipe' column."

Eventually, Pam's dissatisfaction paid off. She was assigned to do *Exciting Confessions'* advice column, "Ask Harriet Sanford." The column always contained a letter from a woman who had given birth without having known she was pregnant, and a call for help from a mother who suspected her husband of molesting their preschool children.

Meanwhile, down other corridors, other Fox-MacKneill editors worked away at *The Fruitarian*, a magazine for food purists. *The Fruitarian* had been the brainchild of the founder of the company, old Arthur Fox, who had lived until ninety on a diet of fruit and macadamia nuts. He had died several years before my arrival, but Fox-MacKneill employees still spoke of him, and his was the spirit that led us.

Old Arthur Fox had been obsessed with fears of "contamination." He insisted that his food be washed in Clorox solution, his clothes sterilized in special cleaning vats. Yet, in a contradictory mood, he might refuse to part with any bodily wastes. He kept things you ordinarily wouldn't want around—there were stories of his Mason jars being impounded at Customs.

His son, Gordon Fox (who would soon become fixated in extramarital passion for me), had no interest in *The Fruitarian*, or, it at first appeared, in any of his dad's eccentric ways. Gordon Fox oversaw the entire enterprise. If he had a pet project, it was drab little *Input*, a magazine for computer programmers.

∾

My first close friendship at Fox-MacKneill developed with Dolores Lester, who wrote the cover lines and edited manuscripts for *AS* and *OS*. I met Dolores in Mr. Marrone's office, where she was reciting, in a flute-like voice, some suggestions for our next issue:

"I Spit on the Sheriff's Grave!"

Marrone loved "dialogue." "I think the spoken word has an immediacy which is well suited to our publications."

Dialogue issued from the mouths of lawman and killer alike, resulting in a "Yes, I Can. . . ." "No, You Can't. . . ." duet.

"I'll Kill, Kill, and Kill Again."

"You Can't Kill a Cop in Pine Bluff, Arkansas!"

Very rarely, there was a yelp from the victim herself: "He Cut My Throat with a Straight-edge Razor!"

Marrone had been displeased with Dolores's original reading, and suggested she try the same title, but express it in the "police voice."

Dolores took a breath and squeaked: "Let's Nail the Texas Torso Killer!"

"That's better." Marrone smiled, and so did Dolores. I learned later that she wanted to be a playwright and thought this might be a shortcut.

Lovely Dolores. Poor Dolores. I still feel sad when I think of her. You can't imagine a more beautiful girl, although hers was a doomed, droopy beauty. With her thin wrists and long, limp, blond hair, Dolores could have played Ophelia at a moment's notice. She was in love with an actor who hadn't called her in two years. "He will call, I just know he will," she kept saying. In the meantime, she had a habit of smiling, and giggling softly at her left shoulder. We realized she was talking to "Bill," only when it was too late.

Poor baby. Well, I'll tell you what happened to Dolores later on. . . .

The person who really colored my experience in publishing was Antoinette "Tina" Rossini, the editor of *Video Secrets*, a magazine that offers inside peeks into the love lives of game-show hosts.

I met Tina Rossini in the ladies' room. Specifically, I was disassembling the toilet paper squares that I had dealt out along the seat, in a manner taught to me by my mother, when I heard a husky voice say:

"Well, finally found a guy who knows how to diddle clit."

I froze. Never, ever had I heard a woman say such a thing. Yet, I realized, as she went on, those were the very words I'd been waiting to hear.

"He knew how to diddle it. . . . He knew which side . . . how hard, and in which direction—semicircle toward the right."

As discreetly as I could, I left my stall and joined the

group of women before the mirror. Tina Rossini was holding forth on her favorite subject. Within two minutes, I knew much of her intimate history.

She had been married twice and divorced twice by men she referred to only as "Creepo One" and "Creepo Two." "Creepo One didn't know I had a clit . . . and Creepo Two didn't care."

I observed Tina in the mirror as she spoke, her bright red mouth going a mile a minute. I guessed her age at late thirties, but found out later she was just thirty. The wear and tear had been hard on her, especially around the eyes.

Something happens to women who have slept with what Tina called "the multitudes"—and it happens around the eyes, I think. Each time they see a new male organ, another line is etched.

People tell me I look younger than my years, and I suppose my lack of experience can account for that, although the marriage left me with one eyebag and a comma next to my mouth. My later loves didn't cause that many wrinkles, but added a certain puffiness to my lids.

The furrow you see on my forehead happened on my first night with Paul Whiting. I must have been so shocked that my forehead never did smooth down. But the real damage—the whistle marks over my lip—from pleading—resulted from my long affair with the National Book Award nominee, Julian D. Sarkoff.

Anyway, Tina Rossini's face was crisscrossed with wrinkles. Her sun-worshiping vacations with Club Med on Guadeloupe hadn't helped either. Permanently tan, her skin seemed shaded by deep, maroon blood.

Not really attractive, somehow that's just what she was: attractive. Her voice was all brass, her manner all jut and bounce. Her breasts preceded her by about four inches, although, later, I was to see them slump below her waist.

There was always sound effects around Tina: her clacking bracelets, her banging clogs. Mostly though, there was her voice:

"Nine million bodies in the naked city," she told me after work as we walked through Grand Central Station. "Look at 'em: nine million bodies."

I looked: Massive numbers of men rode toward us on escalators. "Nine million, and only a few can pass. You could stand here for an hour and not see a good one. I know. I've done it. You got to look, look, look. When you see a possible, imagine running your lips over him. That's the test. If you can get past that, the rest is a snap. But you got to sift through the multitudes to get at the good ones. How many you think I had to go through to get maybe sixteen, seventeen winners? Guess."

"Twenty?"

Tina laughed. She raised her hands to show finger-counting. Opening and closing her hands, she seemed to conduct the crowd of commuters rushing toward us.

I computed, in my head, that she had slept with "one hundred and eighty-seven?"

"And most of them were stinkos. I'll show you my file sometime. I rate everybody—from 'Yccch' to 'Terrific.' Most men fall into a category I call 'Eh.' "

We squeezed through turnstiles. "Eh?" I asked.

"Yeah. That's what I say after one of those: 'Eh.' But I'm getting better at picking them."

We descended to the dark at the bottom of the stairs. Subway trains thundered in, making it slightly difficult to hear Tina:

"How many have *you* had?"

Our train squealed open, and Tina and I wedged ourselves through the one open door. Behind me, I felt the thrust of either an umbrella tip or the Pervert's diabolically pointed penis.

When we hung, side by side, from handles, I confessed to Tina that I had not known that many men. "C'mon. How many?" she pressed. "You can tell me."

I struggled to free the hand pinned to my side. I held up two, then three fingers. "I'm not sure whether to count one."

"Jesus—only three or four. Where've you been?"

Another suspicious jab at my behind made me jump. Something was going on back there.

The Pervert flashed me a salivated gold-toothed grin. I tried to see if he was exposing himself, but a newspaper with the headline "Mother Chews Dog, Lover to Death, then Bakes Pies," obscured my vision.

The train lurched, and I maneuvered my rear end so that it faced a door. "I'm looking for someone special," I explained to Tina.

Another lurch, and Tina and I skidded in opposite directions. "In New York?

"Well," she said, when she'd finished laughing, "if you ever get horny, come with me some night. When I get horny, I go to Mr. Laffs or someplace."

The Loner—at Mr. Laffs? I didn't think so.

While the train stalled, I told Tina that I had to wait for a special man, and that when I was with him, I'd feel a little shiver.

"Um, the pre-orgaz."

"I guess I need a slow buildup."

Around us, the crowd was heating up. Sweat beads broke out on some faces, and one man complained "C'mon, assholes, move this thing already."

"Don't wait for the slow buildup," Tina urged. "There isn't time in New York. I wasted two years on Creepo One and one year on Creepo Two. You have to run through them fast. And don't judge it by how they look. Some of the repulsive ones turn out to be the best. You got to keep an open mind."

The train moved two feet, and people cheered. Then it ground to another stop. "I have felt a few shivers, and a funny, little *unfolding*. . . ."

Tina looked interested. "Has it paid off?"

"Not really, but I know it will. I must not give up."

The train started, with a sudden humping motion, then tore into the Fifth Avenue station. I departed, en route to the Art Students League and Paul Whiting.

That night, in Zum Zum's, Paul sipped his coffee and said, "All right, Alice, I hope you have no regrets."

My blushing and downcast looks at my *apfeltorten* had worn him down.

There was, he went on to explain, a slight problem that would delay us for a few days. I did not want to pry, so I smiled and said that that was fine.

A lover of his reputation, I assumed, had to juggle a sexual calendar. No doubt, he was just rearranging his schedule to fit me in. I learned later that he was having massive injections of steroids to treat an arthritic condition that prevented him from bending over, or from straightening up.

~

At last, he nodded to me in class. And I knew that tonight was our night. I nodded back, having taken the precaution of applying contraceptive cream and a heavy body lotion.

By the time class ended, my knees were knocking together.

I led him up here. I had left the bed made up in my best sheets. (Oh, Darling, does it bother you hearing this? That what follows happened right here in this little bed? Oh, no, it mustn't—for as you'll soon understand, that night was a disaster—nothing like tonight.)

Ravi Shankar played on my record player. I lit some new, sixty-nine-cent tapers.

By candlelight, I undressed, undulating to the Ravi Shankar. Paul, still in his paint-splattered blue denims, sat on my bed and watched. I danced around the bed and managed not to trip, except once, over the cat's water dish.

I recovered, and continued to move to the music, shaking my foot slightly to dry it.

"So beautiful," he said in a new soft voice.

He went on, in a whisper, to compare me to Lily

Pons, to several famous Odalisques, and, in particular, to "In the Hindu Pose" by Matisse.

Paul never stopped whispering. Throughout the next hours, he murmured bulletins: "God, we're divine. The way we're moving. We were made to fit together . . . like this. . . ."

I smiled and nodded in response to these whispers. But something was bothering me, a nagging at the back of my mind. I couldn't let the idea surface while he was there, but I knew I would confront it later. Something definitely was wrong.

At the close, Paul kissed my forehead and made his concluding statement: "We were beautiful."

❧

Then he was gone, tiptoed back to his loft in SoHo.

I lay flattened for a few minutes. Then, sure he had really gone, I sprang up and double-locked my door. *It can't be*, I thought, as I raced around, touching familiar objects. *It just can't be.*

Running about, I touched the most solid pieces of furniture in the room: an oak bureau and an old bentwood rocker. At last, I ended up before my heavy mahogany-framed mirror, there to confront my newly wrinkled forehead, and the truth.

❧

As I washed the dishes from a late snack I'd shared with Paul, I reviewed the outtakes of our evening.

I had imagined that I would need hours, years, perhaps a lifetime to explore Paul Whiting. As it turned out, I could have finished in five minutes.

Actually, the truth was even worse than that: I could have finished before I started. The first shock: when he slowly unbuckled his cowboy belt, and let his paint-splattered jeans fall.

His body doesn't matter, I lectured myself, as he unsnapped the pearl buttons on his denim shirt and revealed the twin droop of what appeared to be furry breasts.

I love his spirit, I love his mind, were my thoughts as I rushed in to kiss his defects.

See, I don't mind these gray-furred flab breasts . . . or this damp crease beneath them. I love your insight, your talent, so this mountainous white belly does not bother me . . . or those brown splotches on your skin.

Oh, poor Love—the wither of age is upon your thighs, also . . . and you wear, here and there, garnet clusters of blood cysts. I suppose those are permanent.

"I love you," Paul sighed.

"And I . . . you."

But what is this coolness? This molded damp? I knew you were old. But cold?

We have come to the bottom: His penis may no longer be alive.

Omigod, face to face with it, I see it lies in a sullen curl. *Why such a crustacean white? How long since it's seen daylight?*

It stirs. Recoiling. Still, that's movement. Hope. It's just been sleeping. Now it's been irritated and rolled over on its side. That's understandable.

Give it time. It will respond.

Moody and inert, that appendage went along, only reluctantly, with what Paul Whiting had in mind. Am I crazy? It's possible. I kept thinking that I was crazy all through that session.

As Paul flipped me from one pose to another, it seemed as if we were working in one of those soft-core films where specific acts appear real to the audience but that the performers know are simulated.

Poor Paul. How I wish I hadn't looked up and caught that expression on his face. I wanted to cry "Cut! . . . I didn't see that!" but I had seen:

His lips twisted in concentration, as when, in class, he had grappled with a dehydrated tube of burnt sienna. The cap would not come off, no matter how he twisted. Instead, the tube pretzeled, leaking oil from its cracked side.

This went much the same way: Paul straining his entire body, but his own thick white tube buckling at the entry.

Poor Darling, I addressed him in my mind, *This doesn't matter. Not one drop.* I cupped his face in my hands and brought his lips down to mine.

He rammed his tongue down my esophagus. What was that? Why do that so hard and deep? Compensation?

Down below, he continued to stuff himself into me, in stages, the way firemen repack their hose. He groaned. I could see what an effort it was. I patted his back. My hand slid, down a cold, wet crevasse. I remembered rock-climbing in rain.

How would this act end? Or would we slip and slide around this cliff forever?

A raucous cry sounded over my head. I looked up: My beloved art teacher's face had knotted . . . his mouth stretched open. . . . What agony.

Then, the plummet down, down . . . into a briny silence.

Pinned under his damp weight, I wondered, *What kind of cry was that? Had he really screamed "Oh, Death!"?*

My poor Love. What men went through. The burden on all of them. *How easy it is for me*, I reflected; *all I have to do is splay apart for at least passable congress to occur.*

I had seen movies. Read books. Now, as the tide of disaster rolled over my bed, I knew what to expect.

The man huddles and apologizes. Says something like, "I'm sorry. I was no good." Or, "I'm not a real man anymore."

Well, the tide rolled in, and the tide rolled out. I waited. Then, at last, Paul, never again the craved-for Paul, but this new clammy Paul, raised up on his palms and stared resignedly down at me. A small pocket of humidity formed between us. Our thighs, ungluing, squealed.

"How are you?" he asked.

"Fine."

"You'll never have it again like this."

∿

Later, during a Muenster cheese and wine picnic on my carpet, Paul Whiting explained, "The anticipation . . . the adventure of the unknown lifted us to the ultimate heights." He went on to say, eating with gusto, "It'll never again be quite so thrilling." He munched a cracker. "Only satisfying."

Then he took the biscuit from my hand and suggested, as if in a daring mood:

"Again?"

∿

Anxious that he never feel inadequate, I committed myself to a three-times-weekly schedule. And so our long, simulated affair began.

∿

𝒲hy three times a week? Well, one of the charter beliefs of our little club was that his sexual desires needed satisfying every few days. "If I don't have you, I feel pent up—restless. I can't concentrate."

A man, he explained, has "needs."

❧

I continued in Photo-realism I, but my enthusiasm waned. In my "Study of a Disconnected Telephone," Paul accused me of injecting my own mood and feelings. In front of everyone, he said I had "slipped into abstraction."

On my four nights at home, I plunged my hands back into clay. How good the terra-cotta felt as it oozed between my fingers. Working nonstop, I turned out several statuettes of goatishly handsome fauns.

The Dream, by the way, continued, with one key difference. I still sat on a lap. The long male organ still unraveled. But when I looked up, where Paul Whiting's sage, seamed face had been, there was only a blank.

Paul was a mistake.

I realize that now, but then I did not fully appreciate the fact. I kept telling myself that our problem would straighten itself out. How we kid ourselves. My own style suffered: I needed a stiffer spoke upon which to turn. A limpness and clamminess seemed to spread from Paul to me.

We went to art galleries, museums, and a party where Larry Rivers was. Paul gave me a Matisse print. I gave him a bathrobe (extra large). Because he found my apartment too depressing, we simulated our affair in his impressive plant- and light-filled loft in SoHo. Actually, it wasn't in SoHo, but closer to NoHo. A long trek for me on the BMT.

∽

While personal happiness eluded me, professional success was almost forced upon me at *Actual Slayings*. Marrone recognized my abilities. I worked on choice assignments: multiple-slaying layouts, and the special feature, "The Cop of the Month."

"The Cop of the Month" was a lawman who had distinguished himself in the line of duty. The editors chose "The Cop of the Month" from a portfolio of candidates nominated by local police departments all over the United States. The winner was awarded an *Actual Slayings* badge, a certificate, and a full-page spread of text and photos celebrating his achievements.

The first "Cop" layout I arranged starred one Dwayne Purvis, Jr., sheriff of Parker County, West Virginia. He had gunned down two moonshiners and confiscated their "white lightning."

As I mounted his photo—Dwayne was leaning against his sheriff's car—I read in the text that his avowed goal in law enforcement was to "bring back the death penalty . . . throw the fear of the Lord into those scum who are destroying West Virginia's decent towns and cities."

We at *Actual Slayings* also editorialized in favor of bringing back capital punishment. "There was an urgency to our stories back when the perpetrators were executed," reminisced Mr. Marrone.

Denny, too, longed for those days, when he could run a handsome photo of the Sing Sing electric chair under the caption: "Mr. Sparky."

Actually, we later ran the "Mr. Sparky" feature anyway—just to keep up reader interest.

One afternoon, as I air-brushed Sheriff Dwayne Purvis's paunch and kidded with Denny, we were interrupted by the sudden appearance of the president of Fox-MacKneill, Gordon Fox.

"What's going on in here?" he wanted to know.

I looked up and saw The Gray Man. His ability to speak without moving his lips impressed me.

"Did I hear laughing?"

Denny and I lowered our heads.

Gordon fixed me with his mentholated stare. "Try to keep it down in here. They're trying to put out a magazine next door."

Gordon Fox dropped in almost every day after that. He stood over me as I worked. His attitude remained disapproving.

"He's dying for you," explained Tina Rossini. "All he can think about is how he's going to put it in you."

During a long hair-combing session in the ladies' room, Tina went on to explain that Gordon Fox became infatuated with a new girl every few years. "You'll see," she predicted, "he'll approach you about 'profit sharing.' That means fucking."

It didn't seem possible, but Tina Rossini was right.

❦

I had entered into a triangular friendship with Dolores Lester and Tina Rossini. Dubbed "The Three Musketeers" at Fox-MacKneill, we met whenever possible: on the coffee line; in Guido's, the greasy spoon on the main floor; and in the ladies' room.

Every morning we traded ritual greetings.

"Hi, do I look fat?"

"No. Do I?"

"No."

"I wish I had your hips."

"I wish I had your chest."

"I'll trade you."

"Any time."

We gathered in the ladies' room as women have gathered at cisterns and menstrual huts, to ask the eternal questions: Do men ever really fall in love? Why are they so mean when we're so sweet? Where are the real men? (In Nova Scotia?)

The married women bemoaned their husbands' failings: "He drinks. He goes out. He gambles. He hits." But, eternalest of all questions: *Who else is there?*

Women without men sometimes mistook men as "the answer." These women worked on getting the men as the others dreamed of getting rid of them. Dolores continually brooded, "Why hasn't Bill called? It's been two years, but I know he loves me. Do you think he was afraid of getting serious?"

"Jee-sus," was Tina Rossini's answer. "Forget that prick."

Two years was a long time to carry the torch, but Dolores kept it from going out. She burst in daily with new developments: "I thought I saw him on the bus, but it wasn't Bill. It was his coat, and his hair—all curly and black."

And, "I dreamed Bill came back to me last night. He stood in my door. He was wearing shining armor. And he said, 'Dolores, I still love you.'"

There were also anniversaries: "Two years ago today, Bill was still with me. We had chestnuts in Central Park and talked to a squirrel."

Dolores still celebrated Bill's birthday—by sitting in front of his picture and communicating "Happy Birthday" telepathically.

She dredged up the heart-cracking details: "He called me 'Button.' He wouldn't have called me 'Button' if he didn't love me, would he?"

"He's a fucking asshole and a prick," was all Tina would say. But she said it softly, and sometimes let Dolores have a fattening cookie.

My occasional conversations alone with Dolores were quite different from those in which Tina participated. With me, Dolores worked more toward a pragmatic course of action to win back Bill: "Should I call him? Send him a funny card: 'Why don't you call me?' Or should I stand outside his building and make it look like an accidental meeting?"

"I don't know, I don't know," was my advice. Privately, I thought Dolores was barking up the wrong tree, but I didn't want to hurt her feelings. I wondered how she could have let herself in for that much pain. Little did I know that Dolores was in good shape compared to the way I would be—lying in state by my phone for the NBA Award nominee, Julian D. Sarkoff, to call.

But that treat was still a week or two away.

The strongest thread in the fabric of the three-way friendship among Dolores, Tina, and myself, was Tina's running narration of the adventures of Old Snapper—Old Snapper being nothing less than Tina Rossini's vagina.

"Well, Old Snapper got some action last night," was her standard opener. "It was just a cocktail weenie, not enough for Old Snapper to really get a grip on."

Old Snapper needed, I learned in a ladies' room confab, "a nice fat braunschweiger to feel full."

"Creepo One had a nice braunschweiger, but he didn't know how to swing it."

Tina described every sexual partner she had ever "enjoyed" in pungent detail. At Guido's lunch counter, as we sat eating their revolting diet platters, Tina told us that her marriage to Creepo Two had dissolved because of a medical anomaly.

"He was half nutted. Only one ball had descended, and this bothered Creepo Two. He worried night and day about having only one nut in his bag. The other one was stuck up in him someplace, and when doctors tried to pull it down, that ball just bounced right back up and out of reach. I spent a whole year telling Creepo Two that it was okay to have one ball—that it was even better. It was unique, you know. Only who was I kidding? I missed that other nut more than he did. I kept squeezing his bag, and it felt real weird—incomplete, you know."

Dolores and I nodded our understanding.

"I left him in a fight over doing dishes. But, who knows, maybe that nut was at the bottom of it."

After her second divorce, Tina had settled into a long affair with a man who wore pinkie rings and worked at a mystery job. "He bought me all kinds of dresses, wigs, jewelry. Every night he wanted me to pretend I was a new girl. So I'd get all dolled up— blond wig, a different style of dress—the works. You know, I felt kind of sorry for him, because eventually I had to take it all off, and there was the same Old Snapper, no matter what kind of package it was in. Yeah. The same Old Snapper."

Following that romance, Tina Rossini decided to "play the field." She scoured the bars, hunting up action for Old Snapper. These days, she preferred to keep her encounters impersonal.

"Met a good one last night," she reported during one coffee break. "Went back to his apartment. He knew how to diddle clit. He diddled it, then played with Old Snapper. Even put some Cool 'n' Creamy pudding in, and lapped it up. Then I licked Skippy peanut butter— the chunky kind—off him. Finally, I put tapioca in my mouth and told him, he could . . ."

Well, I won't go on; needless to say, I was shocked, if fascinated, by the exploits of Tina and Old Snapper. Particularly the tapioca incident, which Tina wrapped up with: "Now, I don't know if I'll give him my phone number."

When Dolores crept into my office later, she whispered that she too had been appalled at Tina's anecdote. "Did you ever do any of those things—with pudding and peanut butter?"

I told her that I hadn't.

"There has to be love." Her eyes shone.

I expressed my own belief that I hoped that was true, but that "Lately, I've begun to doubt the power of love. Still, I think I'll give it one more chance. Then, if it doesn't work out, I'll consider anonymous tapiocas."

She said: *No*, that I mustn't, because when she first met Bill, she had felt "all static electricity between us."

She fluttered her thin fingers through the air to demonstrate: "It went *tchi tchi tchi tchi*. There were little sparks. It happens. You must not give up." She fluttered again: "*tchi tchi tchi.*"

At night, with Paul Whiting, I waited for some sign that he knew we performed a charade. I waited in vain. He never said a word, or even threw a wink—no clue that he was anything less than a tiger in bed. He even apologized one night for "getting too carried away. I didn't hurt you, did I?"

If only he had let down his "illusion," maybe we could have continued, even as lovers, and avoided the disaster that occurred. . . . But he would not confront the reality.

Fearful that I was losing my sanity, I agreed to go "man hunting" one night with Tina Rossini. I was not yet ready to think in terms of "Old Snapper," but I wanted something substantial.

I got it.

Okay, Now, we've come to it. The great love, the ridiculous obsession, the love that brought me to my knees and turned my brains to fettuccine.

Please don't let what I am about to tell you influence your opinion of the literary genius Julian D. Sarkoff. In spite of everything he did to me, I still hold that his novels, *Naked Faces* and *Mortal Coils*, are two of the finest studies of the human condition ever written. Did you happen to catch an off-Broadway play, *Injured Parties?*

I'm surprised. It was quite a hit. Well, surely you read the book for which he was nominated for the NBA Award—his only major nonfiction work, *Turned Off, A History of Alienation in Contemporary America.*

You read "in" it? Well, I really recommend you read it all the way through. The compassion. The insight.

What the *Atlantic Monthly* review called "the suppressed tenderness."

He has written other works, stories and tone poems that I won't go into now but that I sought out in the basements of second-hand book stores and among yellowed card catalogues. Maddened by love, I even went into microfilm. But I'm getting ahead of myself.

Did I say "love"? I didn't mean to. It wasn't real love, clean and sensible, which I now know with you, but some sick force.

He was dark as only Devils are. . . . When I first saw him, he actually wore black leather. There was even a hideous horned amulet around his neck. Smoke seemed to waft up from his head (actually there was a cigar).

I took one look at Julian D. Sarkoff and told myself: "Say hello to trouble. There will be crying in a phone booth over this one."

And—so strong is the gift of prophecy in such cases —that I did, indeed, end up sobbing in a phone booth. Me!

It was Fate, all right. Not Chance. Chance and Fate are not the same. It was Chance that entrapped me in marriage and the world of Sportorama. Chance that led me to Suffern. And Chance that landed me in Paul Whiting's class and bed.

With Chance you have a chance. It may be difficult, but you can decide your own moves. Take a break, forget the whole thing. But when it's Fate, you have to go along. What's the use?

Whenever Julian D. Sarkoff was involved, strange forces wreaked havoc with my life. Fate's heavy hand clopped me on the back of the neck. There were horoscopes (which I don't believe in) that were accurate to the minutest detail. Dreams that were re-enacted in broad daylight. Coincidences (?) Meetings—against which the odds were a million to one.

I discovered that his birthday was the same as my father's. And there was more, much more.

I'm just warming up for this one. Oh, this is still getting me a little. Thank God you're here. We'll exorcise this *dybbuk* together. I'm afraid if I hadn't met you, I might still be having those impossible dialogues in my head. You know the kind—when you have to speak both parts because the other person doesn't want to have anything to do with you.

❧

I should have known better. The stories abounded: He played with women, then left them without warning—usually at some poignant, "blossoming" moment. The women (or girls, for he liked them young and tender) then took to drink, drugs, or acute nervous collapse. There was one reported case of psychoneurotic eczema. He was a vessel of pain and minor inflammation. He hurt.

❧

I would have avoided him if I could. But Fate, and Tina Rossini, walked me, arm in arm, into the bar restaurant now known as Johnny's Steak Casino, but then still called Patty's, and, of course, there he was.

Tina had led me on one or two other "man getting" expeditions. The "man getting" always went the same way: Tina grabbed a man and dragged him home to appease Old Snapper. I took the subway home alone.

In the bars, my leper's bell of loneliness tinkled away. I needed someone, and, of course, that smells worse than Woolworth's perfume. Tina lectured me: "That desperate look is a turn-off. Smile."

I smiled.

If a man did approach, I didn't know what to do. I dropped all conversational balls that were tossed to me. Sometimes, if the man looked nervous, I could chat a bit. But if he was handsome and self-assured, I had to cough and look away. Sometimes my left eyelid blinked on its own.

This was the condition I was in—left eyelid blinking—when I spotted Julian D. Sarkoff.

What I remembered is how he looked around—with absolutely no interest. And his stance—framed in a stucco arch—he stood there for a minute. Braced for something . . . firm and apart.

I was reminded, of course, of "Poseidon," in the basement of the Metropolitan Museum of Art—Poseidon, whose oxidized bronze nudity had (coincidentally?) given me, at age eight, my first information of the adult male member.

I must have made a sound, because Tina followed my gaze, saw Julian Sarkoff, and hit my arm. "No. Anyone but him."

"I like him."

Oh, sure, even in those first seconds, the warnings were there. In Sarkoff's case the warnings were two young girls hanging on his elbows.

I can overlook them, I thought, even though, as it happened, they were very large girls. Show-biz types. Six-foot-tall beauties.

Their faces unmarred by thought, the two girls tossed their hair. They danced slightly, although there was no music. Both girls were iridescent blondes. One girl had painted herself to look wicked: blood-lipped and black-eyed. The other had preserved a milkmaid freshness. I discovered later that both girls were teen-aged Latvian models imported by a famous model agency after an exhausting search of all the Baltic states.

Sarkoff and the girls were joined by a group of short men attired in studded cowboy costumes and safari suits. The blondes leaped toward the shorter men, then fell back to flank Sarkoff. The men smacked Sarkoff's shoulders. Because the men were short, they had to reach up to do their smacking. They looked to be in love with him, hopeful that by being near him they might somehow grow taller and acquire his more vivid coloring.

Oh, that face—inked in the ancestral black, Cyrillic

script. His eyebrows alone marked him a man to reckon with.

"Who is he?" I asked Tina, for I did not yet know the name of the one who would undo me.

"J. D. Sarkoff."

I had to concentrate; then it hit me:

"The writer?"

"The prick."

He moved closer to the bar, where Tina and I sat on shaky stools. Tina went on: "Forget him. Look at that. Those girls. That hideous amulet around his neck. The disgusting way his shirt is deliberately unbuttoned. Those tasteless trousers. You can see a quarter in his pocket."

"A nickel," I corrected. Then I averted my gaze, for the NBA nominee's trousers were on the snug side and defined not only the Indian head side of a nickel, but also Sarkoff's manhood, which even at a quick take I noticed was in interesting shape.

And he can write, too, I thought.

I felt my body tilt, in a sexual tropism, toward him, who was now being greeted by the nickname "Julie Boolie."

Tina pulled me back. "Sometimes he sleeps with two or three at a time. You know what that means."

"What?"

"Fag."

As I watched, the two blondes nuzzled him around the neck. He patted them and motioned to two bar stools. The blondes hopped up on them.

"He's sweet and sensitive underneath," I told Tina. "And you can see he's lonely."

"Ugg. I'm gonna puke. Look at that amulet. It probably has dope in it."

Sarkoff cracked open what looked like a Tahitian fertility god's grinning mouth and sniffed some gas that it emitted. Then, with a snort, he threw back his head and downed a double Bourbon.

You won't need that when you have me, I silently told him.

Tina's voice acquired a rasp. "He hurt two girls I know: Joyce Wupchik and Carol Henning, two beautiful, sexy, bright girls. Joyce Wupchik is the best PR girl in town, and Carol Henning was a Ph.D. in abnormal psychology."

"So?"

"So Joyce Wupchik ended up in Payne Whitney for two weeks. Carol Henning is still standing on one leg up at Rockland State. They say she shits all over herself—and that's with a Ph.D."

Tina's words were wise ones, but they slid off me. Try to tell one lemming not to go off the cliff with the others. Ask a sloth to step out of the La Brea tar pit.

I was a goner.

Here comes the really revolting part: The wicked blonde, the one with the blood lips, jumped from her stool onto Sarkoff's lap. She wrapped her legs around him and licked his inner ear: slow, circular lips—a nauseating display that should never have occurred in public. Yet I knew that if there had been some socially acceptable way to knock her off his lap and jump on myself, I would not have hesitated. I'd have approached him then if Tina Rossini hadn't dragged me from Patty's and out into a damp spring night.

Tina insisted that she telephone Deedee McKay, who had slept with everyone in the East Seventies and Eighties and surely would be able to give the real dope on Sarkoff. "I just know he's a fag or a sickie. If Deedee McKay says so, will you listen?"

I waited outside the street phone booth while Tina called Deedee. Tina motioned me to wait a few minutes: Deedee was going through her Rolodex, or something.

"She had him in '68," Tina called out, then bent her head back down to the receiver.

Just because he wasn't good with Deedee McKay doesn't mean he wouldn't be wonderful with me.

Tina came out of the booth. She looked dejected.

"Well? Well?" I wanted to know.

Her voice was dull: *"Magnifico."*

Magnífico. I ran back to Patty's where everyone waited, as in a sepia print, just as I'd left them: Sarkoff, the Visconti blondes, the subordinate males. As I walked toward him, a song blared forth from some mysterious source, echoing my very thoughts:

> Take the ribbon from my hair
> Shake it loose, and let it fall
> I don't care what's right or wrong
> I won't try to understand
> Let the devil take tomorrow
> But tonight I need a friend

Sarkoff looked up. His hooded eyes flicked over my secondary sex characteristics. Then: a direct stare.

I responded with a shiver, my most soul-racking to date. A rivulet of passion started down my inner thigh.

Terrified, I ran backward out of Patty's.

Sarkoff did not come after me. As I heard from Tina the next morning on the coffee line, Sarkoff had stayed, getting into heated debate with the bartender of the amount of aquavit in the two Latvian girls' drinks.

❧

Well, there would be another night. I was not ready. He was preoccupied.

I will come back in top form, I vowed.

❧

There followed a season of preparation. I worked on mind and body. There is still a muscle on the back of my thigh, that I owe to Sarkoff, and the series of leg extensions that I performed, alone on my living room rug, in order to attract his attention at some later date. More important still, locked in my brain are his literary masterpieces, which I read in a fever.

I was to become more zealous, but I was no slouch even on that first day of my commitment to Julian Sarkoff. Staggering under the weight of his heavy tomes, I went straight from the public library to Marboro's, to see if my new love's latest opus had, by some chance, been remaindered.

It had, and with mixed emotion I paid two dollars less than the publisher's list price for *Turned Off: A History of Alienation in Contemporary America*. The fattest of Sarkoff's books, *Turned Off* offered, in addition to its own bulk, a dust-jacket photo of Sarkoff in a safari jacket and aviator shades, and a list of promising blurbs:

"He writes with powerful thrust, won't let the reader go. . . ." *Publishers Weekly*.

"Shakes up all our preconceived ideas of modern man and his morality. Or lack of it." *Catholic Transcript*.

"The ultimate explosion: Sarkoff can go deep." *Cleveland Press*.

Gee, I thought, *he's going to be terrific*.

Wandering around Marboro's a while longer, encouraged by the Tijuana Brass on their Muzak system, I was stopped in my tracks by a new book display with the banner:

"Unlucky in love? Check Out Your Next Mate Through *Erotic-scopes*."

Skeptic that I am, I did not buy *Erotic-scopes* but read it standing up in the aisle. My first impression of the author, Sybil Rasmussen, was that she was full of what Tina Rossini called "crapola." Then I checked out my husband's sign: Scorpio.

"He'll scuttle over you . . . leave crescent-shaped wounds on your flesh."

A *coincidence*, I thought, flipping on to the tooter in Cancer: "This crab will never leave you alone . . . although he pretends not to be interested."

Hmmmm . . . I moved on to Paul Whiting, in Pisces: "Don't be surprised if this cold fish flops out on the shores of love."

Realizing I should give Sybil Rasmussen a chance, I

bent the spine of *Erotic-scopes* while reading "The Love Habits of Leo"—for Julian Sarkoff, according to his profile in Who's Who in Contemporary American Literature, had been born under the sign of "King of the Jungle."

At first I thought Sybil Rasmussen hedged about Sarkoff: "He's passive and ferocious." Huh? "He's eager and reluctant."

About to toss the book aside, I couldn't help reading: "So you've found yourself a lion, eh? He has a massive head, powerful shoulders, and thick, muscular haunches, no? He looks about him with an air of sovereignty, yes?"

That's more like it, I thought; Sybil continued:

"You will not tame Leo! This beast has the strongest sense of his territory. If you wish to mate with Leo, you must hunt him down in his lair."

Patty's.

"How will he mate with you? You will hear the Lion roar! You will feel his stiff whiskers, his long, sandpaper tongue. He will tussle with you, maul you with his paws. In his lust, he will mount you from the rear . . . the front . . . the side, his thrusts so strong and deep, you fear you will be rent apart. His fuzzy body will crush you. Only the strongest signs in the zodiac dare mate with this wild animal!"

What about me? I turned to the *Erotic-scope* crosscheck and found that it would be "touch and go between the Lion and the Virgin. Perhaps with a strong rising sign, you can hold your own. Remember: Leo loves to be petted. Rub him under the throat, along his flanks, especially his tail . . . and then you will hear your Leo *purr*."

Flipping back to "Pleasing a Leo," I read more: "He loves earth smells, is drawn to high grasses."

Well, who knew?

The last section, "What Leo Will Do to You," made my knees buckle: "He has a big mouth, and this cat loves to use it."

This is Sarkoff, I realized.

❦

On my nights alone at home, I pored over my other required reading: Sarkoff's complete works. Murmuring all the way, *This is it. Oh, yes, yes, yes.* So closely did our subconscious minds work that I seemed to be reading my own thoughts.

I shared all of his interests except high-stakes gambling and casual sexual intercourse. The high-stakes gambling I could accept, but the casual sexual intercourse had me worried.

In his novels, Sarkoff's alterego, Kevin O'Casey, enjoyed sex with prostitutes, teen-age girls, and the mentally disabled. Kevin O'Casey kept, under his bed, Emko aerosol cans to spray into his transient lovers.

How sad for you, my Angel, I thought, reading the recurrent sprayings in *Mortal Coils.*

Meanwhile, a fever heated up my brain.

What would Julian D. Sarkoff be like in what he called "love's arena"? Tender? Rough? Crazed? Would he be like his Erotic-scope? Or like his depressed protagonist?

I learned shortly that Sybil Rasmussen had predicted him accurately; but for the last month of a damp spring, I chafed with curiosity.

❦

Pleading fatigue and overwork, I called Paul Whiting and tried to beg out of our nebulous affair. He insisted he couldn't live without me. "A man has needs," he repeated.

I agreed to see him, but held the line at one simulated session per week. He began to feed me expensive French cheeses, and old wine. One night, he cooked: an authentic *boudin*, blood sausage of France.

❦

Which didn't help my diet—although I could have certain cheeses and meats, if I did not eat them with carbohydrates. I'd been on the Atkins diet ever since I'd read, in *Naked Faces*, that "Kevin O'Casey loved his women lean. He liked to feel their bones."

Well, he'd have to dig down pretty deep to feel my bones, although, I was by no means a fatso. No one would call 125 pounds fat—okay, 128, tops.

Still, since my divorce I'd been eating more, especially when no one was looking. And I now wore a small holster of fat along my hips.

These are holding me back, I thought, grabbing them.

So I threw myself into what Atkins called "ketosis," a rather blah state in which I excreted "ketones" through my pores and other places. I didn't love the thought of those ketones, but I was losing weight fast. Soon, my clothes hung and my wristwatch fell off, suddenly too large for my emaciated little wrist.

There were side effects: a stinging breath, and a tendency to reel down the corridors at the office. I also heard buzzing in my head. I sometimes thought my phone was ringing when it wasn't.

Also: Opponents of the Atkins diet said it turned your brain to a useless pulp in one year. But I didn't plan to stay in ketosis that long—just long enough to see my hip bones. Then I'd swing into "The Cellulite Diet," which worked on an opposing principle but would "get rid of lumps 'n' bumps and the fat you can't see."

I could see "the fat you can't see" if I went looking for it, but I didn't want to squeeze my thighs as advised. Instead, I bought the recommended harsh loofah and followed the prescribed self-flagellation technique.

Oh, brother, I realized, striking out at my thighs with a loofah, *this is going to be a long haul, but Julian D. Sarkoff will be worth it.*

At last, skinny, and wearing a dress I made myself, I returned to Patty's and my appointment with destiny. By this time, it was summer: a New York summer that made my thighs stick and my hair curl. A night so humid, my blood moved only downward in slow, turgid circles.

It won't be long now.

❧

He was there, in black, greeting members of his entourage. Girls lunged up to him, as in spawning season. I watched as he accepted their kisses. With a few apparent favorites, Sarkoff passed a crystal cube back and forth between their mouths.

I sat near him, searching for the right words. *Say something scintillating,* I ordered myself.

At last, I pushed a bowl of peanuts toward him, and said, "Would you care for a peanut?"

He did not turn to me, but acknowledged my offer by saying: "No."

His first words: "No." Not even "No thanks."

I slipped partially off my stool. The bar spun. Unable to think of another move, I sat in catatonic quiet, gripping an empty glass.

Sarkoff passed more sugar cubes on his tongue, and performed perfunctory squirmings with a succession of new, leggy arrivals. With the short men, Sarkoff spoke of the fact that his alienation quartet would undoubtedly be received with that of a lesser author, whose name I heard only as "Jerome."

"I have nothing against Jerome," I overheard Julian say, "but I don't want him in there with me."

During a sudden lull, he turned to me and said, "I'm just going through the motions here."

I knew it.

"This isn't me."

Of course not. I had seen through the disguise at once. The shades, the safari jac, the Hollywood blondes, the amulet, the mystery sugar cube—none of those had anything to do with him, with the real Julian Sarkoff.

He rotated his neck in sovereign anger, then lowered his massive head. A sound such as I've never heard from a human being tore from his throat:

"Arrrrrrgggggh."

You will hear the lion roar.

Then: "I've got to get the hell out of here."

I realized that he had to get "out"—not just of this bar, peopled by socialites, starlets, mannequins, literary loners, and their agents—but also out of this *life*.

Don't worry, Angel—I hurried after him—*I'll save you from all this.*

Outside, although the air hung heavy and still, Sarkoff stalked as if into a headwind. A knot of tension tied his head to his shoulders. Oh, the burden he carried there, all too visible to me, as I stumbled after him. Did he know he was not, after all, alone?

"I'm still here," I advised him.

He accepted my presence. We walked together. My platform Kork-Ease clopped on the pavement—echoing my heart. *It's really happening.* After the weeks of preparation, the reading, the frankfurters without rolls, here I was—really with him.

We roamed without a plan, somehow arriving at a rotted rim of the city. We sat on a piling, and watched the lights of the city tremble on the river.

"Some nights I get so sick of being Julian D. Sarkoff," he began, "I'd love to be anybody else." He raised his hand as if waving good-bye to someone in a bar. "So long, Julie Boolie, I'll see you around, I'm heading down to the Lion's Head. . . . But I can't forget, even for one second, that I'm Julian D. Sarkoff, and I'm on Book Three of my quartet. Do you know what it feels like to be on Book Three of a quartet?"

"Yes."

"I'm not going to be any good for anyone until I've got those fifty thousand words under my belt. Those fifty thousand words come first. Until I finish, I have nothing to give. You understand?"

"Yes."

"All I want is to be alone with my words. But I can't keep people off me." He checked his sleeve, as if someone might still be hanging there. "The women, especially. Every night. It's the same old story. The women all seem the same. They're even different in the same ways, if you know what I mean."

"Yes."

"French girls, Irish, Alsatian, All-American, Transalpine, Icelandic. I've even been with a Ubangi. Same old story. So I now know how to say 'fuck me' in Ubangi *'Uni cuni wikum.'* I guess that's something. From a cultural point of view. But it's no fun making women unhappy, believe me. And you know something?"

"Yes?"

"Women all cry in the same language. Oh, maybe Moroccans put an extra whine on it, but basically the tune is the same."

I'm different. But it was too soon to tell him. Let him discover that for himself.

He rocked, hugging his elbows, and sighed.

"None of it helps the ache."

The *ache. Oh, Darling*, I wanted to say, *don't worry. I'm here now.*

Later, we searched midtown for a special deli, one where he went when his Weltschmerz became unbearable.

"Just going to this deli seems to help." But we couldn't find it. For hours, we roamed wrong cross streets. All the while, I prayed we would never find that deli.

Time stop! I wanted to cry. *Let us wander forever. Give me this moment, this hour. Let me live in it. It is enough.*

"Here it is," Sarkoff said, shoving a revolving door. So eager. Hadn't he delighted in our extra ration of time?

The fluorescent light bore down on us. Once in our booth, Sarkoff slumped, resting his head on the yellow Formica table, which still bore tendrils of dried *Kugel.* He spoke again, in that nonstop style of his, pausing only to order a pastrami on rye. When the pastrami arrived, he ignored it for a long time. He had to tell me what was on his mind.

I wish I could remember what it was—I know only that "time," "death," and "ancestors" were mentioned, and that he came to an abrupt stop and paid me my first compliment:

"You're a great little listener."

I started to say something, but he went on:

"I'm glad we decided not to go the usual route. I mean, ordinarily, I'd have taken you straight to bed, and we'd have done the [he gave me his nibbler smile] *tango*. But this has really been more fun. I'm bored with the other, if you want to know. I'm too tired to ... *tango*."

When did we decide not to go the usual route?

"I can see the end in the beginning. The end is always bad. So I'm starting to think: Why start? The tears, the bad scenes ..."

He bit into a pickle, which forced him to pause. I jumped into the opening: "... the nagging, the accusations, the sense of disappointment, that blah feeling the morning after ..."

"The jealousy, the hostility, the lies," he resumed. He went after some potato salad with his fork.

"The name-calling, the nastiness," I continued.

"Yeah, I'm glad we're skipping those parts."

"Me too."

"So many friendships are ruined."

"Yes, I've ruined a few."

He put down the fork and the half-eaten pickle and reached to shake my hand. "Friends?"

Was it possible? I wondered, setting down my glass of Tab and returning his hard grasp.

"Friends," I whispered. My God, he was *touching* me.

"You know, I can really use a woman friend right now. There's a character in Book Three. She's supposed to be a normal woman, but she sounds like a hooker. May I use you for syntax?"

"You want it fast or you want it slow?"

He laughed for the first time, a roar that made me want to jump across to his side and tickle him.

"You want it plain or you want it fancy?" I breathed.

He laughed again, but his eyes turned serious and flicked over my breasts. I tensed, my nipples stiffening. He scared me when he did that "flick." It reminded me for some reason of his Emko foam cans, the ones he kept near the bed to spray into his one-night-stand girls. Was I in for a foaming tonight, or not?

Much as I wanted him, I might have chickened out if we hadn't gotten stuck in the same sector of the revolving door of the deli. But there we were—wedged together—standing perhaps one eighth of an inch apart, and a spark flew. We laughed—heh heh heh—and he pressed from behind to ease the door through.

"Friends?" he whispered into my ear.

"Friends," I agreed.

Friends? That was a new one. I hadn't considered that possibility. I mean, what would he want to be friends with me for? What could we do together? Take a ballet class? Try on dresses at Alexander's?

Still, he had suggested it, and I loved the idea.

"Can we really be friends?" I asked, walking quickly along with him.

"Sure. There's only one thing I just realized might bother me."

"What was that?"

"Oh, just something technical. You know. Details. Even though I know there are no real surprises. I still can't help wondering, when I meet a new woman: 'Maybe this one will be different, maybe she feels different . . . feels like no other, has some new move, says something I wouldn't have thought of. . . .' "

Wasn't this just the sort of thinking that had troubled me all along? "Yes, me too! It's that curiosity that can never be satisfied without . . ."

"Fucking," he finished for me. As we walked, he reached down and gave my neck a brief rub. "Okay, so we're agreed. We've got to get ourselves past the technical part. There's a way. One way. It's something no one does. But I think we should take a shot at it. . . ."

"Talk our way through?" I guessed.

"That's my girl. No curiosity. No trouble. We're over the hump, so to speak. We can be friends."

Hmmm. "Go into all the details? Size? Style? Timing? Texture? Favorite expressions? Unseen scars?"

Yes, all must be revealed, "so that there is no sliver of curiosity to trip us up. Okay. You first."

"No, you," I insisted.

He escorted me into the gated doorway of a Hoffritz cutlery store. When we were enclosed in that little entrance, Julian Sarkoff told me something personal and explicit, something that would have sounded vulgar from another man's lips. But not Sarkoff's. He could say "fuck" and make it sound, somehow, shy and endearing.

What he told me was a complete surprise. (No, my love, this I won't repeat. Some confidences are sacred. You wouldn't want me to tell another man about you, would you? Then again, there will be no more men. So maybe I will tell you, if you promise to keep it a secret. But later; I must go on.)

I told him something personal (nothing as personal as all this, of course). We exchanged relative data. He berated me lightly: "C'mon. You're leaving things out."

Begging him not to look at me, I told him something unbearably intimate. To speak that way made me ache and unfold between my legs, as if old locks were being turned. (Turned, not opened. You, my One-and-Only, had the key.)

He kept his back to me, so that I would not be embarrassed. Oh, he was sensitive then, he was! I could not even look at his back. I was afraid I'd see his shoulders react. So, as I spoke, I stared through the diamond-paned burglary gate at a collection of flared Swiss Army blades.

When I finished, I heard Sarkoff breathe. I turned. Our eyes met, then deflected.

We tore from the doorway, as if someone had cried: "On your mark, get set, GO!"

We ran and ran. Across deserted intersections, with fixed red lights. Past a small green-veined park. Down a narrow mews. We passed through phosphorescent halos and heard the *ting* of dying moths.

A summer night's wind suddenly buoyed our backs. Garbage can lids and paper bags danced before us. Block after block, we ran. At last, we arrived at a diamond-sprinkled avenue. There: a white high-rise. I thought: a hospital. But, no: This was Sarkoff's building.

The doorman dozed on a high stool. We ran past him into a vast lobby of geometric seating arrangements and Moorish wall hangings.

The main elevator gaped open and empty. We stood inside it and stared straight ahead, like office workers. He pressed the top button and we ascended with a cottoned *whrrrr*.

When we emerged, the air thick at our ears, we found ourselves in a long and silent blue corridor. We walked without sound. Sarkoff motioned: "This way . . ."

I followed him through a lacquered door, past an ashy landing, to yet another elevator. This elevator: dark and narrow as a closet.

The instant we stood enclosed within that closet-elevator, Sarkoff pressed himself against me. Even through our clothes, I felt him.

My thighs weighted, sank. He held me with the pressure of his body. We pressed together, without kissing, forging something.

The elevator rose with creaks and groans, swaying within its shaft, occasionally scraping cement. Then trembling on its cable. At last, the box lurched to a stop and Sarkoff yanked back the gate.

Bowlegged with desire, we staggered through another ashy midstation, past human-sized bags of garbage and pyramids of logs. Snorting, Sarkoff rammed his key into the narrowest door of all.

Inside. We were inside, a dark and private place.

He slammed the door behind us, then pinned my back against the wall. Again, I felt him move through his clothes.

Heaving, we pulled at pants, buckles—everything that kept us apart. We pushed our clothes up, down, off to the side—just enough to find our flesh.

My knees gave way. I could no longer stand. He scooped me up, held me to his groin. My legs snapped around his back. He was into me, fast.

A moaning duo, we staggered on two legs around his apartment, veering into other rooms, bouncing off walls, occasionally resting at ledges or sinktops. The whole while he said things I could not understand . . . sweet nothings. He mumbled them into my hair and against my cheeks.

I saw nothing but one safe section of his neck and shoulder. The rest passed in an inflamed blur. We circled some liquid center. Time stopped. Started. Changed dimension. I felt our bones.

He cried out. I couldn't understand. He dropped me.

As I landed ankle-deep into a kind of goat-hair rug, I understood that Sarkoff had finished. The red blur evaporated. Suddenly in black and white, we confronted each other in a grainy NET-type way—two people with *cinéma vérité*-mussed hair and underpants twisted around their ankles.

We hopped toward a large bed in the center of the room.

"Same old story?" I had to ask.

"Same old story."

∽

The next day, at work, Dolores Lester and Tina Rossini wanted to know: "How was it?"

I told them it was "the most beautiful, touching, evocative, thrilling experience of my life."

Dolores said that was how she felt about her first night with Bill.

Tina wanted to know, "Did he take you home?"

Balancing our styrofoam coffee cups with the pink "Sweet 'n' Low" packets on top, we made our way down the corridor. "Did he take you home?" Tina repeated.

I explained that Sarkoff, drained by the experience, had fallen into a profound sleep.

"Did he give you money for a cab? Or put you in one?"

"This wasn't the kind of thing where you even think about cabs or money."

"Uh-oh," Tina registered her disapproval. "Not taking you home is an indicator. The other indicators are feeding and calling. Did he feed you?"

"Well, there was a chance for a pastrami sandwich, if I'd wanted one. I'm sure he would have . . . I had a Tab."

"A Tab." Tina could be heard at *The Fruitarian*, one floor below. "That's all the hotshot Julian D. Sarkoff got you? A *Tab*."

"You don't think of how much the refreshments cost when something so intimate . . ."

"HAH! You think Sarkoff isn't thinking about it every second? His mind's going like an adding machine. I know his type. El cheapo! Did he say he'd call you, at least?"

"Tina! This is beyond calling. This is more than love, more than sex . . . a kind of . . . mind reading. There's nothing we can't do or say."

"Yeah, but will he call?"

❧

At that moment, I had no doubt that he would. Surely, he could not forget me any more than I could forget him.

Of course, Tina Rossini was on the right track: my Cassandra from the Bronx. Her adenoidal whine of recrimination perfectly predicted the course of my romance.

❧

But I did not know that then as I sipped my saccharined tea and tried to find the words to break Paul Whiting's heart.

Yes, for as soon as Sarkoff had pressed himself to me in that narrow elevator, I'd known: Paul was out. He was absolutely out.

❦

Oh, I will see Paul forever in my mind's eye, standing before his open closet door, one hand on the shoulder of the maroon silk bathrobe (my gift) and the other hand unfastening his cowboy belt.

He turned at the sound of my voice. His mouth opened—a slot to receive pain.

How could I break Paul's heart, tell him I'd given myself, in passion, to another man? A man more attractive. Beside whom he was (oh, cruel words) only a pale carbon of a man.

But I had to tell him something, because never again would I let him touch me. "Darling," I began, "can you hold up on the bathrobe?"

"Don't say a word," he guessed. "I see it in your eyes. Your beautiful eyes."

Did he have to say "beautiful"? Scrunch his eyes and nose into such hurt and supplication? Pouch his cheeks out, like a baby's?

Believe me, I hated myself. I called myself every name I could think of: "Bitch! Hard-hearted Hannah!"

"Was I too old? Didn't I satisfy you?"

"No!" I rushed to him, opening his cowboy belt still farther to show him that wasn't where the problem lay. "You are not old. You are young, young. Younger in many ways than I am. And you've always been good, good, and sweet and kind. My perfect lover."

"Yes, I have been," he agreed, his mouth turning to prune. "I should have realized you would slip away— so young, so desirable. I was going to paint you lying on the couch—with your hair over the armrest and your legs like so . . ."

Like so . . . for Lord help us, we had moved in tandem over to the couch. Paul busily cleared away a heap of black socks, a cat, a copy of *Realities*, and a crackling cellophane that had, I noted, once contained a medicinal suppository.

"God, how I love you!"

"And I you."

(Sweetheart, forgive me. I did love him in a way. Not as I love you, but love in some weaker, tepid form. And just for a few seconds.)

I swear: I didn't mean for it to happen. But he moved so quickly. He took the moment away from me, you understand?

What would one farewell session cost me? Wasn't it kinder to leave him with a kiss?

Besides, I reasoned, as his white member buckled against my labia majora and he tried to pack himself inside: Can this really count? It wasn't as if he could actually enter what was now Julian D. Sarkoff's private study.

No, it didn't count, I realized, parting my thighs and reaching down to do what I could to uncrick the pleats in his penis.

I was so much luckier. I had, only last night, discovered a red mist. Sarkoff and I had sipped an apéritif for the gods. Ecstasy waited for us, as on a buffet. Why be niggardly and deny an old fellow his partial pleasures?

Oh, what was it, anyway? I reflected, playing his flaccid flesh as I would a small accordion, *What has happened here?* One minute ago, I wore a dress and stood two feet away. He wore paint-splattered jeans and was opening his closet.

Now, we lay upon the couch. An appendage—enough dough to fashion maybe one cruller—is in my hand. My own little envelope of flesh lies parted.

A matter of a few steps across a parquet floor. A few ounces of clothing tossed aside. A change in respiration and body temperature.

What's it all add up to? It'll be over in twenty minutes and we'll be eating cheese. Why make a production of going along, or not?

(Dearest one, I was wrong, wrong to think those thoughts on the couch. Because more happens there than I just said. Paul was right. There is a mystery. Something not from us. We invade some other dimension when we lie naked together—even when one of us is pleated.)

Why did I cry? I don't know. I cried on his chest hairs, matting them into gray swirls. I cried and I writhed. Faster than ever—to disguise the truth that bobbled between us.

The last time, the last time. That's what I kept thinking as I kissed his defects. *The last time.*

I ran my lips over his paunch. *Good-bye, paunch.* Then nibbled an occasional fleshy cyst that dangled near his armpit. I traced every diverted capillary along his thigh. With my tongue, I lingered at the crimson brooch of blood blisters near his navel—just to show these were not factors in my leaving. *Good-bye, cluster. Good-bye, liver splotches. Good-bye . . . good-bye . . .*

Finally, I said the Big Good-bye: taking him whole into my mouth. Thinking: *Perhaps he'll rise for this occasion.* But, no, he rolled out.

(Forgive me, I had meant to save this act for you . . . but I swear to you, as I looked past Paul's belly to the back of the blue sofa, I begged my True Love for his understanding: *See, this is only an act of resuscitation.*)

Anyway, he rolled right out. But Paul Whiting had decided to return the compliment, and he dove head-first between my raised knees. He peeked up, his face framed moistly between my thighs, and declared that he would stay there until I changed my mind.

He went at me with a perseverance I would have thought limited to rodents at work on kitchen screen doors. We were there for hours. His beard grew in and scratched my thighs. At last, at a quiet, dark hour, Paul perceived that he could not persuade me.

It was really over. *Finis.* He sat up on his wrinkled

knees. I leaned back against the armrest and contemplated the change in him: new droop to his cheeks and breasts. Tears and sweat beads coursed down his face and pelted his belly. His eyes, watering, met mine, and he said,

"May I have my Matisse back?"

"It's just a print."

"To remember you by . . ."

It was not the monetary value, but the sentiment.

"*Bien sur, chéri,*" I whispered, not sure why I was speaking French. Perhaps we need a different language at such times?

His wet face beamed. With a hop, he straddled me in a new way, one that made his pleat not so noticeable. He quickened toward what I sensed was, for him, an impassioned finale. His high whimper sounded, and I braced myself for the words that had always shaken me, made me want to embrace him, pleat and all, forever:

"Oh, Death."

Could I bear it? How cruel I was—putting my *plaisir* ahead of his need. Shallow. Fickle. Vain. Dum-dum. Here, squashed against my thigh, was a man whose soul struggled to enter mine.

I must keep seeing him.

"Oh, Death," he whimpered.

For the last time? Perhaps, that was why he cried out more loudly, with better enunciation than his standard whimper. I asked him: "Could you repeat that?"

He repeated what he had whimpered.

Rotten man! I pushed him off me and sprang from the couch. I never wanted to feel his skin again. All these months, he had not been crying "Oh, Death," but "Odette."

"Forgive me, *mon petit,*" he begged. "I have always loved her. Some men have only one great love. . . ."

"I thought I was your great love."

"One great love . . . then a series of smaller ones."

"And that's what I was—a smaller one?"

"You were the greatest of the smaller ones."

I inquired as to what was so memorable about Odette when "that was twenty years ago . . . in Paris. Par-*ee*."

"Oh, but she comes to the States every spring, and we . . . well, I won't go on. . . . I don't want to hurt you."

"Hurt me."

Naked, with all his parts drooping like wax down a candle, Paul stood before me. "Well," he said, with a smile that annoyed me, "it's as if twenty years never passed. We are young together. We can't stop."

The pages of my mental calendar flipped back. I tried to keep my voice sweet: "You were seeing me in April. Does that mean you were sleeping with her and me?"

Paul bent over and pulled on his paint-splattered jeans. "The one doesn't steal from the other."

You said it.

As I stamped about the loft, collecting my belongings, I kept repeating my one line: "I can't believe this."

He followed, bleating, "What was I to do? Turn away my old love, my oldest and dearest love? A woman who gave me my manhood . . . taught me all I know of women . . ."

Not much. For a moment, as I scouted for my other shoe, I debated telling him just how poor his tongue technique was. He thought because he applied himself with pucker and drool that he was some kind of *artiste*. Well, he never really got to me there. And he made it look and sound like work, always sentencing himself to hours of it, as in,

"I'm going to dee-vour you for two hours."

The great lover.

As I pulled my knit dress over my head, I heard:

"I thought of telling Odette it was over, but it would have killed her. Twenty years, remember. I couldn't do it. I tell you the truth. I tried, but the words stuck in my mouth. So, what was it? One or two nights to save a woman's heart?

My breath felt hot under the acrylic cloth, but I wasn't ready to pop into view. Paul continued to address me. He described their ritual dinner at Lutece, how they ordered one goblet of an ancient brandy and sipped it—sloshing from his mouth to hers. They had been drinking, not just that ancient brandy, which had been around since Louis XIV, but also "La Belle France!"

Why didn't I cut him off? Why did I stand there, suffocating? Why didn't I, for once, call a spade a spade, and ask him, "Did you ever really get inside Odette?"

Oh, I was burning, baby, you'd better believe it. All this time, for almost a year, I'd kept coming back for more simulated sex, afraid of hurting *him*. And his inert penis had not been mine alone—he had been slipping it against someone else too! Oh, I wanted to tell him, "You don't have to feel sorry for Odette. What would she have been missing?"

I'd bet anything: Odette had been taking him on out of pity. She probably made the whole trip each year because she thought that was the only time Paul would ever get any solace. Poor Odette—*Shlepping* herself by freighter, I learned, across the Atlantic Ocean to get to a cricked penis. And I'd thought I had it rough: a crosstown bus, and a short hop on the BMT.

Yet I bit back these words. I felt some odd reluctance to inflict pain—even on someone who had cried out for another while we simulated sex.

Choking, I pulled down my dress, buttoning one button too high, so that the dress hung askew.

"So now who will I make love to?" Paul was whining as I ran for the door.

Wait until next April.

I took his stairs two at a time. My feet pounded the dark pavement of NoHo. Blind, I ducked down into the BMT, rushed on board the wrong train, and was whipped out to a warehouse district in Astoria.

While waiting for the local back to Manhattan, I caught a rusted reflection of myself in a gum machine.

Who was this person, so pinched and pale, with white tracks down her blush-on?

I had to tell her:

"He didn't care. He didn't care about you at all."

❧

I went home and waited for Sarkoff to call.

❧

The silence crackled. My phone had been ringing while I was out. Sarkoff had been trying to reach me.

"Thank God I've found you," I thought, adjusting the dial under the phone to Loudest, so that I could take a shower.

My thoughts were all addressed to Julian Sarkoff now. Mentally, I told him what had happened with Paul. He was sympathetic.

Cheered, I shared a few anecdotes from the office and a vignette of the bum I'd seen in NoHo. The bum, I mentally told Sarkoff, had been shooting a beer can into a trash basket, as if he were Walt Frazier.

Sarkoff could get a story out of that. Wasn't this wonderful? All my experience could now be tossed into the NBA nominee's literary hopper. I made a mental note to be more observant—to catch nuances of weather, and the appearance of a crocus in hard earth, stuff like that.

I didn't start to worry for several hours. Secure and casual, I stepped out to the hall to empty my garbage. I even made a few phone calls, tying up my line for at least fifteen minutes.

"The Late Late Show" came on; I watched, then hung around for "The Star-spangled Banner." Dressed and ready to meet Sarkoff, I sat on the living room rug. After an hour of this, I undressed and turned out the lights, except for a small bulb, which lit my path to the phone.

Make-up still on, I lay in state on my bed. I listened

to produce trucks roll into the ethnic vegetable neighborhood below me.

I'm beyond this, I told myself. *I shouldn't be waiting for a man to call.*

Why not end the suspense and call him?

"Because if you call him," Tina told me, "you're saying, 'Hi. Fuck me over. I care about you, even though you don't give a damn.'"

Tina wasn't actually with me, but I knew that was what she would have said.

No question: It would be better if he called me. Then I'd be safe. Sure. I'd know he really wanted to see and sleep with me again.

I recalled a time when my phone had been broken. I could make calls, but not receive them: My phone didn't ring for two months. I felt unwanted. I did not realize it was out of order until my parents called long distance and had the police check my apartment for a body.

Perhaps it was out of order now?

I tiptoed to the phone and lifted the receiver. A dial tone. *Damn.* Using the hem of my nightie, I dusted the phone, then set it back on the table.

It rang in my hand. *I knew you loved me!*

"We'd like to bring sirloin, london broil, and other choice cuts straight to your freezer," a woman offered. Fifty pounds of beef for the same low price that had brought me only chopped chuck in the past. Her voice trembled. I had the feeling she didn't really have it to be a successful sirloin solicitor.

I explained that I was almost a vegetarian, to save her feelings, and thanked her for her offer.

After the meat woman's call, I lost hope for sleep, and resigned myself to an all-night vigil.

Well, I still had my work. I pulled out some of my commercial projects: tie-dye scarves which, cleverly knotted, could be worn as halters.

If I didn't have this, I thought, painting on a hummingbird design, *I might start to fall apart.*

Work had saved me before. *Be more ambitious.* Why

stop at tie-dye scarves? Why not fashion a wrap-on blouse, with the same hummingbird pattern? Now, that would be a project, something to test my patience, bring me out of my emotions.

Yes, I realized, painting on a bunch of cherries, my work was progressing. Soon I would have enough scarves to market at a boutique. Then I could return to my great project, the stone sculpture. On all fronts, my efforts were rewarding.

In fact, what had I been so shaky about? What was the production? I could call Sarkoff. It wouldn't mean any more or less than that. No power game. Just a human communication.

Was it too late? Not for a night owl, which he was. And he'd be sure to be home. What if . . . No, not in bed with someone else, her head near the receiver . . . the two of them looking and giggling. *Stop that.*

Go ahead. Call. He'd be delighted. He probably wore himself out dialing while I was at work, or at Paul's. That had to be it. He called and called, then gave up in despair. Perhaps he's lying awake, wondering why I haven't been in touch.

"Hi, just thought I'd give you a ring," I rehearsed as I walked back to the phone. "Just thought I'd give you a ring." No. Not a ring. Too much like wedding ring.

"Hey, whatcha been doing?"

Worse. Sounds inquisitive. What has he been doing?

"Remember me?" *Terrible.* Of course he remembers you.

"Hi, just thought I'd see how you were getting along." *That's it.* Casual. I could care less.

I ran through it twice, and laughed—for vibrancy—before dialing. Casual. Casual. "Hi, Julian? Alice. Just thought I'd see how you're getting along there . . ." *Where you made love to me standing up.*

His phone rang. My heart pounded. *Stop, heart!* My ear throbbed. *Stop, ear!* My mouth dried up. I croaked: "Hi, Julian?" when I heard his voice cut in:

"No, this is not Sarkoff. You have reached his machine. You want him, and this is wire, plastic, a technological mockery. Well, be assured. Sarkoff is alive, human, and in pain. Call back later or leave your message after the sound of the buzz."

I gasped and hung up. I dialed back instantly, to hear his voice, so deep and tender:

"No, this is not Sarkoff."

I listened again, and hung up—gently—without leaving my message: *Take me in your arms again.*

❧

The next morning, at *Actual Slayings,* I pasted a photo of the police chief where the killer's face was supposed to go, over the caption—"He thirsted for wine, women, and blood."

"A serious mistake," said Mr. Marrone, when he called me into his office. "I'm surprised at you, Alice. Your work has been excellent until now."

I shuffled my feet on the green carpet. "I don't know what's wrong with me. I can't seem to keep my mind on my work."

"You'll be more careful."

"Yes."

❧

On the third full day of no call, Dolores and Tina found me in the ladies' room, where I was applying Erace to the shadows now ringing my eyes. Sarkoff shadows.

Tina literally said: "I told you so."

Dolores touched my shoulder. "Sometimes, when they're really moved, they never want to see the girl again."

❧

On the fourth day of no call, I started to slump to the floor of the elevator. Tina caught me. I was surprised at the strength in her arms.

When we stood outside on Forty-second Street, under a baking sun, she said, "You're killing yourself over a prick who only bought you a Tab."

"No . . . ," I protested. "I was just woozy. I think it might be this diet. I haven't had a carbohydrate for five weeks. Maybe if I went into a cafeteria and ordered a whole bowl of turkey stuffing, or maybe some kasha . . ."

"Don't do anything crazy. . . . You look great now. Your arms are sticks. You have no ass. Don't ruin your diet for that prick."

I begged Tina not to call the NBA nominee "that prick."

"He's wonderful," I told her. "I'm sure he's just waiting for the weekend. Lots of people don't call on weeknights. They save it for the . . ."

"Wise up!" Tina took my elbow and led be toward the 104 bus stop. "That prick doesn't give a damn."

"You don't know him."

"I know writers. Writers should be read and not fucked. They'll all try to give it to you up the ass, 'cause they're all latent fags, hung up on their mommies. That's what makes 'em write. If they could fuck straight, you think they'd put a word on paper?"

The bus rolled into the stop, blasting exhaust in our faces. "Run!" Tina shouted.

I ran. "Why am I running?"

" 'Cause I'm taking you to a shrink." Tina held the rubber doors open, and I wedged in behind her. She dropped two tokens into the box. "My treat."

She told me that she knew this bargain therapist and that this bus would take us to him. "He's ten bucks less than anybody."

We got off at Seventy-ninth Street and walked to a constricted row of brownstones. Tina stopped in front of the narrowest: a mere sliver of a building, impacted between two others. I read the shingle: "Dr. Peter Lasky, Psychologist." His office nestled below street level.

"I don't want to go down there." I balked on the first step.

"Look. I went to him, and he fixed me in two weeks. I'm talkin' from experience. I was hung up on a writer —a stringer for *Arizona Highways*—and he was a real pain in the ass, in every sense of the . . ."

"You don't understand!"

I told her again of my feeling of mystical communion with Julian Sarkoff. "He's in the air I breathe . . . the proteins I eat . . . I see his face floating before me. My thoughts are all for him."

"He hasn't called you."

That did it. I threw myself down the steps and banged the brass knocker. Let me in!

❧

My work at the office improved. I pasted up two "sniper" layouts, positioning seventeen victims where it had seemed only fifteen would fit. And it was my idea to superimpose a clockface over the slay scene to indicate the "timetable" of the massacre.

At home, I completed two hand-painted scarves, then began to eye my suggestive hunk of granite. That rock had been looming over my bed long enough. Somewhere within it was my *chef d'oeuvre*. If only I could tackle it . . . create the form I dreamed of . . .

❧

Although I slept well (insomnia is not my problem: waking up is my problem), I suffered from disturbing dreams:

I'm on an amusement park slide: wide and wavy. Although in real life such slides are metal, this one is padded, like a mattress. I roll down it, over and over, until, at the very end, I land breathless, on a man's dark, heavily muscled chest. "Who is he?" I wonder, and I squint up, trying to see him. A small cloud obscures his face. (In all my dreams the man's face has been a blank. Now, Darling, that blank is you.)

Another disturbing dream: I'm at a party, hoping no one will notice I'm not wearing a dress, but only a shred of cloth. I sit so that my private parts will be as concealed as possible. The party is very chic, and I'm the only one there in a shred.

A man (blank-faced) approaches me, and he is the only one who notices I'm almost naked. But he lights a cigar and laughs. His question "Where've you been hiding?" is unmistakably casual.

∾

This is the stuff that I have to bring to Dr. Peter Lasky's bargain basement. "This was my girlfriend's idea," I told him on that first visit. "I can't afford a long haul. I feel silly coming here anyway, without real problems. But there is a temporary little situation . . . maybe you can ease me past. But I can't spend more than a hundred for the whole package. If you can't fix anything for that, I'll stick to 'When I Say "No" I Feel Guilty.' What did you think of that, by the way?"

"Suppose you just talk today. Not make any decisions. Expect any fast answers." He leaned back in his swivel chair.

I took a hard look: He seemed as good as a more expensive analyst. Maybe a little young: only in his thirties, with a wispy pale brown beard. Come to think of it, that beard looked a bit sparse. Was that a pink rash shining through?

Perhaps the rash was keeping his price down.

"You know best," I deferred, and settled into the patient's armchair. Yes, armchair. Dr. Lasky had no couch. A little disappointment. I had secretly looked forward to a couch.

"Begin anywhere you like," he invited.

I took him at his word, and decided to skip my childhood. I didn't feel that Max and Sophie Smilgiewicz were to blame for the present situation. And my up-bringing had been such a setup, anyway. There was no way I could tell Dr. Lasky about my family without diverting him from the real problem:

"Do you think it's better to call the man, or wait for him to call you?"

"You're interested in a specific man?"

"Yes."

Then I thought: Why not level with him? Take a shortcut to mental health. "I slept with this man Monday night. Today's Friday. That's Monday, Tuesday, Wednesday, Thursday . . ." I held up my fingers. "Five days and he hasn't called."

"And you believe you'd be happy if he called?"

"Uh-huh. It would solve everything. I'd never ask for a single thing again. Just call me now. I don't ordinarily sleep with a man on the first night. I'm just not made that way. But I did with him, because he was special, and I didn't want to lose him on some stupid technicality."

I turned my face so I was hidden in the armpit of my chair. "He touched something inside me. I felt our bones. Is this love?"

Dr. Lasky didn't answer.

"Maybe you've heard of him? He's so special. He's a writer, the most wonderful one in the world. Julian D. Sarkoff."

Dr. Lasky took up pen and paper for the first time. *"Mortal Coils* and *Naked Faces?"* he asked.

"You read them! Aren't they the most wonderful books in the whole world?"

He wrote something on a pad, then flipped through a small calendar. "I want you to come twice a week instead of just once."

❧

Had I done the right thing—letting Tina push me into therapy? You can see my situation: One stand-up session, a few unintelligible endearments in my hair, and I was committed to a heavy psychoanalytical schedule, spending God knows how much money, money that could have gone for new outfits and art supplies.

What was Dr. Lasky doing for me? He hardly spoke. His eyes—their whites showing under the faded blue irises—looked sad and hopeless.

Still, in order to fill the vacuum, I'd rattled on, and surprised myself a few times—especially when I said "lonely" instead of "only," as in: "I'm lonely interested in him."

I did confide in Dr. Lasky that there were a few minor problems. "Sometimes I'm not sure if I've given the correct name when I've made a telephone call. I think maybe I gave another name . . . especially my surname. Sometimes, I have to hesitate before signing 'Berry.' Also: If I have to borrow a pen, I'm afraid I'll say, 'May I borrow your penis?' I have a similar problem with 'I need a fork.' And then there's the screaming. I've never done it. But I worry that I might start, you know, in public."

Dr. Lasky nodded and told me that my hour was up. As I went out the door, I turned and stressed that these problems were not urgent ones: "They're just there, in the background. I don't spend much time on them."

❧

Was Dr. Lasky's silence the help I needed? Perhaps. After only two weeks, I felt better. At the office, I continued to let the work absorb all my energies.

One night, at home, I took my first chip into the big quarry stone. That first cut was made blind. I simply took a breath, shut my eyes, and struck.

When I stood back and opened my eyes, I saw form: The haunch of a well-developed male.

As I hacked out a tendon, the telephone rang—right up my spine. I hit my hand with a chisel.

Damn. The first minute I put him out of mind.

Okay. I can handle him now. Deep breath. Casual. No need to run to the phone. It's a fact: The phone rings ten times in one minute. Anyone would let it ring five times before giving up.

So slow down. Let him sweat it out.

I hung over the receiver, my hand poised. The receiver trembled in its cradle.

No time to fool around.

I grabbed it.

∾

Through three windowed walls, I could see what Sarkoff called "his city." Inside, I could see his world, the apartment that had been veiled in red mist on my first visit.

Decorated in "Macho Moderne," the vast penthouse was divided into "areas" rather than rooms. Surrounded by waves of goat hair, the bed on which I now lay floated like a giant aircraft carrier. Off to the left, I could see a suede conversation pit.

Roped off from the rest of the main room was Sarkoff's work area. Within what looked like a prizefight ring were his typewriter, a camp chair, folded towels, a supply of liniment and Bourbon, and a punching bag.

That's where he writes, I realized.

I craned my neck for a closer look, but Sarkoff himself lay diagonally across my belly. He had fallen deep into that stupor that hits men right after . . .

(Does that happen with every man on every woman? Or is mounting me so enervating?)

Anyway, I was thinking, *Oh, this most precious time, the time to hold the one who has given his most awesome gift. My lover. My man. My father. My son.*

I would have relayed these ideas to Sarkoff, but he rolled onto my rib cage and cut off my breathing.

My gasp must have awakened him, for he sprang up on all fours. His head snapped toward the door.

"Who's there?" he yelled.

"Nobody, Angel . . . it was just me."

He remained poised, in midpush-up position, his

palms on the mattress. Then he looked down at me as if for the first time. A comma of a smile tugged his lip. His voice sounded soft:

"I missed you. You were my reward."

"For what?"

"Five thousand words."

❧

Later, Sarkoff explained the relationship between sex and his work. "I either leave it there," he waved toward his work area, "or," he smacked the king-size mattress, "I leave it here. You understand?"

"Yes."

"I left a whole novella here once." He smoothed a pucker from his Missoni-striped bedsheet. "But I was younger then. Didn't mind throwing one away. I can't do that now. Time . . ." He held his head in that way that was becoming familiar. "Time. Death. Well. Do you understand?"

"Yes."

"And there's something else you should know: I won't do any calling."

I must have whimpered, for he pulled me closer. I felt the heat of his body, the strong heartbeat within. . . .

"No. You will do the calling, if there is to be calling. Until I have those fifty thousand words, I have nothing to give. All my strength must go"—he waved again to the prize-fight ring—"there."

He let me go and stretched out his broad, dark body, and sighed: "I'm one of the real monsters. Stay away from me."

"No! No!" I cried.

"I'll be awful . . . no good for anyone . . . until I have my quartet."

"You're not awful," I argued. "You're wonderful."

We both dove under the thin sheet at the same time. We crashed heads. Slightly dazed, I insisted that he was the wonderful one.

When he didn't answer, I guessed that I had won.

〜

The next day, on my lunch hour, I announced: "I'm treating you all to diet burgers at Stark's."

Tina and Dolores pressed closer to me in the elevator.

"He called!"

〜

The diet burgers arrived with mounds of cottage cheese and canned peach halves. We forked aside our peach halves. As we quaffed tall, artificially sweetened glasses of iced tea, I confessed that Sarkoff and I were deeply in love.

"Did he say 'in love'?" Tina wanted to know.

"Well, not right out. But he came close. What he says amounts to 'in love.' "

How could I tell the girls all the clever ways Sarkoff devised of not saying "in love"? Even in passion, he would scream to the ceiling: "I like you!"

But I held myself in restraint also. When I dove to new mushroomy depths of him, I whispered, "I'm fond of you."

"You see," I explained to Tina and Dolores, "a great writer like Julian D. Sarkoff must turn all the clichés upside down."

What I didn't say: Often, he turned *me* upside down. In our love scenes, I often found myself facing his feet. I remember begging his big toe: "Tell me we're friends."

And he, the darling, murmured to my instep:

"Yes. We are."

〜

Dr. Lasky was not impressed. He had developed a cough, for which he sucked a menthol green lozenge. As I recounted my amours, Dr. Lasky spit lozenges into his wastebasket.

"He's so adorable."

"Specifically?"

I had to make Dr. Lasky understand: "The way he says 'Yeah, yeah' like some street kid. And his sidelong glance—that's really cute. And his hug. And what he says when he hugs: 'Oh, Al—what a mess, what're we gonna do?' At least, I think that's what he says. His voice is all choky. His chokiness is what excites me. I'll take his chokiness over anyone else's enunciation, anyday. Oh, and his *l*'s are wonderful. All buttery. 'Lollipop.' It's nothing when I say it. He puts tongue on it. 'Lollipop.' Ummmm. Oh, and you'll love this! His eyebrows shoot up like French accent marks—circumflexes—when's he's surprised. Is that where French accent marks come from—eyebrows?"

Ping. Dr. Lasky spit another lozenge.

"I'm not getting this across to you, am I?"

He waited.

"All right." I'd been holding back. Something irresistible: "He has two brown wrinkles across his belly."

❧

How I loved that belly. Sarkoff's spirit might be elusive, but it was housed in some pretty solid flesh. After a month of my cooking, I had plenty of his hot Mediterranean skin to hang onto in what he called "the love hold."

Our time together had settled into a pattern.

Sarkoff broke, as he put it, from work each night at nine. I'd call him then and ask if I could come over with a casserole.

Some nights I'd hear only his recording: "No, this is not Sarkoff. . . ." And I'd know that meant he was working straight through, in what he called "a white heat."

Most often, though, he'd tell me: "Okay. I'm drained anyway." And I'd rush crosstown, with my Corningware steaming up a plastic D'Ag Bag.

After he put away one of my casseroles, he would take me on in "love's arena." We made love on his vast bed, submerged in his hairy carpet, and on the multi-levels of the conversation pit.

One night, we ended in the trapezoidal shadow under a steel coffee table. I rested my head on his warm belly, where it sounded as if he might be having trouble with my chicken tetrazzini.

Indeed, he soon began to thrash and moan. He flailed his arms, knocking aside our romantic debris: the Johnson's baby oil, Kama Sutra cream, frankincense sticks, and a just-bought pair of "tiger-stripe" panties.

"Arrggggggggghhhhh," he roared, his first roar in weeks.

I rubbed him under the chin and scratched his side whiskers. He groaned again. Seeing the problem was serious, I reached down and tickled that chamois-soft pouch between his legs. But he continued to groan and thrash. I heard his teeth.

"Something's wrong," I diagnosed.

I offered the usual remedies: Bourbon, Alka Seltzer.

"No, no. That isn't going to do it. This is no good. I'm happy. And I can't work when I'm happy."

"I'm sorry. I know it's my fault."

"I need to be in pain."

"Is there something I can do?"

"Yes. Understand. This is the way I am. I have to get away. Someplace where I can work. I have to feel lonely, cut off. . . . I have to be caught up in the nausea of creativity."

I sat up, bunking my head on the coffee table. As I cried, he patted my hair, and repeated: "Poor little Al. Poor little klutz. Always bumping her head. Don't be sad. I'll come back."

"When?"

"Ummmmmm . . ." He exhaled a long breath. "Eight thousand words?"

෮

The postcard came from Vegas. On the glossed side: Caesar's Palace, spurting fountains. I savored the moment before turning the card over to read my first message in the great writer's own hand:

> Muchas grazias for packing my suitcase. Supply of shirts holding up. You were a dear to roll my socks into little balls.
>
> Hasta la vista,
> Julian.

Mucho as I hated that card, I knew I would have it for the rest of my life. I already had a plan to laminate it. Meanwhile, I slipped the card into an old Valentine's candy box, where I keep my other love letters.

Opening the red heart-shaped box was my major mistake, because I dumped the contents on my bed, and shuffled through that little pile of paper that is all I have to show for my romantic past.

～

Would you like to see what my nostalgic juices have to flow on?

The box happens to be under the bed. Here: Pick a card, any card, at all.

Ah, what have we got? A little wrinkled restaurant chit, from Mister Chows: "Next time in L.A., give me a tinkle. 213-435-9078."

I wish I could say I've forgotten the man who slipped that to me, as I waited to get my umbrella. But I remember him—his greased tan, his Lacoste shirt—just as I remember all my admirers.

What have you got there? Oh, forget the business cards—all from pants manufacturers. There's only one from a maverick film producer—Unicorn Productions. Who ever heard of them? Oh, where is that card? He did pencil in the margin, "You got legs, kid."

That's something.

Oh, look at this. I'd forgotten. "Pick up Gatorade, Absorbine, Jr." That was from Robert.

Wait a second: Let me see that yellow scrap paper first. I think that was from the tooter. I don't know if I want you to read that one. I said I would keep no secrets? Well, all right. If memory serves, it begins: "Dear Fire Pussy . . ."

I told you not to read it. Don't look at me that way. I didn't write it. Is it my fault?

Here, check out these call slips and index cards. Those are from Stony Brook. They all say, "Meet me after class."

The Modigliani card, from the post card rack at the Museum of Modern Art, is from Paul, of course . . .

Hey, here's another Sarkoff card . . . from Rio. . . . But that's later on in our romance. No peeking.

Would you like to see my carton of nonromantic mail? There are several letters from girls, all describing sexual trysts in outdoor vacation spots. There's a pretty good one from my old college roommate, Joanie Lipshitz, describing her rendezvous with a Ugandan. She had come to his village to bring civilization, in the form of the Peace Corps. As I recall, Joanie begins, "I never knew what a man really could be like until I met Kwami. Remember the jerks and frat slobs at Stony Brook? They didn't know how to handle us. I always had trouble coming. Last night, Kwami made me come eight times. It's being in love: with an honest, natural man. Simple as that! I will stay on here in Bwatzilli Junction, even after my tour with the Corps ends, for Kwami has asked me to be his 'kwitzzuna.' The only question is: Will he be able to get Abe and Golda Lipshitz to accept three goats and a pig as my bride price? Ha, ha."

Someday, I'll have to tell you more about Joanie Lipshitz. Her story has some bearing on my own. How lives, once parallel, can become hopelessly crisscrossed!

Give me the rubber band. I want to put this box back under the bed.

Oh, look what else I found under here: the Kama Sutra cream. There's still plenty left. You promised me a rubdown, if I remember. I think I could use a massage, right about now.

If you'll just rub that cream into my back . . . concentrating around the lower spine. I have a little twinge there. . . . I'll tell you about the increasingly wild tangents I took while Julian Sarkoff worked on Book Three (he said!) in Vegas.

∾

Ah, don't you have the nice light touch. Ummmm. . . . You won't hold these sexual adventures against me, will you? I'm rather ashamed of them . . . but you're here to love me more than I love myself, right?

I can't start with my night with the Dogfood King. I have to work up my nerve for that.

Anyway, that came toward the end—during Sarkoff's trip to Rio. Let me think: Did I pick up that boy in the Purple Pantaloon when Julian went away the first time? No, that was during the second trip.

I remember, Gordon Fox! Sarkoff had been gone for a week when Gordon Fox invited me to lunch and that whole nasty business started. . . .

Blame Tina Rossini. I would never have gone out with Mr. Fox, if Tina hadn't told me I was a fool to be faithful to Julian Sarkoff.

"He's working," I told Tina one morning as I stood in line for the coffee wagon. "He went to Vegas to work on his quartet."

"Work!" Tina snorted. "He's up to his eyeballs in all that topless pussy!"

How accurate her prediction was, I discovered purely by accident when I rooted through Julian's secret file box later on in our love affair. . . .

Tina Rossini had also foreseen that Mr. Fox would sound me out on the subject of "profit sharing."

"Profit sharing means fucking. He'll take you to a dimly lit restaurant, so no one who knows him from

Prickhaven, Connecticut, will spot him. Then he'll hit you with the proposition."

"I don't want to go."

I didn't like anything about Gordon Fox: not his grim gray mouth, or his slippery gray suit, or his way of sliding soundlessly into my office. His ruthlessness was known: how he loved to catch workers reading, sleeping, or otherwise enjoying "company time." His favorite management ploy was to fire people just before they became eligible for senior benefits.

"I hate him," I told Tina as we sipped coffee in the *Actual Slayings* office, where we used a corpse layout as a placemat.

"Yeah, so do I." Tina stirred her bitter coffee with a stick. "But who else is there?"

No one.

"And look at it this way—it's a free lunch."

❧

And so it came to pass that I sat in a rattan-screened booth at Nirvana. Unable to return Mr. Fox's blue stare—his eyes had the eerie, artificial color of a certain Popsicle I knew—I stared down at a lazy susan of chutneys.

No good could come of those chutneys. . . . Chutneys dipped into, not out of love, or even in companionship . . . but chutneys consumed in the interest of corporate evil and officious lust.

Forgive me, Julian, I thought, dunking a curried chicken leg into mango sauce.

(Of course, now I realize I should not have begged Julian's forgiveness, but yours—and so I do that now. Please, please forgive me for everything that followed. . . .)

Mr. Fox delivered a short pep talk in favor of profit sharing. To demonstrate the financial principles involved, he moved salt and pepper shakers around the tablecloth. "This is how my conglomerates interlock."

He performed another tricky move: bringing an ash-tray into play. "I'm not boring you, am I?"

"Oh, no, it's fascinating." I dug into some pretty yellow rice. (Forgive me: It was delicious.)

How will he make the transition from profit sharing to sex? I wondered, quaffing some perfumed darjeeling.

"Everything in life is an investment. You put in time, money, yourself. Then . . . ," he paused, and I realized: *Here it comes.*

"Then," he reached for my hand, which had been grasping out for more chutney, "you get a return."

His blue eyes froze. I tried to confront them, but a blood speck in the left eye frightened me. I stared down at my green curry.

"You have to make sure the return is high enough. Now, in my marriage, I get a return. But I'd say it's only coming in at 6, maybe 7 per cent. That doesn't justify keeping myself in there for twenty years. . . ."

I made a move for the chutney, but his cold, dry hand held mine too fast.

"I think I might get 10, maybe 11 per cent, if I deposit somewhere else. . . ."

I began to cough.

"Nervous?" He smiled. He set down my hand. "This is a big occasion for you, isn't it?"

I coughed again.

"It's like a fantasy: This restaurant . . . a lunch with" —his thin mouth stretched again—"with your 'boss.' "

He assured me that he could see how overwhelming it all was from my point of view.

"You're very cute, you know that? All wide-eyed and trembling. I noticed you that first day. I shall have to keep from getting too fond of you, you know. I don't want you to delude yourself. Whatever happens, there is no chance that I will leave my wife."

Another warning. I had quite a collection now. All the men I knew had warned me. It was funny, I thought, sitting in that rattan booth, that they warned me only on certain subjects—more or less romantic ones. They never warned me of anything that might really put me off—such as nose-picking, or leaving the bathroom door open while they took a groaner or worked the crossword puzzle.

I giggled. Imagine Mr. Fox saying: "I must warn you, I'm going to let one go after this Tandoori chicken."

"You have such a cute little laugh," he complimented.

"Listen," I said. "About the profit sharing. I don't think I can get involved in it. To tell you the truth, I've been profit sharing a lot lately, and I'm a little tired." I drank some ice water to cool my throat.

Here goes nothing, I thought. *Hello, unemployment.*

"Let's be frank," I went on. "What you want is for me to slip off to a hotel with you and profit share for an hour. But I can't because I have to stagger my men as it is. I won't offer you any false hope, because I don't see my schedule opening up."

We just stared at one another, both shocked by my speech. *What am I doing?* I wondered.

A turbaned waiter brought the check, and Mr. Fox paid in silence. Also in silence, we rode in a cab back to Fox-MacKneill.

"Well, thanks for lunch," I said at the elevators. We parted company—I thought—forever.

ⸯ

The next day, I found an envelope on my desk. A pink slip? I ripped the letter in half, then pieced it together to read: "No one ever said that. You're a delicious, naughty little girl. Lunch?"

ⸯ

I tried to call Sarkoff at Caesar's Palace. The Caesar's Palace operator sounded smug. "He isn't taking any calls."

Sensing that I was about to board some sexual express with Gordon Fox, I left an urgent message for Julian to call me. I waited all day and all night.

He never returned my call.

Sitting by my Princess phone, I thought of the sweater I had knitted for him and sent to Caesar's Palace, where I imagined him catching a chill from the air-conditioning. Although he was outwardly strong and powerful, I knew Julian to have a tender constitution. He caught colds easily, and I had thought . . .

Now I remembered he must have received his sweater, with the special personal motif of rolling dice, at least three days before—and there was no response. Okay, even if he hadn't loved it, he might have said . . .

I jumped up, kicked off my shoe, and threw it at the wall. That's what I do when I'm upset: throw my shoes.

"Why should I be kind?" I asked the wall. "No one else is. Go ahead. Be a bitch. Drink human blood."

∽

The next morning, I waited until almost eleven before sending a message to Mr. Fox.

"Busy for lunch. Sorry, Alice S. Berry."

For extra hurt, I wrote the note on *Actual Slayings* stationery.

∽

When I came back from a greaseburger lunch with Tina and Dolores, we all saw the bunch of violets on my desk.

Tina whistled. "You got him on the shore. Hit him on the head with a rock."

∽

And so the series of torture lunches began in bilious earnest. I could not lunch with Mr. Fox every day:

That would make it hard to torture him. I mustn't seem eager for the food. So I spaced our lunches: one accepted invitation for every three rejections.

The ratio of pain worked to my advantage. He did not dare press for "profit sharing." Instead, his cold exterior cracked wide open, and he began to implore me in a squeakier voice:

"All I want is to hold your hand—just let me hold it."

I forced myself to say, "I'm eating. *Please.*"

His appearance also changed. His gray silk suit lost some of its sheen, and his own blue eyes became ringed in red. What had been an icy reserve now thawed into drool.

"I have to have you," he said finally, one afternoon as I munched a sparerib at a sequestered palm-filled African restaurant. "What do you want?"

I doused my meat in more sweet 'n' sour sauce. "Nothing you can give me."

Mr. Fox stared down at his own plate—filled with an exotic pork stew, which he'd only been able to pick at. "What is it? Do you want gifts? A bracelet? I'll take you down to Gimbels Jewelry Department. . . ."

Gimbels? Didn't he mean Cartier's? I had to laugh. Even my bitchiness could only produce cut-rate results.

I did better with style. I caught on quickly that Mr. Fox wanted to suffer. The smallness of his requests— He went from "I want to look at you" to "Just let me touch your hair"—tipped me off.

"Don't mess my hairdo," I told him.

"I'm sorry."

I almost shrieked. Was the world crazy? I didn't have a hairdo. Nothing, not King Kong or Hurricane Lulu, could possibly disarrange my tresses, which have resisted all straighteners, rollers, and conditioners on the market.

"I'm sorry, I'm sorry," Fox kept repeating. "I won't ever mess your hair. Please don't be mad. Don't stop seeing me."

"I can't make lunch for a month," I told him, right away. "Would you get my coat."

~

Yes, Fox suffered. But was I happy? Our daisy chain of pain reached all the way to Las Vegas, where Julian Sarkoff held me looped to him as neatly as if he had me back in his dark, narrow elevator.

Oh, why didn't I hear from him? Had he forgotten? At home, I could not face my hunk of quarry stone. What was the point of artistic endeavor when you had no one to hold you at night?

My nights were bad. I bunched the three pillows into human form, and, by pretending these were Julian Sarkoff, I could drift into a deep but troubled sleep. He returned to me in dreams leading me down aquamarine corridors and into a subterranean cave. There he'd enter me, but just once (perhaps this aspect was picked up from *Exciting Confessions*); then, shining with the glazes of my love, he'd withdraw, laughing. Forever.

~

"What does this mean?" I asked Dr. Peter Lasky.

He was about to tell me, when he was seized by violent sneezing and coughing.

"Your cold is worse," I observed.

Dr. Lasky nodded. "I can't seem to shake it." He opened a box of lozenges and began to suck on them.

"Here, try these." I held out a box of pleasant Honey-Glycerin cough drops, which I had always carried in my purse for Julian.

Not wanting to upset Dr. Lasky while he felt ill, I changed the subject to something lighter.

By the time I left, he was laughing and looking much better.

~

The next day, I found myself wandering without a plan into a downtown section of the city that specialized in dusty books. The dusty books lined the street, with signs blaring their cheapness: "Any book fifty cents."

Purely by accident, I paced the dusty-book streets for an hour, then darted into a shadowed stairwell that led to a cool but airless cellar.

Students who had seldom been exposed to sunlight wormed their way among dark and moldly tunnels. A few boys crawled ladders to get at cracking leather tomes on hard-to-reach shelves.

Obeying an instinct, I crouched, sniffing, and moved on my haunches along the bottom rows of dusty books. And there, with one unerring move, I grabbed a decayed volume entitled *Gather Ye Rosebuds*.

The book had been covered with plastic to hold it together. The plastic, in turn, had become a cataract of grime. I wiped at the back flap. My hands came away black.

But at last I could see him whom I must now admit was my beloved. Julian D. Sarkoff.

My tears splashed, cleaning away more of the grit that obscured those tender features. *Oh, my darling,* I thought, clearing a view of his eyes, *this is you.*

Instinctively I had known that the safari-jacketed Julian on *Mortal Coils* was not the real Julian. Even the aviator-shaded Julian who grinned from *Naked Faces* was only an imposter.

Here, at last, was the real man. Or boy—for his thin white neck and dewed eyes had still the look of a young scholar, as did his sweater, innocently balled with fuzz, helplessly rolled up at the wrists. He wore unflattering glasses; taped at the bridge with adhesive.

What happened, Angel? I begged the now clear and shining face.

"You want that book, miss?" a sweating person demanded from a ladder above me.

I nodded. *More than I've ever wanted anything in my life.*

"A quarter."

And so for a quarter I sold away my sanity and my heart, for once I held *Gather Ye Rosebuds* to my chest, where it soiled my white shirt, no other man could exist for me.

❧

Fate goosed me up the stairs, out to the blinding street. Blinking, lost, I stumbled into a man of substance and strength. He steadied me and I looked up . . .

Into the twenty years older, thicker, sadder face of him who was pictured right there against my breast. "Julian!"

He looked at me and I looked at him. And forget everything that happened before. The real trouble had just begun.

We knew we had something to do with one another.

❧

Led like puppets on the string by that mystical being whom Julian referred to as "The Great Promoter," we walked slowly along the parched avenue.

"Where have you been?" he asked me.

"Busy." *Lying on the carpet with my hand outstretched for the phone.*

He explained that he had just flown in from Vegas the day before and that he'd been trying to reach me. Because I wanted to believe him, I did.

❧

On the floor of my apartment, my head rebounded against the parquet. Right over there. (Love, this doesn't bother you, does it? That Julian Sarkoff made love to me on the floor just a few feet away from where we now lie?)

Never before had even Sarkoff taken me with such

intensity. We wrestled and writhed, trying to avoid the sharp little feet on my end tables.

I could feel him. Really feel him.

Once, in our earlier trysts, Sarkoff had poised himself in midthrust and demanded, "What does this feel like to you?"

Because he refused to continue until I told him, I'd hemmed and hawed and said: "Not what you'd think. More amorphous. Like percussion. Vague and liquid."

Well, now I could redefine those sensations. As he thrust sideways, then to and fro, I felt he was setting my margins farther apart. If an X ray could be taken (one was later), I felt sure it would define every irradiated crease, and a down-curved smile upon his nether face.

As he surveyed some new boundary, I almost screamed. It was exquisite, and almost unendurable. I was too, too tenderly aware.

(That day I called it love; within a few weeks I learned there was a medical explanation.)

Afterward, as a dying summer sun striped our bodies through my venetian blinds, Sarkoff held me and said I could have the key to his apartment. "We'll be more comfortable there," he rubbed his back. "On the carpet. You'll also be wanting to get in with groceries."

❧

My joy knew no bounds. Five pounds lighter, I flew for weeks. The grocery sacks felt solid and safe within my arms. I could hardly wait to leave work, go to a Safeway, the liquor store, and then on up to what I could almost call "home."

Tina Rossini caught me in the elevator and tried to warn me. "You have the key to his apartment, but not his mailbox. That's trouble."

I brushed her aside, as I did the now rheumy-eyed Gordon Fox. Fox waylaid me in the corridors, and begged to reinstitute our lunches. Every time I refused, he fell deeper into his now declared "love."

There was no way to get rid of him. Perhaps if I suddenly cried: "You're the one! I love you!" he could have turned on his heel. But I couldn't say those words.

I could see real trouble building when he snatched up a Kleenex with which I'd blotted my lips and asked if he could keep it. "All right, Gordy," I said, calling my victim by the name his father and nanny had favored.

How sad, I reflected, watching him fold the old Kleenex and walk with his now uneven gait toward the executive men's room.

~

If I felt sad for Mr. Fox, that was but a shadow on my sun-dappled path. I fairly skipped along the streets of the city. Strangers hailed my new mood: "Hi, smiley . . ."

"Hey, beautiful!"

"Happy lady!"

I chatted for five minutes with the checkout boy at Safeway, and he said, as he rang up my order, "You've really brightened my whole day."

In the ladies' room, I urged the others not to despair. "There is love. Julian is wonderful."

Dolores, applying eyedrops for a duct problem, expressed renewed hope that "Bill will come back to me now. I just know it."

Only Tina Rossini, in a mist of harsh hairspray, glowered disapproval.

"Bill is a shit, and Julian is a shit." She outlined her lips with Love's Hot Shimmer.

~

I spent almost every night at Julian's apartment. One or two nights, he needed to be alone. I understood, and went home to throw myself into laundry.

As a semiresident at his apartment, I had certain rights but was denied others. I had the heavy brass keys to both the entrance and his own door, but not the cute little silver one for the mailbox.

My name did not appear anywhere.

Yet the kitchen was mine. "Do what you want in there," Julian invited.

His was the kitchen of a man who had lost all hope. The clever gadgets, rusted by disuse, indicated only that there had been some optimistic start at least four years earlier. Now, the refrigerator breathed decay. Last year's lettuce lay bagged in a blackened rot, much as the "decomposed remains" I had to work with at the office. Cheeses had sprouted hallucinogenic whiskers. An unidentifiable fruit huddled brown and shriveled in the vegetable bin.

There was also a mystery vial of clear and evil fluid, which I poured at once down the drain. Julian told me later it was worth a thousand dollars, but he did not seem angry. I guess he didn't want that poison in his system any more than I wanted him to have it. So when I found a stash of cubes, I tossed them into the toilet, too.

The bathroom was a divided territory. I had rights there, but within limits. I had to promise to hide all my "female junk" in a cabinet under the sink. I did so, thinking, *I'll move it up later, when I can have shelves of my own.*

The only section of what we called Sarkoffville that was absolutely *verboten* to me was the roped-off area, where Julian did his writing. "Nobody goes there but me," he warned.

I agreed, but felt a powerful pull. The first time Julian took a long shower, I leaped over the rope, stayed inside for one second, then leaped back out.

When he emerged, a towel wrapped at his hips, he looked suspicious.

I tried to stay out of there, but, as you'll see, the attraction became overwhelming and may well have destroyed me. If only I had never seen the strongbox he kept there, under his typewriter stand. . . . Well, that was later.

❧

At night, he murmured those unintelligible endearments. I could never quite understand his words, yet they excited me more than anything I'd ever heard.

My passion was real, even if my climaxes remained somewhat questionable. One night, as we finished making love in the conversation pit, Julian saw through me: "Are you faking?"

I blushed, and nodded.

"Are you *blushing?*"

My face was on fire. "No," I told him. "This is fake blushing."

I felt his belly shake. We both laughed.

"You've got a great act."

"Ummmm. . . ." He nibbled at my earlobe: "Let's take it from the top."

And from then on we did just fine.

❧

I spun into Dr. Lasky's office. "I won't have to come back here!" Instead of taking my seat in the old vinyl armchair, I did a half-remembered pirouette around the desk. "I'm in love! I'm in love!"

Dr. Lasky hunched over in a racking spasm. I leaned over and patted his shoulder. "Still sick?"

"Things aren't going well."

"What's the matter?"

"I'd better not get into it. . . ." He looked up at me, and I noticed for the first time that sad yellow bubbles hung on his eyelids, like permanent tears.

"Your happiness worries me," Dr. Lasky said, pointing to the chair. "Sit down."

To oblige, I perched on the armrest. "Listen, there's no problem. I love him and he loves me."

Some fluid eked from Dr. Lasky's eyes. He fixed his stare upon my face.

"Okay," I broke, sliding back down into the seat. "He hasn't said the words yet. But I *feel* that he cares. And it's just a technical thing, those little words. . . ."

❧

"Hasta la vista!"

Sarkoff turned and waved before running to board an Aeronaves flight to Tijuana.

I pressed my body against the glass shield that prevented nonpassengers from following their loved ones. Nose and breasts flattened, I strained to watch Julian's tall, strong back for as long as possible. Then he and his Olivetti turned a corner and disappeared into a tube.

❧

Tina Rossini heard me crying within my stall in the ladies' room. "Stupid," she yelled from the other side, "don't cry over that pompous prick!"

As she lectured me, I could see her feet, yellowed and horn-nailed, supported on blocks of wood and bound in plastic straps. Her feet braced; she held her ground.

"This 'one man at a time' thing is passé. You have to sleep with someone else. Always keep one other on the back burner. Look at you: You're locked into all that emoting and nausea; you're a prisoner in a toilet stall, for God's sake!"

❧

I conceded that her ideas had validity. It was agreed, when I emerged, that I should have a one-night stand "As a prophylactic against falling in love."

To find a new outfit for me, we went to a mass try-on room at Alexander's. Surrounded by shivering protoplasm, I cautiously slipped on an overt black Arnel number, which Tina Rossini had selected as a "man getting" dress, a dress that says "Yes."

Women on both sides of me were wedging into too-narrow French jeans. In the mirror, I could see a thin black girl tying on a "santy-pants," in accordance with the hygiene rules for bikini fittings. She stood in confusion, the giant paper towel jutting out of the miniscule yellow crotchet bathing suit bottom.

"Shhheeee-it," she said to herself. Then, turning to us, "Am I okay in this?"

Tina appraised her. "You can go a size smaller. I wish I had your stomach."

"I wish I had your tits," laughed the black girl.

"I'll trade you. Anytime."

"You're on."

~

In the dress that said "Yes," I walked alone, that night, into the Purple Pantaloon. For a "swingles" bar, the Purple Pantaloon looked empty and still. A light show played across the bare walls. The tables and chairs awaited an army of available, carousing men. Fat candles, trapped in plastic net, sat unlit.

The juke box blared out my own mood: "Town Without Pity." I walked along the bar and tried to make a snap decision concerning the three men who sat, at wide intervals, in what must be "swingle" readiness.

"Remember," Tina had instructed, "you want someone meaningless, someone you can forget right away. Once you go to bed, and it's no big deal, you'll never look at sex in the same dopey way again. You know, it isn't a matter of life and death."

It isn't? I'd been truly surprised.

I ruled out the first man: unshaven and weary. His despair, I felt, even as I passed, was profound. *That wouldn't be meaningless.*

The second man, young but bald, gave me a wet smile, revealing a toothpick between his front teeth. He wore a T-shirt with the message, "69 Breakfast of Champions."

That's too meaningless.

Then I saw him: An absolutely average fellow.

He wore neutral colors: a beige shirt and chino pants. *That's him.*

I popped up on the stool beside him. The bartender, a rather cute fellow with a moustache, approached, and I ordered "an orange juice."

My throat felt scratchy. I was afraid I might be coming down with something. *But I won't let sickness stop me,* I thought, taking some vitamin C pills from my purse.

"Can I have one?" my guy asked. "My nose is all stuffed up."

And so it began. As I doled out the vitamins, I flashed him my most obvious "C'mon" smile.

He held out his palm for a long time. I regretted I was carrying my most expensive units—1,000 mgs. For this total stranger, 500's would have been good enough.

Already, I didn't give a damn about him.

We chatted awhile, exchanging lists of movies we'd seen. I had not seen any of his, and he had not seen any of mine. *Good. Nothing in common.*

He told me his name was Tom, that he was new in town, and that he came from Indiana. "My dad," he confided, "raises hybrid popping corn."

Uh-oh. Something personal.

His eyes wandered to my breasts, which were as prominently displayed as my breasts can be. I realized that Tom was having trouble making the transition from popping corn to sex.

I decided to help him out: "Corn stalks are either male or female, aren't they?" I spoke from knowledge gleaned during my visits to my former in-laws.

Tom's dull brown eyes gleamed. "You bet. That's the big problem. Crosspollination. If we don't watch out, the wrong corns will mate, and we'll get a lousy kernel."

I leaned forward in what I hoped was a seductive

way. "How do you keep the wrong corn from getting it on?"

Tom grinned, pleased to be on the right track. "We tie little hoods over their tassels."

◆

This led, in no time at all, to an invitation to see his apartment. Again, I remembered Tina Rossini's advice: "Don't take him home. He'll eat all your food. And if he's a lousy lover, as most of them are, the memory of him is going to stink up your place for a long time. So go to his apartment, where you can get out fast."

"My room's so small I don't even have a real bed in it. But I got a couch that turns into a bed." Tom grinned.

Smile, I ordered myself.

"You 'n' me could have a real rompout up there."

"A rompout sounds terrific," I gagged.

Tom stood up. Surprise: He wasn't going to be all that easy to forget; I guessed his height at six feet eight.

◆

Suddenly Lilliputian, I stumbled onto the street alongside him. We took a too-bright bus uptown. Was that a cold sore starting on his lower lip?

Silently, I prayed to God or to Julian: *Stop this*.

They didn't.

As inevitably as I would one day lie in a grave, I ended up on Tom's converted couch. Tom sat beside me. I didn't look, but heard the *pffft* of his flip-top beer can.

After a few minutes, he set the beer can on the floor, and lunged, knocking me flat out on the metal-ribbed mattress. His beer-wet mouth covered my face with spittle. Even as I discreetly tried to wipe my cheek against his shirt, I wondered *How did he get me so wet so fast?*

"You got me hot right away," he said, moving into

second gear. His hands wrung my breasts as if they were handballs. I almost cried out in pain.

Mistaking my little sound for enjoyment, Tom blew noisily into my ear.

No falling in love here, I congratulated myself.

"Stand up," he ordered.

He stood and I stood, I at eye level with his steer-horned belt buckle. His penis, under khaki, pointed toward the door. *The right direction to go.*

Save me, I begged his cracking walls and floral linoleum.

My hands fell to my sides. I felt cold all over. I watched as Tom pulled off his T-shirt, then his pants. I heard his belt buckle hit the floor.

My senses were heightened. The sound of his buckle, his breathing, attacked my ears. I could even hear an argument in the next apartment, in Spanish, a man yelling at his wife over lumpy *pollo.* Outside, a police siren screamed, and brakes squealed around the bend.

The only sense that failed me was touch: When Tom touched me he raised only goose bumps. I pulled off my dress and let it fall. As I looked down, I could observe my breasts as if they belonged to someone else. Formerly my favorite parts of myself, they now struck me as unattractive, the nipples a bit downtrodden.

"Hey, you got a bod," Tom remarked.

"So do you."

And so he did: At six feet eight, his torso and legs went on forever, like linguini. The squiggle of his man-hood seemed small in comparison. Would he really be inside me, this skinny giant from popcorn country?

Maybe I already knew him too well. He was no longer a stranger. So this experience wouldn't set me free. Maybe I should just leave.

"Oh, man, I can't wait to get in you," Tom announced, prodding my shoulders so I fell backward upon the wavy mattress. He dove on top of me. Because of his extreme length, he had to position his palms on the mattress on a level with my head, instead of near my shoulders, where other men had rested their weight.

He hung over me. His penis sliced at my thigh. I assumed the Open position.

His penis pointed to the right. In a detached way, I wondered if it would continue to point that way inside me. As he lowered himself, the shaft corrected its angle, as automatic as the arm on my record player.

Let it happen, I told myself.

And perhaps I could have let it happen, if he had not, in a surprise hop, moved his entire torso up, so that he now aimed directly at my mouth. "Wynch you do me, first?"

I stared up in disbelief.

"I like the girl to suck me first."

Oh, do you?

"Gwan, it's good for you."

His bubble-gum colored glans head bobbed in agreement. "High protein," he explained. "Gwan. It tastes pretty good."

Then why don't you have some, Tom?

Out loud, I demurred.

Tom went on to say that back in Indiana, where he had enjoyed celebrity status on the Indiana State basketball team, all the girls had quaffed him and extolled the flavor of his elixir. He was better than a vanilla phosphate, sweeter than a *piña colada*, frothier than a meringue.

I shook my head "No," bumping my nose against his penis, which now waved in disagreement: *You don't know what you're missing.*

"Okay," Tom conceded, "I guess yer frigid. I'll just ball you."

As he set his new course, I snapped my legs shut. "Uh . . . I think I've had a change of heart."

Tom held his position, using his penis as a lever between my thighs.

"I know I should have said something sooner. I shouldn't have come up here with you. But I really thought I was going to . . . but now, I can't. I'm sorry."

"You know I ought to rape you?"

I agreed that that was what he ought to do.

"Shit." He rolled off me, sat on the edge of the bed, and retrieved his beer can. "I'm never going back to that dump again. The last girl I got from there had hair on her tits."

Sigh. Burp. Tom motioned to a mini basketball hoop that hung on the back of his door. "Wanna shoot some baskets?"

He threw me an orange puff ball. We played one on one. He was an excellent player. Nine out of ten. And he was robbed on the tenth. I didn't think my six out of ten was that disgraceful, considering I didn't get to play that often.

After a shower with harsh deodorant soap, I announced that I was leaving.

"Well," he said, "it wasn't a total waste." He had dressed again, and he absently scratched his crotch through his pants. I had noticed he had a problem there: some old scar tissue and new chafe marks. I supposed that was the "jock strap itch" I had heard some mention of at Sportorama.

Oh, what do I know of men and what they suffer?

"I'm really sorry, Tom."

I stood, ready to leave his doorway. He leaned over me and grinned: "Shit. I hardly ever get laid."

"Well, thank you for a lovely evening, and for not raping me. I really appreciated that."

"Heck. I'm not that kind of guy. You know why I didn't?"

"Because you're sweet and gentle?"

"Because yer white."

"Oh, well . . . um. I'll be running along now." He made a weak gesture toward his hip pocket. "You want me to take you home?"

"That's all right."

❧

My heels clacking pavement, I skittered along Ninth Avenue toward my building. I walked near the gutter, as I'd learned in "Defend Yourself!" an *AS* Exclusive, and in my hand I clenched my house key, ready to scratch my attacker's face.

It was well past two in the morning, and only a few winos spiraled by among the trash cans. My doorway gaped black and dangerous.

I had to force myself to step inside. *Look over your shoulder to make sure no one is behind you.* I looked, and there he was: dark, his face shadowed by a hat.

"Please," I blabbered, "I want to live."

He laughed. I caught the familiar timbre of his voice: "Julian!"

❧

"We can't stay apart like that," he said, holding me in his bathtub, where we lay in low suds.

I agreed, but wondered why he said that. Who had ever kept me from him but *him?*

"It was awful. I couldn't enjoy Tijuana, usually one of my favorite places."

He looked tanned and rested, but swore that he hadn't been able to sleep without me. Vowing affection, he turned on his Jacuzzi and let new strong tides swirl around us.

❧

We entered a new stage. He let me keep clothes in a spare closet. Sometimes he invited men friends over, and I served their meal, or just snacks of cheese tidbits and wine. He referred to me once or twice in company as "Mamacita."

❧

I came to know him, as you only know a person you live with. I knew his night groans, and his morning "brain aches." The brain aches were different from headaches: "They start in deeper, right in a back section of the brain, the section I need to finish Book Three."

Julian always started the day with a detailed description of what was bothering him. This "Tsuris du Jour" might be a brain ache, or some new nausea connected with his work.

"I'm not going to be any good today because . . ." was the way he usually launched our breakfast conversation. The truly bad days stand out in my memory: In August, a flyer from Book-of-the-Month Club arrived—offering a gift bonus of Julian's collected works for $2.25. The low price didn't bother him, so much as the italicized warning: *Sensitive readers may be offended by explicit language.*

"Sensitive readers! My ass!" was Julian's response.

There was another bad day in September, when Julian heard, from his agent, that his play *Injured Parties* had been retitled *Bootsie*. And a worse day in November, when he was told *Bootsie*'s option had been dropped.

The worst day came in December: Writer's Guild West informed Julian that he had not sold enough material in the past eighteen months to entitle him to all their benefits. As a result, he had to mail back his prescription drug card.

"This finishes me," he said, slipping the celluloid card into an envelope.

I did what I could to comfort him.

༄

"There's nothing too terrible that we can't share," he told me one night as we lay joined.

I looked up surprised. I hadn't expected Julian to start talking in complete sentences at this stage of our union. His breathless sweet nothings had always endeared him to me.

"What are you thinking about while I do this to you?"

I shook my head.

"Come on. You can't shock me. Are you pretending I'm someone else?"

"No." *Are you pretending I'm someone else?*

"You know what I think about?" he asked, continuing an insistent thrust. "Or are you too middle-class to want to know?"

"No. I'm not too middle-class."

I smiled, hoping he could not see me in the dark. In my parents' home, "middle class" was still something you aspired to.

His voice took on a fantasy tone, and his eyes focused above my head. "We're at a party. A book party. At the Top of the Sixes. You look very sexy, very desirable in a long, clinging, white dress."

He concentrated: "I watch you from across the room, as I autograph copies of my new book. You turn your back on me. Your dress is so tight. I can see the cheeks of your ass. And there's no panty line, so I know you're not wearing anything underneath."

I tried to match his breathiness: "I haven't got a thing on underneath."

"You turn, facing me, and bend over to pick up a meatball *hors d'oeuvre* that has fallen. You spear the meatball with a toothpick. As you bend over, I see your cleavage—even the tips of your nipples. Your breasts almost spill out of your dress."

I began to lag. "Does anyone else notice this?"

"No. Everyone is looking at me. Nabokov is talking to me. I watch you walk to the other end of the room. You enter the cloakroom."

"I enter the cloakroom."

This is picking up, I thought. *I guess this is a side benefit to sleeping with a literary giant.*

"There is a kind of dutch door—closed on bottom, open on top. You lie down on the floor of the cloakroom so no one can see you . . . although people are standing a few feet away."

"Isn't there a hatcheck girl?" I had to ask.

"No. She left. I walk to the cloakroom and climb over the dutch door. In so doing, I step on the train of your dress and rip it. Your lower limbs are exposed to me. You look away, shy and embarrassed."

You got me there.

"I open my pants and you see the Penetrator."

That got me.

"Oh, yes. I see it. Oh, what do you do now?"

"I take you right there. Still standing: Everyone can see me from the waist up. No one can see that I'm holding you to my loins. You're hanging there just below the edge of the door."

I asked if Nabokov was watching.

"Only disinterestedly. Pronounce that *NAH-BO-KOV*. The conversation still swirls around me. Everyone is talking about my book. I smile and nod politely. No one guesses what I'm doing behind that dutch door until . . ."

"Until?"

"Until you're so excited by what I'm doing to you that you can no longer control yourself." He panted. "Even though there are eighty-seven people in the room, and many of them are from the New York *Times Book Review* section, you cannot help yourself. You make a sound."

A warmth that had risen in my thighs began to ebb. "A sound? What kind of sound?"

"A scream. Almost a scream. Like this: EI-YEEEEEEOOOOOOO!"

Under my breath, I repeated, "Eeeeiiiiiooooo?"

Sarkoff's breath came in staccato pants: "Everybody hears you. They run to the dutch door. They see you hang from my groin . . . your legs wrapped around my waist."

His eyes bulged. His head went back. Cords knotted in his neck.

Who is this? I wondered. *I've never seen him before.*

"EEEEEYEEEEEEEEEOOOOOOO! *Everyone can see us!*"

They cannot.

I wanted to say, *Please come back, be the man you used to be.* Instead, I launched a series of violent thigh vibrations. These paroxysms, although phony, continued long after I wished them to stop.

What were these new shudders? They weren't orgasms, but more like orgasms in reverse, each spasm more intense and painful than the last: Sarkoff had unsprung the deepest chord within me, and I lay desperately thwanging.

Finished, Sarkoff collapsed on top of me, with his elbow tugging my hair, it seemed, by the roots. I whimpered.

"Ummm, great fucking," he mumbled into my hair. "Now, tell me what *you* were thinking. Come on. I'll understand. Anything."

The thwanging inside me sharpened. I could picture all my organs irradiated in neon. "I was wishing," I whispered to the safest section of his body, his neck, "I was wishing you could say you loved me."

"Jee-sus." He rolled off me and hunted for his cigar. "That old thing. Why'd you drag that in?"

He found the cigar and peeled it. "Come on, Al, tell me something that will turn me on."

❧

Was it only the night before that we had walked with our hands in each other's pockets through the first fallen leaves in Central Park? Only last night when he had explained the importance of time?

"Look," he said, as we stood under the sodium lights installed to discourage muggers, "these are the hard facts and figures: I'm thirty-seven and a half years old. With the history of thrombosis in my family, I'll be lucky if I'm around ten years from tonight, fifteen at the outside. You know what that leaves me? Maybe 3,650 nights left to go. I can't waste them, throw them away just to be polite."

"I feel the same way," I assured him. My fingers had found a hole in his pocket lining, and I couldn't resist tickling him a little.

"You're what? Twenty-six? With any luck at all, you'll go to seventy-five. Hell, maybe more. Women live forever. There are whole crowds of them over a hundred—knitting and watching TV. And how many hundred-year-old guys? There's only one, in Russia. What I'm saying is that you, Al, have a minimum, *minimum* of 18,250 nights. You can afford to throw away one now and then, maybe even kill a week with some deadheads at Club Med in Guadeloupe. . . ."

This last referred to an invitation I had mentioned. Tina Rossini and Dolores were going and had invited me along. I had said I wouldn't go without Julian.

"I can't lose a week there," was his reply. "And I don't think they'd be such hot company."

Later, he would see Tina Rossini in one of her leather outfits and say, "She's got a nice pair." And I, turncoat bitch, would say, "They sag"—which was just one more thing I would look back upon with deep regret.

But that came later, when I was whooshing down the greased slide.

I asked Sarkoff about all those nights he spent watching the Knicks. He gave me his cute "eyebrows up" expression. "Those nights? Those aren't wasted!"

And the nights "shooting the shit" at Patty's, Elaine's, The Lion's Head, and other bastions of the *homo sapiens literati?* He had totaled up, if eyewitness accounts could be trusted, at least four thousand of those.

"Those were okay," he reflected. "Those were okay."

I asked him about the time with me. Was that wasted?

In answer, he brushed his lips across my forehead and said, "Hey, come on," which I took to mean . . . well, you know what I took it to mean.

❧

My mistake. And can any mistake scald your insides and make you want to dive under water like the mistake of believing someone wants you?

~

A warning thwang in my belly sent me, one week later, to a Park Avenue gynecologist who specialized in ushering thin-hipped society mothers through delicate pregnancies. Pam Richards, at *Thrilling*, had been ushered by Dr. Lawrence Parkness, and she swore he had the lightest touch and warmest speculum in the business.

While sitting in the waiting room among the head-tossing society *prima paras*, I flipped through the latest issues of *Baby World* and "Do You Know the Warning Signs?"

Know them? I read on: I *had* them. Of the seven deadly danger signs listed, I could tick off six. The only thing I didn't have was the hoarse throat.

I'd been hiding from my own body's distress. Now I had to face facts. I had *sores that would not heal*. I'd bumped my knee on my desk two months ago, and I could still see the mark.

Worse still was the situation with the mole on my inner thigh. I could swear that just last week that mole was an inch to the right. *Change in a mole*.

Before I could dwell on the other signs, I asked Dr. Parkness's nurse if I could see the doctor right away. *Better set my mind at rest. He'll be able to tell me that it's all my imagination.*

~

High in the stirrups, I spread, as instructed, for the distinguished, silver-templed Dr. Lawrence Parkness. "Lower, please," he requested.

I inched my pelvis to the edge of the obstetrical table and splayed my legs even farther apart.

Not my best angle.

Dr. Parkness's pale face, seen between my thighs, frowned in professional detachment. I wondered: *"What's he thinking?"*

Fresh-shaven, his skin gleamed with a pale baby-blue moisture, the result, I guess, of fifty years spent peering into uncertain cervixes. Was he finding me plebeian in comparison with the fragile fillies he usually examined?

"Hello, I'm Jane's reproductive system," someone announced. "I have two ovaries, shaped like dried Anjou pears. . . ."

Who spake thus?

Afraid for a terrible second that it was I, I looked wildly around the white-enameled room.

There, in a corner, so still I had not seen her, was a woman, holding a cassette. Dr. Parkness explained that his nurse would play educational tapes during my visits.

"Each month I release an egg . . . no bigger than a speck of dust . . . and begin the long, tiring journey down those long, twisting tunnels called the Fallopian . . ."

Dr. Parkness inserted his pink-gloved hand into "love's domain."

"Let me know if you feel anything when I press."

His rubber fingers traveled within me. I wanted to catch the expression on his face, but Dr. Parkness had ducked below a white drape. In an attempt at modesty I could not fathom, the drape covered my stomach and knees, while my pudenda waved in the breeze.

Dr. Parkness's voice sounded thick, muffled under the cotton: "What seems to be the problem here?"

I didn't want to mention the thwanging right out, or that Sarkoff felt like a fire poker when he thrust inside me. So I hedged and said:

"I've been nervous and upset. I find myself feeling as if I might start crying, for no reason."

"Ummmmm. . . ." He had an echo, now: "Ummmmm."

His speculum, warm as promised, joined his rubber fingers in my sacred amphitheater.

"Do you bleed after marital relations?"

"No." *Not so anybody'd notice.*

"Feel anything when I do this?"

He pressed.

"No."

Now, in another direction.

"No."

I said "No" several times, then felt something which caused me to scream.

"A little sensitive there."

"That was it. You plucked it. The thwanging part."

I told him the rest then: that I had sores that wouldn't heal, and a mole crawling all over my thigh. "I've been drinking a lot of diet soda lately . . . and Sweet 'n' Low in my coffee . . . and even my hair conditioner, I read that it causes . . . you know . . ."

Dr. Parkness straightened, and peeked dewily at me from between my thighs.

I held him with my legs. These doctors will brush you off with iron pills if you don't tell them everything —"Look at me. Look at my eyes. The whites. They're *yellows*. . . ."

"You can get dressed now, Mrs. Berry."

"It's *Ms*."

"Ms."

❧

We reconvened in his consulting room. Now that I was wearing a suit, I felt somewhat silly. Surely, I was worried about nothing. I shouldn't have even mentioned the mole. Who knew where on my thigh it truly belonged?

I didn't like Dr. Parkness's opening line, delivered with a white card: "This is the address of the lab."

He explained there would be tests. "I took a smear too."

"I thought I felt something." Like a Popsicle stick.

He kept his voice casual: "You'll get a post card in a few days. If it says 'Positive,' call for an appointment with my nurse."

"I'm in the middle of an intense relationship with a man," I blurted out.

His marbleized eyes rolled. "I know."

～

After my blood was taken and filled a glass spinning wheel, I headed for my demihome, Julian's apartment. A small cape of dread hung across my shoulders. *He'll make me feel better*, I thought, wedging my brass key into his lock.

The apartment waited, more soundless than I'd ever found it. The goat-hair rug prickled as I moved to the great raft bed.

On the pillow I thought of as "my" pillow there was a typed note:

Mamacita,
Went crazy over new lead. Must think things over in Rio. Take Care. Will return with 1,000 words.

Hasta la vista,
J.D.S.

～

There is a symmetry to our situations. One person balances another. The next day, I sat within rice paper screens at Benihana Palace with Gordon Fox. After we had both opted for chicken teriyaki, a young, thin Japanese boy with a headband and wild eyes began his kamikaze cutting and stir-frying. As I watched his blades slash pink chicken flesh, the boy seemed to return my interest in him.

I felt a shiver. Stopped it. I've had some strange shivers, but I do have my limits.

Food, oddly enough, had never tasted better. I supped a hot onion broth and downed my clay thimbleful of sake. Fox watched me, his gill lips in a smile.

His hand gripped mine, forcing me to drop the porcelain soup ladle. "Do I seem different to you?"

I looked up from my bowl. "You do have a different quality."

"That's because Gordy has good news for you."

Good news? I laughed. What could be good?

"I've left Marcy," he almost sang.

Marcy. I didn't know any Marcy. Then I remembered: "Oh! Marcy!"

At this point, the young samurai chef beheaded a broccoli. I nodded my appreciation.

"It wasn't easy, but I did it." He spoke in an alarming new voice, the cackling voice of a parent to a child: "You didn't think Gordy could do it, did you?"

The chef bowed and departed. I was sorry to see him go.

"It's going to take a while with Kerry and Matthew, but I'm sure, in the end, they'll accept"—his eyes filled —"us."

I dropped my chopsticks. *Kerry? Matthew? Marcy? Us?*

Mr. Fox went on to say that Marcy had taken it hard, but would be appeased by a large settlement and ownership of their vacation house, The Palms, and their small yacht, *Bluebird*.

"It's Kerry who worries me. He's the vulnerable one. Matthew? He can kid around about anything. Take the punches and roll. But Kerry, he's stuttering again. This morning it took him a half hour to ask for toast. *T*'s and *d*'s trip him up. He can't get 'Daddy' at all anymore. And his teacher called to say he peed in a milk container during snack break."

From container to container, in three generations. What a legacy, I reflected.

Fox drained some sake. "Even King is affected; he used to be paper trained."

Our waiter reappeared with a dessert menu. "Ice cream? Kumquats?"

I felt sick. "No, thank you."

Fox beamed, and pulled an attaché case up from beneath the table. He smiled as if he knew his next words could only delight me: "How'd you like a roommate tonight? Bet you never believed I'd leave my wife for someone like you. None of my friends in Connecticut will believe it."

Someone like me.

For the next ten minutes, I used the word "really" more than I've ever used any word in my life: "You're *really* nice. *Really* kind. *Really* attractive. *Really* generous." But I'd always thought "ours was a *really* professional relationship," and "I *really* don't see how it could be anything else."

Bitch! I called myself. I should never have started these lunches. They weren't free lunches. I had to pay. Worse, Marcy, Kerry, Matthew, and King had to pay.

He plucked a wedding ring from a folded hanky. The ring looked old and worn. I imagine it had come off an old, worn finger.

"I used soap to get this off . . . Marcy's finger had swelled."

"I'm really sorry . . . but I can't go with you. I'm sorry."

I was. Never again, I swore, never again be so unaware of what someone may be filling into their own private vacuum.

"Don't give me that," he hissed. With a quick but not wide gesture, he tossed the wedding ring onto the stone table, near some mustard sauce.

Sensing more to come, I backed up and grabbed my purse. I almost made it out the folding screen without hearing his parting shot:

"Filthy twat."

༄

The next day, New York lay glazed under a freak ice storm. Winds of new intensity blew the autumn leaves prematurely off their branches. The Gulf & Western Building swayed. At Penn Plaza, windows shattered, raining fine glass upon pedestrians.

On West Forty-second Street, outside The Juggernaut, the police erected barricades and ropes to aid

Actual Slayings and *Thrilling Romances* employees en route to their tasks.

I liked the ropes. *Why aren't these here everyday?* I wondered, gripping them in a wrist-over-wrist motion. A few times my coat billowed over my head and my feet skidded out from under me. With effort I straightened up, and dragged myself inch by inch toward the building.

Work will take my mind off my problems.

I had to concentrate on something besides Sarkoff in Rio, my lab report, and what Gordon Fox had called me in Benihana.

As I took my place in an elevator crammed with stiffened, red-faced *AS, OS,* and *Fruitarian* workers, I felt my spirits ascend. How petty my personal problems now seemed against this backdrop. I felt a twinge of guilt: There was a job to be done, and I was already an hour late.

In my absence, no doubt, a pile of corpse layouts would have accumulated. Pulling off my coat, I ran to my office.

A girl, freckled and blond, looked up from a spread on car trunk victims. "I can't fit these in," she was saying to herself. When she saw me, she looked up with polite interest. "Looking for someone?"

"Who're you?"

She introduced herself. I didn't catch the name, only that she was from Office Temporary Service. "They brought me in to replace some girl who couldn't handle the . . ."

"Me!" I yelled. "Me! My job! My desk!"

At this precise moment, Denny, balancing two coffees and a platter of prune danish, walked into the Art Department. His face screwed into an apology: "I talked to Marrone. But the slip came from somebody upstairs. It was in your box yesterday, but you didn't come in and pick it up. Where did you go after lunch?"

I shook my head.

"Al, let's face it. Your work had been slipping. I tried

to cover for you. But you goofed with the police chief. And there was a severed breast on that 'Louisiana Slasher' layout. You didn't draw an arrow toward it, and several readers wrote in to complain."

"Where was it?" I demanded. "Where was there a severed breast? That's just an excuse. . . ."

Denny whipped out the stat. "It's the crumbly thing on the floor."

"Anyone could have missed it."

"Well, maybe not 'anyone' should be assistant art director at *Actual Slayings*."

"That cut, Denny."

"Look . . ." He set the danish down before the Office Temporary girl, who began to nibble. "Look, Al . . . you know I love you. We all love you. But the word came down that you got to go. Your ass is kicked, baby."

"One little mistake?"

"You missed another one: In 'Ohio Prober Nails the Sock Strangler,' you wrote 'his sock became an important clue' under the picture of the medical examiner. Marrone has to print a retraction: 'His sock was not a clue.' "

I didn't want to hear any more. I reached across the Office Temporary girl's shoulder and snatched up my personal effects: a small terrarium and a hand-sculpted ashtray.

"We're a unit here, Al," Denny continued. "And we just don't know where your head's been at lately." He went on to toss the thin lifeline of free-lance artwork, if not here, for *Real Killing*, a new magazine Marrone was aiming at a "more urban" market.

～

Was it an hour later? I found myself tumbling headlong down a fungoid gray stairwell, seeking sanctuary in the ladies' room of a subway-level Horn & Hardart.

I rushed into its miasma and faced the lipstick writing

on the wall: "Suck My Pussy—453-6789." And "CALEB DAVIS IS A SHIT."

You can't get away from it, I realized.

For several seconds I confronted my reflection. *How're you doing today, Alice?*

Not so hot.

Yet I was surprised at how well I looked, if a corroded mirror can be trusted. *You've seldom looked better,* I encouraged my mirror image, across whose forehead I could read:

"Want a real woman? Call Shirlene: All nights only. 897-6543."

I thought for a split second of calling Shirlene, "shooting the shit" with her. There was a basis for friendship.

Instead, I pulled off my coat and lifted my sweater to see how my breasts were doing.

They looked okay. They were still there, anyway.

I felt for lumps, and found some.

Figures.

I struck several attractive poses. My waist looked very small. I'd finally lost all the weight I would ever need to . . .

If only I could make love now; I would really like to touch and be touched. . . .

My terrarium looked dry. I held it under the faucet. It drank.

A sudden clang from one stall alerted me. I was not alone! I straightened my clothes.

From the other side of a stall came a banging and a muttering. I looked down and spotted a set of elephantine ankles wrapped in Ace bandages. Beside the ankles rested a still life of bucket and mop. A deep voice muttered:

"Lookin' so fine, so tough . . . like they wus real ladies. On'y I'se got dair numbah. Dem's makin' messes. Ah try to run a nice, clean place. An dems don't even pull de chain. Dem's too fine."

She appeared: black, behemoth. She moved heavily to the radiator, retrieved a small wrapped sandwich from among the gratings, and checked to see the cheese slice between the bread.

"Wal, dey didn't get mah lunch. Dem's so fine, so tough . . . but dey see that samwich, I won't get to eat foh all de tea in China!"

She replaced the sandwich and resumed a slurpy mopping of the tiles around her feet.

Women must help each other more, I thought, and said I'd like to finish the job. She looked suspicious: hurt. I felt sorry: What I'd done had bitten into her pride.

"Why don't you weigh yourself?" she suggested, in what I took to be a conciliatory gesture.

I stepped onto the scale: an antique job with a fat, oval face and a fortune window.

"Be shoh an' read yoh fortune," the mop lady said.

And I knew that the mysterious forces that had steered me of late would assert themselves again:

This fortune was the real fortune.

My weight—170!—was way off; but not the message, which the huge black woman read over my shoulder:

"You gawn to meet an interesting stranger."

❧

There followed several days in which I wandered the city. I had no place to go. Sarkoff's apartment felt haunted, and I was afraid if I stayed in there, I would hop over the ropes and crack into the strongbox—the strongbox which I now felt contained the secrets of his essential being, secrets that could free him to really love me, or provide me proof positive that he didn't give a damn, and so set me free to start looking, once more, for the Loner.

When I went to my apartment, I found roaches and a postcard. I didn't have to turn this one over. It was faceup, like the ace of spades:

Your test was positive. Please call.

❧

My heart beat against my coat. I saw again, for a split second, the back of the sanitation truck, the words on the asphalt: "YOU ARE DYING."

I started to call the doctor, then changed in middial and called Seminole Village. I caught myself, just in time, before Sophie or Max could pick up and innocently say, "Halo?"

What was I doing, calling them? Killing them. This was what they needed, this was what would keep their pacemakers on the right beat.

On my last visit, they had showed me confetti electrocardiograms: "The real ticker tape, huh?" Max had sighed.

"Don't read it," warned Sophie.

"I'll just read yours," countered Max.

∾

I thought of Dolores, then remembered that she and Tina Rossini had gone to Club Med on Guadeloupe. "Come back with tans" had been my last words to them.

∾

And where was Julian Sarkoff? In the land of the string bikini. Working on Book Three.

∾

I went to a movie, and the Pervert sat beside me. As Liv Ullmann floated across the screen in a Bergman fantasy, the Pervert placed a raincoat between our seats and proceeded to rustle underneath.

I would have liked to see the Bergman movie, especially since Liv Ullmann was licking her lips in an expectant way and beckoning to her family physician, but the Pervert's rustling distracted me.

I changed seats. He followed. I left the theater. He followed.

From a pay phone, I confirmed my appointment the next morning with Dr. Lawrence Parkness.

As I spoke, the Pervert opened his pants and pressed his yellow, hooded penis against the glass.

❧

The Pervert accompanied me to the brownstone on West Seventy-ninth Street, where I descended into my bargain basement for mental health. As I ducked down the steps, I heard his refrain: "I know how to do eeet. I know how to do eeet. I do eeet so good."

❧

Dr. Lasky had his head down on his desk. He peeked up over his elbow when I entered. More white showed under his eyes. Christ taking a break from the cross.

"Are you okay?" I asked.

He shut his eyes and nodded. When he opened them again, he seemed to give me a slightly accusing look: "You haven't been coming."

"I'm sorry."

"A lot of my patients don't come anymore. I don't think I'm helping them."

I rushed to the other side of the desk. "That's not true. You helped me. Remember how I was when I came to you . . . the nightmares, the delusions . . ."

I stood before him and urged: "Look at me now."

He did, And then I remembered how awful I felt. I saw myself in his pupils.

We exchanged the look between lifeboat passengers who know their little boat will not be found. Dr. Lasky smiled then . . . at least his wispy moustache moved. I smiled too.

❧

$\mathcal{D}$o you want to hear about the worst one now: the dogfood king?

~

Well, I may have a little wine with this. Although I recovered from it long ago, I warn you: This is pretty raw.

~

I told you I'd been thinking about that strongbox in Sarkoff's roped-off area. Well, I'd done more than think. I have a little confession. I poured wax in the lock.

I hated myself for doing it. That's just the sort of low, snoopy thing I can't stand. But there it is, I did it.

No excuses. And I'm sorry, especially since what I found in the strongbox sent me out in the night on a sexual rampage, thinking all the way to Flo's, *I'll show him. I'll show him.*

Who's Flo?

Oh, I guess I forgot to mention. Flo isn't a person. Flo is a bar.

Can I really tell you this one? I can't believe I did it—that I became involved, however briefly, with . . . Well, I'm getting ahead of myself.

Judge me, if you must.

Understand only, that on this particular occasion I was searching not for love, but for the death of love. Okay? I lost hope for a few hours . . . lost my belief that I would find you. Forgive . . .

Let's get into Flo's. . . .

Picture a dark bar on what's called the fashionable

East Side—a bar, so dark it's even darker by day than it is at night. There is one leaded ruby lamp somewhere in the back, and that stains the main room with a carnal glow.

People come to this warm gloom not for the drinks, which are weak, or for the food, which is sinewy, but for the darkness and each other.

Flo's is a place where men and women meet only once. So what was I doing there? In a weakened condition, no less?

I'll tell you, in a minute. First, I want you to feel as I felt when I walked in there. I was my own robot. A robot in a Tapemeasure markdown cashmere dress, and unstable shoes.

As always in a public meeting place, I felt physically aware to the point of pain. I choreographed my own actions:

Walk. Sit down. Order a drink. Face the door. Smile. Look approachable.

Under my own remote control, I slid onto a bar stool. I lit a cigarette and crossed my legs. When the barmaid leaned over I asked for "Cinzano on the rocks, with a twist, please."

Needing an extra gesture, I rubbed my knuckles across my nose. Later I rattled ice cubes. Much later, I drank from an empty glass.

From somewhere, another record voiced my very expectations: "Strangers in the night, we were two strangers in the night . . ."

Beside me, two beautiful girls (they were beautiful in the dimness, anyway) exchanged diet and medication tips. The girl next to me, a St. Tropez blonde whose teeth flashed white against her tan, recommended body-wrapping. "You don't lose weight. You lose inches."

The other girl, her tan so dark she blended into the mahogany paneling, expressed doubt: "I don't know. I think it's just water weight. Drink two glasses and your hips come back."

This conversation ended as the two girls looked up at the door. I turned and saw the silhouette of a man.

Take him, I ordered myself. *No matter what he looks like. No matter how disgusting.*

That was the plan. You see, I'd decided to sell myself. Just this one time. To prove something.

I had to stop looking for love. Stop saving parts of myself. No one much wanted them. The one-night stand hadn't been a bad idea. But it had failed. Now I saw why: *not extreme enough.*

If a woman sells herself even once, she's a "hooker." To most men. Therefore, my Cinzano thinking went, by selling myself to one man, I can end my need for the approval of all of them.

Good girl. Bad girl. I'd always been described as the former. Time to try the flip side, wouldn't you say?

I'd learned early that any man who called me "nice" was going to put my guts through the mangle. The first boy to touch me, really touch me, you know . . . he taught me that much.

Jimmy Halpern. Best friend's brother. His fingers were calloused. The callouses felt terrific.

Because I was fourteen, I whispered that maybe he should stop touching me. He stopped. And you know what he said then?

He said, "Thank you for stopping me. I'm glad. Now we can go steady. I wouldn't have wanted you if you let guys do that. . . . You would have been secondhand goods."

Secondhand goods.

I didn't say anything that night, but the expression burned a hole in my brain. The next time he called, I said, "I have mononucleosis and can't kiss anyone for six months."

I haven't had much fun since with a man who used the expressions "good," "nice," or "innocent." Robert was always going on and on about my virginity, how he wouldn't have married me without it, how he'd discard me should the sacred seal be broken.

So the hell with "nice." The hell with it forever.

Okay. You want to know what was in the strongbox? An Emko foam can, for starters; and a stack of American Express receipts, from restaurants in Vegas, Tijuana, and Rio. Most of the restaurants were "El" something or other. El Toro, El Boro, El Manuelo.

Take two guesses what J. D. Sarkoff had been doing with an Emko foam can and his El Boro, El Toro companions. Not working on his novel of alienation.

Okay. I knew I knew. . . . I knew inside all along.

I'd shut my eyes to it. And maybe all the El Boroing wouldn't have mattered if I hadn't found the chapters in which "Kevin O'Casey" enjoys the slick service of "a dead-eyed" call girl more than those proffered, for free, by his "slightly plump and skittish girlfriend, Alice Snookerman."

I minded the "Snookerman" almost more than the part with the dead-eyed call girl. Well, I could be as dead-eyed as the best.

Another reason I was here, crossing my legs at Flo's, was my sociological interest. Part of me wondered, *What do men really buy?*

I hoped to find out. It bothered me a bit that the man who bought me would not appreciate these motives. He would think he was buying "a piece of ass." Oh, well. Somehow, any way of saying "Fuck men" involved doing just that.

Flo's reputation was "class." According to Sarkoff's description, everything was understood but not stated. No pimps. No haggling.

At the end of the evening, one hundred dollars would pass hands. Sarkoff had said, "You'd never know they were hookers..."

No satin hotpants. Or plastic boots. No double-decker Dynel falls.

Which was something of a disappointment: Maybe I wanted to wear a double-decker fall and plastic hooker boots. After all, haven't my loves all said I'd be such a wonderful whore? And hadn't I, at the age of ten, allowed a small person, name of Billy Singer, to look up my dress in exchange for his Davy Crockett hat?

Maybe there was hooker in me.

Find out.

Also: Forget about Dr. Parkness's diagnosis. "Something is not quite right," he'd said only that morning on my return visit. "Let's see how crowded they are at Doctors Hospital."

Oh, let's.

Doctors didn't have a room, but would call when they had an opening. Dr. Parkness explained that surgical procedures were indicated in my case. "You look premalignant."

The diet soda! I'd known it all along. Those Tabs had rushed right down to my cervix and were, even now, coursing along with Sweet 'n' Low to sear deadly lesions along my private parts. I thought of all the other poisons I'd imbibed so that I could have a cute figure. This was the inevitable result.

Dr. Parkness went on to reassure me that even if, once he was "in," he had to go ahead with a hysterectomy, my life would not be all that different.

"Many women feel that once their reproductive systems are removed, that they are no longer *real* women. Oh, that may be true, biologically, but hormone treatment can keep your beard growth light, and your voice needn't drop too far down the register. And your big question probably is: 'What will sex relations be like after surgery?' "

That's my big question.

Gill-like creases appeared beside Dr. Parkness's mouth. "I'm happy to say that many women enjoy sex *more*."

"You think it will come to that?" I had to ask.

"Well . . . a bad report while in surgery"—he waved his hand to the window, as if all my organs would go that way—"and it's best to do a thorough cleanout."

Dr. Parkness checked his watch: My time was up. He walked me to the door. "Don't look so scared; these days we don't even cut through the abdominal wall. With a young woman like yourself . . ." His eyes traveled over my body.

Does he want me? I wondered.

". . . I do what's called a 'plastic'—go in through the natural orifice and pull the affected parts out that way." He patted my head. "No scars; you can wear a bikini."

My first tear glided down my cheek. *Wear a bikini.*

෴

I wore my best dress, the Tapemeasure markdown, to Flo's. Because of the "class" reputation, I'd ruled out my snappier outfits—too flamboyant, might offend the sophisticated clientele.

Underneath, I was heavily lotioned. My only precaution: a dab of antibacterial, spermicidal jelly. Unfortunately, my insides burned with hurt. But I would have to overlook that.

So thwanging, premalignant, and jellied, I awaited my first "john."

Is that him? The other two girls and I checked out the man who had just entered. Short but wiry, he led with his head. His attaché case suggested corporate law.

He moved briskly to the bar and ordered a J&B. I didn't like his mouth, which had a wet overhang and promised slobber kisses. But—

I can get past that.

He offered the St. Tropez blonde a light. Their gazes latched. They moved off to a table.

He hadn't wanted me.

The dark girl, against the paneling, rattled her bracelets. She muttered something I didn't catch.

It seemed hours before the next prospect arrived. Tall, oddly wide through the back (was he concealing a hump?), this man lurched over to us.

I took my cue from the dark girl and avoided meeting Humpy's eyes.

I observed him in the smoked mirror over the bar. His nose was long with a bump (matching one on his back?). Hairs curled from his nostrils. His eyes squinted into crescents. Was he a whip freak compensating for jibes he'd endured during his lurching, humpy childhood?

He stood closer. I smelled wet tweed. He smiled, ill-fitting denture whistling into a new place.

I appealed directly to my God: "Come on, not him. This is too great a test. This isn't what an average hooker has to confront on a typical night. This is one she would remember forever."

"Remember your part of the deal," God replied.

"Okay. Okay." I did remember. "You're making it tough on me, but I'll do it. In a way it's better that it's Humpy. This will set the record straight."

Omigod, what kind of Humpy-back penis does he have?

"Would you like to have a drink at a table?" he invited.

I was about to say "Yes" when I realized he had spoken to the dark girl. *Even Humpy didn't want me.*

Laughing into my now empty glass, *Did anyone want me?* I sucked at the glass rim and gave in to curious imaginings. What would Humpy have been like? Perhaps unbearably tender, to compensate for his own lifetime of pain?

"Hey, does anybody here know how to make a Harvey wallbanger?" someone asked. Then I felt him slide in behind me, his damp hand already on my own. "An how yew?"

Thank you, I thought, then looked up.

He wasn't awful, really. Neither was he wonderful. In truth, he resembled Spiro Agnew: a chuck steak wearing a suit.

"Hi, yourself," I said huskily, only it came out *Hunnnnhhhhh.*

A red face beamed back, the eyes squeezed shut.

"Are you from out of town?" I screamed.

"Missouri."

"Show me," I laughed. A mistake. I couldn't stop. Missouri didn't mind. He smiled and nodded until I could come up for air.

I calmed down enough to think: *He's the one. This is it.*

As he discoursed on the disadvantages of being in New York—"the dirt, the traffic, the crime, the noise"—I mentally addressed him:

"You're my ticket to sexual freedom. My coworker in an existential experiment. You will free me forever from the bonds of hope."

"I'm in for the dogfood convention," he was saying. "Sure had ourselves an excitin' day. You wouldn't believe the new products—moist, dry, semimoist, and how humanlike. Looked good enough to eat mis-self. . . ."

"How interesting . . ." I leaned toward him. "I had a dog."

"An what'd you feed it?"

"Table scraps."

Missouri banged his fist on the bar. "Table scraps! That's the worst thing! Makes 'em fat 'n' lazy. Finicky."

He went on to describe the nutritional benefits of his company's dogfood. A name brand, which he had founded on the basis of his pioneering experiments with new, synthetic formulas. "We don't have to rely on the bone meal so much."

Why, I wondered, did my sexual missions usually lead me into the food industry? Did Fate tie me in with chow? Or was this so central to life that one could not cross too many strangers' paths in America without falling into fodder? Missouri worked with test dogs. "To find out what makes 'em grow, what makes 'em happy. I've raised four generations of dogs on completely chemical food." He reached into his pocket. "Lookit here."

He held up a colored slide and flashed his lighter behind it. I could see several black-and-white springer spaniels, their pink tongues lolling in innocence. He put the slide away and pulled out a small sack of gray crystal. "This here's all they've ever eaten. Pure chemical diet."

"No steak?" I cried.

"Steak is a learned taste. Shit, they never had it, they don't miss it."

Missouri warmed to his subject, ordered a Coor's, and went on to explain a dog's protein needs. Still concerned over the springer spaniels, I interrupted: "How about a bone? Couldn't they have a bone?"

"Never. That's our goal. All chemical diet. And kin you keep a secret? We're working up a human line, too."

"You are?" I drew him out. Perhaps our meeting was not random. Or my sexual mission not the real mission. Could I have met anyone other than this man tonight?

Destiny had led me here to Flo's. I was to find out more, as a consumer's Mata Hari. I smelled corporate rot in the air.

With a soft smile, I drew Missouri into deeper conversation. "Tell me more about this synthetic dogfood . . . and did you mean that this chemical diet could be given to people too?"

"Why not? What's the difference between what I whip up in the lab and what you pull out of the ground? Synthetic food's *better*. People have the wrong idea about organic food; they don't know what they're digging out of their gardens. Natural foods are full of toxins. Green peas can kill you. . . ."

I had become engrossed in his speech when Missouri tweaked my nose and said, "Hey, darlin', I must be borin' yew. . . ."

I convinced him to return to his subject. "I try and try and try to git just the right mix of amino acids and trace chemicals but," he sighed, "it ust doesn't . . ." Suddenly, angry Missouri shoved his beer mug down the bar. "Aw, hell . . ."

"What is it?" I touched his red hand. "What's wrong?"

"All right. All right!" he boomed. "Let's talk about it! Let's get it out in the open! Let's not shy away from it!"

"What?"

"Okay," he agreed, as if ending an hour's argument. "Okay. Let's talk about it. It happens. We know it happens. But nobody'll talk about it. Well, I say, let's bring it out in the open. Call it by it's rightful name: Coprophagy! That's right. *Coprophagy!* Dogs'll do it, dogs'll do it. They'll eat THEIR OWN SHIT. Their own shit, goddamnit. Their own shit. Yew know why?"

"No. Why?"

His tiny eyes gleamed. Tears?

"To spite us."

∾

"Why me, Lord?" I asked, downing another Cinzano. "Must I go ahead with this plan? How about—I wait for another guy? Maybe another night?"

God did not reply. And I'm not a quitter. Committed to Missouri, I would not chicken out. I moved with him to a leatherette booth, at the rear.

He had his problems, but I could not respond to: "We tried to get an animal to attend the convention, but the last one, a schnauzer, puked all over our decorations."

All this while, I had not forgotten that we were leading up to sexual congress. But Missouri veered off on so many tangents, I kept thinking, "Where is this leading us?"

At last, Missouri bridged the gap between animal and human husbandry. "We have a mating farm," he chuckled. "And would you be embarrassed at the work we do there. You know anything about the male dog?"

He pulled out a ball-point pen and scribbled something on a Flo's red paper cocktail napkin. "Looky here."

I looked: He'd drawn a large, erect, dog penis. "See the bulbous part? It isn't like, pardon me, the human penis. The dog kind gets sort of stuck in there. Sometimes for as long as half an hour. The kennel men have to reach in and ease it in and out, in and out . . ."

Missouri used this anecdote to jump-start another: "I

207

was in Greenwich Village last summer, saw a couple of, pardon me, *humans* copulatin' on top of a car. I don't know about yew, but I wasn't raised that liberal." His hand dropped below the table. "Yew about ready to go, darlin'?"

I nodded.

He paid for our drinks, and rushed to hold the door for me. Outside, dusk and rain had fallen together. Hobbling to keep under the shelter of Missouri's trick umbrella, we half-ran to the Americana Hotel, where we could become one.

In the vast marble lobby, giant cutouts of St. Bernards greeted us: "Woof. Woof. The dogfood industry welcomes you all."

Another man with a meat face hailed Missouri: "Lloyd! Lloyd!"

So now he had a name. I had to make love to a Lloyd.

The other man wanted to fill Lloyd in on what he'd missed. "The guy from Lassie Recipe gave a really dynamite talk on packaging. He admitted their secret has been Slipability. And you should have seen it come right out of the can."

"They use the white liners, don't they?" mused my man.

"Better believe they do. Makes the chunks show up real purty. But mainly, it's Slipability that put them way ahead. They ran a marketing survey to find out what most women hated about dogfood. Ninety-nine per cent said 'digging it out of the can.' Because, then, what can they do with the spoon? Wash it in the dishwater with all the human forks and spoons?"

Missouri wagged his head. I could see he wanted to get deeper into the subject. But to show he still desired me, he let his hand drop to my left buttock. "Where they've really got us licked," he said, "is in the odor department. Our wet line still stinks."

"Yew in a hurry?" asked the other man. "Let me buy yew a drink."

Missouri's hand hesitated on my bottom. "Maybe just one."

~

In the Royal Box, I sat between the two gentlemen. Their words, buoyed on beer breath, sailed over my head. "Ray Carpenter is working on something for city dogs. Did you hear? If he's really got it, it's a goldmine. *Low residue.*"

Missouri hooted. "Don't have to walk them city dogs no more. Hell, feed 'em low residue!"

I revised my prayer: "God, kill me. Let me die right here. Enough!"

The men argued over distribution. "Why aren't the supermarkets putting us where we belong? Why aren't we next to dog collars, rubber bones, leashes? Huh, why aren't we?"

" 'Cause someone's grabbed that key spot. I say: Go for the corners. That's the point of purchase. That's where Mrs. America stops. She sees . . . she touches . . . she buys!"

I'm learning something.

"Holy shit, yew know what time it is?" He winked at me. *Won't be long now . . . honey.*

~

In his turquoise room on the twenty-first floor, Missouri loosened his belt buckle. "Scusie," he said, moving toward the john. "I'll be right out."

I stood, paralyzed by the window. What should I do? Strip? Stand there, hands on hips? Perhaps one foot on a chair? Or lie on the bed and spread my legs to receive the Dogfood King?

Being me, naturally, I stood there. Missouri took an agonizingly long piss. I could hear him stop and start. The pauses, and the sighs that bridged them, had me worried. Did he have a disease?

"Darlin'," he called out, "could yew do me one small favor? I didn't get a chance to eat. Could you order me up a cheeseburger, with fries, lettuce and tomato, rye toast, no butter, and coffee?"

❧

I was saying "fries" into the phone, when Missouri reappeared, in striped boxer shorts and a T-shirt. He seemed to be stuffing himself deeper into his boxer shorts. "Be a sweet thing, would yew, and see if they've got any chocolate cake."

After I hung up, Missouri took the phone. He asked for the long-distance operator. As he spoke, he ran his hand up and down my leg, then pulled me down on his lap.

"Honey," he said into the phone, "where yew been? To the mall! Whatch yew been doin'—spendin' all my money? I'm jest kiddin'. Go right ahead. . . . What am I workin' for, anyway? Jimmy 'n' Carol bein' good? Yew tell 'em, 'Wait 'til Daddy gits home.' "

Still cradling the receiver, Missouri planted wet kisses along my neck. I could hear squeaks from the phone's perforated mouth: his wife.

His breathing changed. His other hand crawled toward my panty elastic. "Look, darlin'," he said to his wife, "this is goin' to run up the bill."

She continued talking, and he spun the phone receiver on its cord. Her squeaks filled the room. When he held the phone back to his ear, Missouri made a kissing sound goodbye and winked at me.

This is what he's buying.

❧

"I want to see you walk around the room like that."

Naked, I paraded around the bed. Missouri lay back against two pillows. I could see his hand working under the blue-striped shorts.

"Walk over by the window. Bend over. Oh, yeah, darlin' . . . ummmm. . . . I knew yew were the one for me as soon as I walked into Flo's. . . .

I can get through this, and when it's over I'll be different. I won't be saving myself for my True Love. (Darling, forgive me!)

"Oh, I'm gonna screw the livin' daylights outta yew, darlin'. . . . C'mere and let Daddy give yew a big kiss. . . ."

❧

I'm sorry. I know this is rotten. But I have to stop here. I thought I could tell you, but I can't. It was just too awful, although not what you'd think. Let's just say something happened. And I left the Americana with a hundred dollars, which I deposited in a can marked "Help Muscular Dystrophy."

❧

Maybe I can tell you the rest later. I need some more wine, and so do you.

❧

The crazy part was, when I went home, I fell in love with Julian Sarkoff all over again. You wouldn't think I would, would you?

But I opened my mailbox, and there was this card, from Rio, and one line scrawled across the back:

"I am the lonely only."

I fell back, shut my eyes, and laughed in relief, for only I would recognize that line, from a poem Julian Sarkoff wrote in the fourth grade and that I had to go to an outlying borough to find.

"So there is love," I thought. (Mistake.)

❧

"Julie," I whispered, "do you believe in God?"

"Does he believe in me?"

We lay in Julian's bed. I'd returned to his apartment. He'd returned to me. His body heated mine with a Latin intensity.

"What do you think the chances are for a life after death?"

"Zilch."

He yanked the covers off me. I curled into a small ball.

"What's this? What's this?"

I broke down and told him about Dr. Parkness and that I might have the Big One. He sat up, and let his legs dangle over the side of the bed. His toes dug into his high carpet.

"Hell, we all got a sentence on us. When the Great Promoter in the Sky sends you into the ring, he sets the odds up against you. Ashes to ashes. Crap to crap. What's it all add up to, anyway? That I lived, wrote a couple of books, maybe even a quartet. I made the front row laugh . . . I made 'em cry. Maybe I made them sweat for their own selves, while I fought it out for them in the ring. Who really knows?"

I crawled around the bed so I could see his face. "Hey," I whispered, "I'm the one who may be going out on a stretcher. . . . Why don't you talk about me?"

"We're all going out on the stretcher, baby. Life is a fast fight. We don't know how many rounds it will go. . . ."

"I know," I told him. "That's why I think it's important to be in love's arena."

He just looked at me for a long minute. I forced myself not to seek out the safe section on his neck, but to confront his black and burning eyes. "You're in love's arena, huh?" he finally said.

And then, because I could no longer hold back, I came out with it: "I'm madly in love with you. I always have been."

("Madly" was the only correct word in that sentence,

212

Darling; but you can see I was *in extremis.* You have to be in love when you're facing death.)

The author of *Turned Off* quoted from his own work: "An hour before execution can be worth a lifetime in stir."

And (forgive me), the next hour *was* . . .

∾

Après les amours, our bodies lay flung about the room. I ended slung over a chair. Sarkoff sprawled face-down in the goat-hair rug. After several ragged breaths, I dragged myself over to him and tapped his bare shoulder. "Did you really mean what you said, just before, when we were under the drapes?"

"Unnnh," he mumbled, getting *flokati* in his mouth. "I meant it."

"Will you still love me after surgery?"

"Sure."

"If I grow coarse hair on my upper lip?"

"Naturally."

"If I come back with a deep, gruff voice?" I used a deep, gruff voice to give him the idea.

He sat up and hunted for a cigar. "I love it."

"Even if I'm unable to participate in normal intercourse?"

"Oh, especially then."

I asked him, then, why he had taken so long to use the words "I love you." "If you could love me with a moustache, a deep voice, and all that, why not right away? Why didn't you want the peanut I offered you in Patty's? Why did you ignore me so long?"

Sarkoff found his cigar, peeled it, and lit up. Smoke rose over his head. Dark, and covered only with his own brown pelt of hair, he sat there naked on the furry floor, and I thought, *primal man.*

His forehead furrowed. I was pleased to see him consider my question. "I think I know why," he finally answered. "Maybe, just *maybe* now, it took a real gut thing to make me see it." He scratched under his left pectoral. "Maybe I'm only good at big emotions, not little ones." His eyes narrowed, obscured by Cuban smoke.

"Funny. I never had this precise thought about myself before. I must write this down. 'Good at big emotions, gut things . . . not little ones.' You got a piece of paper?"

I rooted around for one, but also reminded him, "You were talking about your love for me."

He scribbled: "Good at big emotions, Kevin O'Casey could not engage himself in the minor fights. . . . He saved himself for . . ." Sarkoff looked up, his satyric eyebrows rising. "Maybe this is why I can move crowds when I speak or when I write. But I have a little trouble with small talk. Introductions, that sort of thing . . ."

"I want to hear more about your love for me," I interrupted. "Are you in love, or do you just love me? Did it hit you suddenly, or sneak up on you?"

"Uh . . . I guess you could say I sort of *backed* into it. . . ."

Even my thwanging seemed less acute. Just a vibration deep within me. But I could ignore the sensation as Julian's hands cupped my cheeks and started a slow, circular motion. I cleared away the paper, pen, a few empty glasses, plates, ashtrays, and an unguent jar. When I cleared a space, I felt I might be in for the ecstatic experience of my lifetime.

As he lowered himself into me, the telephone rang. We both screamed and split apart. Julian answered: "It's for you . . . the hospital."

❧

"I hate hospitals," Julian said as he walked me into Doctors Hospital. "How they perfume and sanitize death. The stink of antiseptic . . . I can't breathe in here." He stopped in the middle of the polished entrance hall. "My leg won't move."

He demonstrated, trying to lift his left leg with both

hands. "Oh, it's this old childhood thing I have about hospitals. This is bringing up a lot of old pain and nausea. I am physically unable to go on. . . ." He set down my small airline bag. "Listen, Al, I've got to get out of here for a while. . . ."

I didn't say anything, just looked at him.

"Shit. You're an expert. You know that? You make me feel this big." He held up his fingers in a pinch. "That lost-waif look. Damnit to hell."

I picked up my small bag.

"What'd you do? Understudy my mother?" Sarkoff tried his leg again. The leg would bend but not step forward. He tried walking backward, and that was fine.

"You think this isn't killing me?" he said, moving back out the revolving door. "You think I wouldn't give anything in the world to go in there with you? You think it's as easy as holding your arm and going upstairs?"

"It's all right," I told him. I followed him into the revolving door. Stuck in the same section, our bodies almost touched, as they had that first night in the revolving door of the deli—the night we had considered becoming friends, then spun round in the other direction. *A mistake?*

"Maybe if I went back and did some work . . . even a paragraph. Then maybe I could go through this with you." He suddenly crushed me into an embrace. Our bodies heated the small, wedged space. "I was going to surprise you with a vacation trip afterwards . . . but this will be better. I'm going home, and you know what I'm going to do?"

"What?" I breathed in his smoky aura and started kissing his eyelids, his cheeks, his chin. . . .

"I'm going to take two Valium, work, do some leg exercises, and work out in the gym. Then I'm coming back. I can beat this thing. I guess what we're learning here is that when the chips are down, Sarkoff comes through. . . . So don't worry, kid . . . I'll be there when you need me."

"You'll be with me, hold my hand?"

"Try to keep me away."

"I'm scheduled for the morning."

He kissed my forehead and tousled my hair. "*Mañana*, baby . . ."

"*Mañana?*"

"Well, I have to get up for it. It's not going to be easy. I have to relive, even if it kills me, every reason I have this thing about hospitals."

Another patient wanted to get into the hospital then, and the revolving door began to revolve. I clung to Sarkoff for an extra minute, then squeezed myself back into the hospital.

∽

As I recited answers, through a glass shield, to the admitting clerk, I concentrated on the fact that Julian Sarkoff would be coming back in the morning, that I was not, after all, a "lonely only."

He had whispered something into my hair, as choky and indecipherable as his first murmurs. I had not understood his words, but my stomach had taken a nonstop elevator.

"You don't have any coverage?" asked the woman, broadfaced and brown, behind the window.

"No."

She whinnied, showing gold in her mouth.

"Then this gonna cost you an arm 'n' a leg!"

My parents had been right: Security was everything. I should have gone into the Board of Ed. The HIP. The fringe benefits.

"Mother's name?"

"Mama."

∽

I shared my room with another woman. She lay across her bed, her body curved back in an arc of terror. Her mouth hung open, and her eyes stared upside down at the wall behind her.

"Is she all right?" I asked the nurse.

The nurse, who looked like a kid out of school, smiled and said: "Oh, yes. She's making a beautiful recovery." The nurse looked at me. "Are *you* all right?"

I felt I might cry, so I bit my lip: "My TV isn't working." I pressed my remote control and pointed to the set, aimed at my bed from on high.

"See. Nothing happens."

The nurse explained that the set was only a dummy. I could have the real one for an extra five a day. "The dummy is there to make you want the real one."

"It does."

I put in my order at once.

❧

I met my "group" in the corridor. A band of bath-robed, paper-slippered shufflers, we were to trudge from blood and piss labs down to X ray. Some rolled metal stands before them. Many of the shufflers had concealed hookups under their robes.

Although I felt fine, except for an occasional twinge in my vulva, I shuffled as slowly as the others.

❧

That night, as I lay cranked high in my bed under a sign, "No food for this one, goes to the OR in the morning," Dr. Parkness appeared. He wore a tuxedo. A miniature golden person seemed hidden behind the doctor.

"This is Dr. Wook Yung Soo, your anesthesiologist." Dr. Parkness beckoned, and the figurine rolled into view.

She bowed.

I gasped: *I'd seen her before.* The oval face, carved from ivory; the oblique gaze. *Where? Where?*

"You wish awake or asleep?"

Was there any question? "Asleep."

With butterfly gestures, she rolled me onto my side,

217

parted my open-backed cotton gown, and pricked me with a long, thin needle. "Make you hoppy. Close eyes. Think only hoppy thoughts."

I closed my eyes and immediately billowed skyward on some sweet zephyr. My lids weighted. *What had worried me?*

"Oh, what does it matter?" A delicious cool rivulet started in my toes and swept up to my private parts. Another shiver.

~

This is it, I realized. My bed rocked gently. I checked the rise and fall for a while, then decided to roll with it.

A rattle sounded. I turned my eyes and forced my leaden lids to lift. I had almost forgotten: The living cadaver in the next bed.

Some sound escaped the open cave of her mouth. In spasm her back arched, and her fingers splayed wide on the covers.

I imitated her, then fell back upon my pillow. My bed changed direction and gently bobbed me closer to the door.

With Nureyev grace, a white-robed orderly drifted into the room and with elegant arm stretches hooked up my real TV. "You'll get good reception from now on. . . . You can watch all your programs."

"Bless you . . ." As my eyes opened and shut, a succession of images illumined my screen. Children danced with a frog as big as a man. Couples jumped up and down, embracing, as a brilliantly shined, high-snouted car rolled, driverless, toward them.

They all spoke and sang, but I heard them as if from a distance. Squeaks and tinkles emanated from the small box on the pillow near my cheek, where the young orderly had placed it.

"Bless you," I repeated, as he toed lissomely from my room.

Another presence replaced him. A black behemoth,

encased in white linen. She pushed a large wagon and sang with melodious depth: "Downtown . . ."

"Oh, when you're sad and you're feelin' so bad, you go downtown . . ." She rolled her wagon over to my roommate's bed. Still singing, she tossed a copy of *Viva* onto the frozen corpse's chest.

". . . downtown . . . ," she trailed off, and sighed. "Well, maybe she git to it later."

To my surprise, I sniffled and started to cry. My body curled so that I bit my knees. She noticed:

"Yo sure are one sad chick."

I whimpered.

"Girl, you got to get yisself together!"

She shuffled over, her wagon wheels creaking and offered me a choice of *Vogue* or *Harper's Bazaar*.

"Please . . . just leave me alone."

"Girl, lissen to me! Look at dat chick in de nex' bed. . . . Don't dat make you ashame?"

I looked from the frozen corpse to my new friend. She shone with unearthly radiance. I had seen her before: on a subway . . . in a ladies' room.

"I've seen you before," I told her.

"I'se all over. An' I seen you too."

"Who are you?"

"Ah'm known bah miny names. Roun' de hospital, most folks jest call me Serafina." She checked her loaded cart. "I got sumpin' foh you."

"What?"

"Ah been watchin' you, and Ah think it's time yoh got a break. But yoh got to promise to do sumpin' foh it. . . ."

"What do I have to do?"

"Doan interrupt. Let me tell you whut you gitten fust. One, yoh gitten a new color TV." She held up her hand: Her palm showed pink. "Doan cry wid joy yet . . . dat ain't all. Two, yoh gitten a whole new wardrobe." She read from a card: " 'from Georgio's of Beverly Hills . . . and dat showcase include a whole new look by . . . Eve of Roma!' Three, ah'm goin' to tell you whut yoh got goin' foh you . . . so you kin stop goin' crazy, wonderin'. Yoh got some good shit. Yoh a nice-lookin' chick, wid a good shape, and nice, big laigs."

"And I don't need to lose weight?"

"Yoh a little healthy in the ass, but dass awright. Lot a mens like dat. An' doan worry 'bout dem orgasms. Yoh gawna have de biggest, de bestest orgasm dat ever wuz. . . ." She held up a cautionary hand. "Control yisself. If you know de answer to de nex' question, you win de gran' prize." She paused, then in a new, loud, mannish voice, demanded, "WHO WAS ELIZABETH TAYLOR'S SECOND HUSBAND? YOU GOT THIRTY SECONDS."

I pounded the bedcovers, racked my brain. "It was . . . it was . . . Nicky . . . no . . . no . . . no . . . it was, oh, I knew this . . . it was MICHAEL WILDING!"

"Das right. You win de gran' prize. And yoh need it . . . 'cause yoh don have a lick o' sense 'roun mens. Yoh bin layin' yisself wide open, honey. But from now on, yo gawna be o-kay, 'cause Serafina goan to give yoh sumpin' thass gawna hep. . . ."

She rummaged through her trays. "Where is dat damn thing?" At last she pulled forth a long steel handle. I strained to see it: a metal detector, complete with headset, such as those used by scavengers on the beach.

Serafina donned the headset, then demonstrated, running the detector, like a vacuum, over the wall.

"Yoh run dis ovah de man's body . . . lak dis. An' if he's full a shit, yo hear dis: 'Beep! Beep! Beep!' " She emitted a long, piercing series of beeps, her body heaving.

I lolled back on my pillow. How wonderful! How fantastic!

"Yo gitten all dis, an' maybe de extra bonus, if yoh do one thing."

I straightened and nodded. "Anything."

Serafina pulled off the headset and smoothed down her hair. "Yo got to start fighten' back, girl. Yo cain' lay down and give up no moh. De worl' ain't dere to make it easy on yoh. De worl' owes yo nuthin'. . . . Yoh got to git up on yoh own two feet. Ah heard you." She raised her voice to imitate my own piping one: "Thass awright. I understan'. Less be friens. Whatever you want, sweetheart."

She moved closer until her round face obscured the room. How beautiful she was, as she boomed:

"DON' YOH TAKE NO MOH SHIT OFFEN DEM MENS!"

I nodded. She was wise.

"But doan yoh dish none out, neither! YOH HEAH?"

More clearly than I've ever heard in my life.

"So okay," she settled back on her heels. "Here's yoh bonus." She handed me a heavy, fresh magazine, wafting new ink. I looked: Lauren Hutton, on the cover . . . holding . . . could it be?

"Oh . . . oh . . ." I moaned in delight.

My Naiad. On the cover of *Vogue*. It was almost too much. My ribs contracted. Tears sprang to my eyes. *My life had meaning.*

And there was more. Serafina didn't allow herself to grin, but her eyes brightened. "Okay. Here's de big break. YOH DON' NEED NO OPERASHUN! Dat doctor a yours come in here, dis bullshit detector go wild. BEEP! BEEP! BEEP! Yo is OKAY. Now git yoh ass outta dis bed. . . ."

I sat up. The room spun. Serafina straightened her wagon and prepared to roll. She touched her hip in a tired way. "Serafina got to git herself down to the lounge. Mah dogs is killin' me."

Her girth blocked the door. She looked at me. "Gwan, chile. Git yoh ass outta heah! Whatch yoh waitin' foh?"

❧

Who can explain such magic? Not I. Weak-limbed, I managed to get into my street clothes. My feet were heavy, my head was light. . . . But miracle of miracle, my thwanging had ended.

To make certain, I touched myself inside, and forced myself to mimic the pressure and motion of a male member. And do I have to report? I felt no pain.

I might have continued this self-examination, testing with two fingers, perhaps even three, but I heard a stretcher rolling down the hall toward my door. Withdrawing my finger, I realized I better do as Serafina had advised: haul ass.

The city was mine. I ran through a sharp winter night. The air pinched my cheeks and tweaked my nose. My eyes saw with clearer than twenty-twenty vision. The streetlights wore double halos. People and cars radiated extra outlines.

Julian, I love you, but I'm not taking any more crap, I rehearsed, running toward his building. How long had it been since Julian and I had run, together, through these same streets, across the small park, to his moon-scaped street on the rib of the island?

Nine months. I held my stomach, stopped, then ran harder, faster. . . . *Julian, I love you, but I'm . . .*

The lobby was the same as on that first night. The doorman snoozed. The geometric seating arrangements created the same right angles. Again, as if by my wish, the elevator door opened as I approached.

I followed the same route: through blue corridors, an ashy midstation, the closet-elevator, then, at last, his door. I turned my key in his lock, then rushed inside. . . . *Julian, I love you, but . . .*

The lava lamp cast molten forms against the walls. In the shadows, furniture crouched.

I saw a large beast move, under covers, across Sarkoff's bed. Bunching and undulating: a science-fiction caterpillar.

"Julian, I love you. . . ."

The caterpillar hunched, fell over, and curled into false death. Its skin peeled back, and Julian D. Sarkoff appeared, orange-skinned, his teeth and eyes flashing white.

"Julian?" My eyes adjusted to the hot-toned dark. I saw him shoving someone under the covers. Strands of silver hair kept spilling into view. Sarkoff kept stuffing the hair under the sheet.

"No! I can't believe it!"

"It's not what it looks like," he said.

The girl popped out of the covers, and he tried to push her head back down. But she resisted. "Joolie Boolie!" Her voice cracked across his shoulders.

I'm glad I'm seeing this, I told myself, my mental camera clicking. I want to imprint this picture in my head so that never again, for *one second*, will I ever entertain an affectionate thought about Julian Sarkoff. He'd finally done it—something so unspeakable even I couldn't miss it. "THIS IS IT! While I could have been dying!"

"There's an explanation. She knocked on the door. I had to let her in." He took a deep breath. "She's a Jehovah's Witness."

"I'll bet."

He fumbled under the pillows and pulled out a leaflet. "Look, *The Watchtower*."

The silvery blonde glared at him, then said: "I'm never going to see you again as long as I live. . . ."

He murmured something into her hair. She nodded. Then, wrapping herself in a sheet, she made her way to the bathroom.

Sarkoff and I were alone.

"I don't expect you to understand," he began.

"I won't."

"This is my way of reacting to death, to disease. It was a frantic reaching out. . . . We make love not to each other, but to ourselves, to drown out the tumbrels that roll through my bowel and through my soul. . . ."

I recognized this last line from *Mortal Coils*. "This proves that what happened to you . . . really affected me . . . got me in the gut." His lip twitched. "Or would you have rather had a Hallmark card and a bunch of dyed daisies?"

"Look," I said, "I'm leaving . . . but why don't you just level with me, since this is surely our last conversation? I know she's not a Jehovah's Witness."

Sarkoff pulled the blanket and tied it toga-style over his shoulder. He moved toward me as through the Forum. "A Jehovah's Witness? No, not in the actual sense. Although, perhaps we are all Jehovah's . . ."

"What a crock," I cut him off. "You'd never let one in . . ."

"In times of stress," he shrugged, "a man will turn to . . . You know, I've never worked through my religious feelings, only certain, in my own crazy way, of the power of a romantic and mysterious ALL . . ."

"STOP! I'M SICK OF YOUR BULLSHIT!"

His words hit me rapid-fire: "She's the lead dancer in a topless revue at Caesar's Palace. I met her almost a year ago . . . on that first trip I took. Her name is Sissy Farlow. She says."

This I could understand. "Then you were just playing around?"

Julian's harsh face relaxed, in an expression I'd never seen. His lashes blinked against his cheeks, and he shook his head. "She's really terrific. A terrific girl. Smart, too. And you know the best part about her?"

"Tell me."

"She never read any of my books."

Julian lifted the edge of his mattress and pulled forth a small box. "She thought I was just any guy. And you know what she taught me to do?"

"What?"

He shook his head again. I could see he couldn't get over this. "She taught me how to use these . . ." He opened the box and pulled out several striped drinking straws. "They come in flavors . . . the syrup is in there, somewhere. Chocolate and strawberry. I prefer the chocolate, and Sissy likes the strawberry."

To demonstrate, he bent the straw. "You put the straw into a glass of milk, and sort of twist it, suck hard, and then you get the flavor right through . . ."

"Why didn't you tell me that you were doing all this?" I asked. "Why did you turn to me with that 'lonely only' business?"

I shall remember his answer forever.

"I didn't think Sissy would want me. I mean, she could have anyone. You know Vic Damone? He's always referred to as 'the crooner.' He was after her."

Vic Damone? Not even Frank Sinatra.

"I wish I were dead," I said.

"No, you don't."

"That's right," I agreed. "I wish I were alive."

I walked, slowly, in a circle. My hand touched the ropes that sectioned off Sarkoff's writing area. "You know . . . I really bought what you said. Time . . . death . . . you know. Your 3,650 nights to go . . ." I noticed his manuscript stacked high beside the old black Underwood. "I thought it was very important. Book Three. Love's arena."

Now, I couldn't look at him. I rested my head and elbows on the ropes. "I'm tired . . . tired and embarrassed . . . because I really thought everything of you, and you want to sip flavor straws with a girl who'd rather be with Vic Damone. I can't even get mad at you . . . just at life . . . at love. . . . I can't be angry with you just because you don't really care about me."

Sarkoff had moved to the ropes. I peeked up at him through my hair. He met my eyes. He spoke in another voice (the real voice?): "I told you I had nothing to give."

"And you delivered. I know . . . it's my own fault. I was the idiot who had to try. Who asked me? Who asked for heated towels and special health salads? I just wanted to give them to you. You seemed so unhappy. Your shoulders . . . I wanted . . . I wanted . . ."
Damn. I couldn't even get through. My rib cage drew in sharply, and my chin went into a high tremble: "I

just wanted to . . ." here comes the sob ". . . bring you a little sunshine . . ."

He punched himself in the gut. "You think this doesn't hurt me? This is no fun for me!"

I lifted my head from the ropes. "Now wait a minute! Listen, I'm the hurt one here. Don't twist this one around!"

"No. This is harder," he argued. "You know I'm a vulnerable guy."

"I'm more hurt than you are."

Julian kicked the wooden base of his platform bed from Loftcraft. "Why does it always end up such a fucking mess?"

"Because we're in it."

He laughed. And I cried again. Who else would laugh with me? Wasn't that why I loved him?

"Don't blame yourself, Al. It's me. I'm the monster. I know. I'm self-centered. Inconsiderate. A prick. I hate women. I'm a fag."

"You're no fun to fight, Julian: You say everything before I can. . . . That's not fair!"

"Women always say the same things to me. So I know what to expect. 'Prick' and 'fag' are the usual farewell remarks."

His great shoulders slumped. I stopped myself from moving to him. "This is crazy. But I don't think so."

"You don't?"

Okay. I did it. I made a fool of myself all over again: "I still think there's a little well of . . ." my voice wobbled ". . . sweetness in you, deep down. I guess you're on guard against anyone getting to it. I think that's why you want Sissy. I feel bad that I couldn't . . ."

He spun around, showing his lower teeth. "That's the worst thing anyone has ever said to me! A little well of sweetness????? You're really killing me with that!"

With his old *aaarrrrwwwwggggh!* he charged the wall, butting his head. Between butts, he begged: "Call me a bastard. Call me a prick. Anything but a little well of sweetness."

Sissy Farlow must have heard the racket: She ran,

in a wet washcloth, right over to Julian. "I'll call you a prick," she offered. Only she didn't pronounce the *r*, so it came out "pwick."

"Thank you." Julian stopped head-butting and stood grinning at Sissy Farlow. She told him off, in no uncertain terms, using her tongue to punctuate her remarks.

I must remember how charming and refreshing that is.

As Sissy twitched by, Julian gave her a playful spank. Sissy looked at me. A sad realization passed between us. I realized she didn't like her part any more than I did mine.

I changed my mind about Julian. "I'd like to call you that, after all." I hunkered down on all fours and bayed: "PPPPPPPRRRRRRRRRIIIIICCCK!"

Julian threw back his head: his very prominent Adam's apple bobbed. "Now," he laughed, "now, my Love, we can really begin. This has touched off a new intensity. Sometimes it takes the idea of the third person to create a bond between the first two. With a stranger there, you find out who is the Couple. I think I just realized it may be you and me, after all." Sissy Farlow started to cry. Her washcloth slipped, and I saw, from the hard jut of her bosom, that her breasts were silicone.

"I hate you," she said to Julian. "Vic Damone wanted me."

Julian said: "Don't think I don't find all this depressing."

"Oh, you!" I yelled. "You're the cause! If you're going to be a prick, you could at least do it with a little *joie de vivre*. Be a happy prick!"

"I've gone from 'a little well of sweetness' to 'a happy prick.' . . . That's what I've got to be all my life. A happy prick?"

"Yes," I continued, "and please do it someplace other than New York. If you have 'nothing to give,' please don't give it at Patty's anymore. Don't bang on bars and say you have an ache. Don't say 'lonely only.' "

Julian went to his writing table and jotted down some

notes. "Where should I go? I want to get all this down. . . ."

"Go to Tahiti! I don't know. Why not just stay in your room? Line it with cork. Get some halfwit to come in to take care of you. . . ."

I leaped into the prize-fight ring. Julian's eyebrows shot up. . . .

"Yes! I'm in here now. And I've hopped in here before! And I just want you to know that you shouldn't feel too smug, too satisfied at the damage you've done. I want you to know: YOU'RE NOT THAT GREAT IN LOVE'S ARENA! You never really knocked me out! In fact, every time I was about to go over the edge, your fantasies yanked me back—That stupid party. With NAH-BO-KOV."

Sissy hopped over the ropes too. "What does 'phantasmagorical' mean, anyway?" she asked.

"I'll tell you what it means: He's full of . . . full of . . . SARKOFF!"

Then, almost unknowing, I picked up his black Underwood, and, with superhuman strength, hurled it at the NBA Award nominee.

"Hey, hey, hey . . ." He ducked. "Easy with that. I have five hundred words to go. . . ."

"OH, GO TO HELL!!!!!!!!" I said, and then *I* went there.

&

I sat in a chair for three days, then remembered Serafina's words: "Yoh got to stand on yoh own two feet!" So I turned to the only thing that had ever helped: my work.

I swung chisel into rock and didn't stop for six months. Dust grayed my hair. Grit stung my eyes. A fine powder sifted to my ankles.

I worked night and day. Nothing stopped me. The phone rang. I never answered. *This is all that matters.* I didn't change my clothes. I slept only on top of the bedspread. I ate only raw hotdogs.

Hack out your own life, Alice!

At last, there it was. Completed work: the hulking quarry stone turned into something, which, I admit, resembled "The Kiss." The difference: Rodin's lovers come together, my lovers tear apart. Their stone faces (referred to later, by critics, as tribal masks) turn in about-face. The eyes shut in hurt. The mouths open in rage. Only the loins remain joined.

This work I titled: "Asunder."

❧

"Asunder" sat, if that's the word, in a NoHo gallery all summer. Men and women in sandals stood, licking cones, to decide whether it was erotic or not.

Then, surprise: "Asunder" was sold. Not to the gallery, or a collector, but to a new high-rise co-op, Blumenthal Towers, which needed to "fill in" an oversized lobby.

I watched, with mixed emotions, as workmen inserted a fountain on the heads of my tormented duo. Ah, well: a start.

❧

And so, my Beloved, that is my story. Until tonight. Until you. Oh, Fate does pull in her drawstrings, and our people end jumbled together at the bottom of her bag.

There are follow-ups: My husband sues for "defamation." The tooter sends a postcard from Chicago: He has married the widow. Paul Whiting comes around, with a bouquet of anemones too long out of water.

Dolores calls Bill, and he does not remember who she is; now, neither does she. Tina Rossini and I visit her in Payne-Whitney. Tina Rossini can no longer "man-get": She has herpes simplex II, and Old Snapper is out of business. *Actual Slayings* has died.

And Julian Sarkoff has sinusitis. Book Three is a critical and commercial success, but he can't enjoy it because he *was* reviewed, as he had feared, with the other "alienation" expert.

❦

Me? My sex life took a savage turn. I decided to dispense with the romantic ideal, and head straight into sensation. Okay, I confess—I indulged in orgies. Which is to say that there are no holds barred. Wretched excess of the flesh: I am raw and frayed afterward. There is nothing I will not try.

Alone.

Well, not totally alone. A few weeks ago, I bought a hygienic device. I swear: I had no ulterior motives. But the advertising, the directions were so lewd and suggestive. The girl, smiling, holding the pulsing jet against her cheek. And the object itself: Why did they design such a nozzle? To lead innocent showerers into temptation . . .

The thing attacked me the first time I tried to use it in its legit role. It plunged into me: I was trying to take a bath. But it wouldn't let up: thumping, humming, and spurting.

Ridiculous, I thought, until I leaned back and shut my eyes. Then I remembered stories from mythology of girls impregnated in mountain streams. Spirits can live in water. Goatish, male spirits.

And so one or perhaps a group of these faceless spirits took me, in playful force, right in my own bathtub. And my back arched against the rubber mat, and I gave myself to spray.

And do you know what I really cried when I could no longer bear the hot-cold crystal spasm? I cried, "No! No! No!"

❦

I cried "No!" because, deep down, I ached at the empty place. I still believed there was a *you*.

Don't you think that now I can love you more, because of all that's happened? I do. I think I had to have that marriage, those men, that nozzle to appreciate the real thing.

∽

Um. I can't stop touching you. Let me use some of this cream. I owe you a rubdown.

Just relax. Your arms will be better at your sides. *There.* I'm warming the lotion in my hands.

Oh, what a nice muscle you have there. From jogging? Let's see . . . I'm having a hard time deciding what part of you is my favorite. . . ."

Other girls have loved your behind? I'd say it has its strong points. I'm more drawn to your upper back. It has a pleasing breadth to it. As if you could carry someone for miles.

Your skin has a pebbled feel to it. Interesting. Like stucco. Am I touching you with just the right amount of pressure? How's that? More between the shoulder blades? Ah, I'll just keep doing that, then. . . .

Up and down, round and round. Did you know you always rub in the direction of the heart? Oh, yes . . . you'll notice . . . everything I've done is toward your heart.

There we go. The grand finale. From the tips of your toes . . . up, down . . . round and round.

Okay, you can roll over. I'll do your front.

∽

My goodness. You're excited. Oh, yes, I see you are. . . .

Oh, feel my heart. It's pounding.

You look . . . Oh, how you look . . .

I really feel you. Don't stop. We're really going someplace. This is it. No, no . . . Yes!

OH, YES, I LOVE YOU FOREVER.

∽

Well, we're still here. I guess I went on the record then, during the red-out? Well, that's okay, isn't it? I don't want to pretend to love you any less than I do. . . .

This is it. The real intimacy. We're home free. Never again, the old business of one person wanting more than the other.

That's what causes all the hurt. Most times, the two people miss each other, in some way. The odds are maybe a million to one against.

We're the lucky ones.

There's a poem that just says it:

Love, let us be true to one another . . .
for we are here as on a darkling plain . . .
where ignorant armies clash by night. . . .

I forget the rest. But you get the idea. We have to hold each other tight, while the world presses wild and terrible against our windowpanes.

The miracle is it only takes one other person. Only one other person. To keep out the cold and the dark. To make dreams come true, to honor the great trust.

Feel. Down here. Between us. How warm.

This is the only warm place in the city tonight. The only warm place in the world.

Oh, no . . . don't get up. . . . Whatever you want, let me go get it for you. More wine? A soda?

I'm coming with you. I can walk with the blanket around us.

Where are you going?

Out? Outside? Out *there?* What do we need out there? We have everything right here. Are you hungry?

I was going to make a salad. The lettuce is wrapped in paper towels. The radishes are cut into rosebuds. There's some dressing in the refrigerator. You *can't* go—

I make my own vinegar!

What do you mean, it's late, you have to go? You wouldn't leave me now?

If you leave now, I'll think you're never coming back. I know it's irrational (isn't it?), but that's how I feel.

How can you do this? After everything I've told you ... I can't believe it—You're "moving on"?

～

Your other shoe is under the bedspread.

～

You have to go. So go. I understand. Boy, do I understand.

Don't say you'll "call me." I can live without hearing that.

No, I'm not going to cry. Don't tear yourself apart thinking that I'm going to cry the minute you walk out the door. I wouldn't give you the satisfaction. I wouldn't cry over you. I might moan, but I won't cry.

Because I can see now that I was wrong about you. You were a mistake.

How could I think, even for one second, that you were the one? He would never act like this.

I sensed it all along. That's why I held back. Thank God, I had the sense to hold back.

The warnings were there. I overlooked them, but the warnings were registering right along. . . .

That wild light in your left eye. Okay, "eyes of blue." But a white streak in one eye is strictly weirdo. Siberian husky.

I started to wise up after I got you up here. It wasn't that you drank all the wine. I didn't mind that. But when you went to the bathroom, you left the lid up. Okay, I understand: The lid will be left up, in a long relationship. But the first time? That's how you start a romance?

When I walked in there and saw the lid up, I should have known the whole story. You just didn't care. Didn't give a damn.

So—splatter.

I didn't mention your splatters: I was afraid that might shatter the mood. And the mood, I thought, was everything.

Even when you gave me that awful massage, I didn't say a word. How can a massage be awful?

You didn't even warm the lotion in your hands. Just squirted it on me. Cold. A little cold dribble. I should have known then that you could care less. . . . A few lousy chops down my spine—so perfunctory! You barely touched my shoulder blades. Couldn't wait to get it over with, could you?

And you know something? For once, I'm going to complain. For once, I'm going to open my mouth—I worked so hard giving you your rubdown, I think I really injured something in my back. I can hardly straighten up. To save you the worry (I thought you could worry) I didn't scream when I tried to get off this bed.

I've never had this before, but something tells me it's a slipped disc.

What kind of guy are you—coming up here, splattering, using cold lotion on me, and then just walking out?

You want to go, so go. I'm not stopping you.

∾

I hung up your jacket in the hall closet.

∾

How could I have mistaken you for The One?

There is no One. I know that now. No ultimate other person. Intimacy does not exist. If only one person at a time believes it's intimate, then it's not, is it?

∾

I think I saw your glove on the chair.

234

❦

I did everything to you, and you did everything to me, and it's nothing . . . and, I'll tell you something— NOTHING IS NOT ENOUGH!

Oh, no. Not for me. Not for this woman.

Go ahead. Get dressed. Walk out. I hear my wine sloshing in your belly. That's my body lotion on your back.

I'm learning. I'm learning. I can live without hope. That should help me out in the future.

❦

How do I know where you left your wallet?

❦

No more indifferent men. They can get along without me.

I'm finished with them.

❦

Did you look on the bureau? I saw something there.

❦

Oh, boy, I thought I hit bottom before. I didn't know—that was only the lower mezzanine. This is the real bottom.

Okay. This may be bottom, but I can use the bottom . . . as a . . . as a springboard! You have to touch bottom to kick off and shoot back up to the surface.

I can come up. On my own. Looks like I've always been on my own. Love someone? Who do we even know?

Love, let us be true to one another . . .
for we are here as on a darkling plain . . .
where ignorant armies clash by night . . .

235

Oh, I must laugh. A darkling plain would be cozy after this. There are "ignorant armies" there. Sounds as if there might be someone on your side.

Terrific. Fly me to Darkling Plain. Club Med can open a branch there: "Club Med Comes to Darkling Plain . . ." Enjoy Dover Beach.

❧

Lock the door, please. It's a police lock. Just slide that rod into the holder on the floor. I'm going to bide my time here for a while. You've given me a lot to think about.

There's a sweetness to giving up.

I'll have more time, now. I don't have to go out and look for the Loner. I am the Loner.

No true love. That was the lie.

But even as I'm giving up, I'm also thinking—*maybe giving up is the answer*. When you give up is when he finds you. He senses a sincere giving up. He knows that's the time to rush in and hold you.

I'm not looking for him anymore. But let's face it, I'll accept a draft.

Somehow, despite all evidence to the contrary, I still half believe he's out there. And should he find me, you can bet I'll have something to give him. Something I'll just pull out of the hat. Something from deep down. Something no one ever got. Because, as anyone can see:

I'm a great little saver.

❧

THE BIG BESTSELLERS
ARE AVON BOOKS

☐	**The Thorn Birds** Colleen McCullough	35741	$2.50
☐	**The Bermuda Triangle** Charles Berlitz	25254	$1.95
☐	**Lancelot** Walker Percy	36582	$2.25
☐	**Oliver's Story** Erich Segal	36343	$1.95
☐	**Snowblind** Robert Sabbag	36947	$1.95
☐	**A Capitol Crime** Lawrence Meyer	37150	$1.95
☐	**Fletch's Fortune** Gregory Mcdonald	37978	$1.95
☐	**Voyage** Sterling Hayden	37200	$2.50
☐	**Lady Oracle** Margaret Atwood	35444	$1.95
☐	**Humboldt's Gift** Saul Bellow	38810	$2.25
☐	**Mindbridge** Joe Haldeman	33605	$1.95
☐	**Polonaise** Piers Paul Read	33894	$1.95
☐	**A Fringe of Leaves** Patrick White	36160	$1.95
☐	**To Jerusalem and Back** Saul Bellow	33472	$1.95
☐	**A Sea-Change** Lois Gould	33704	$1.95
☐	**The Moon Lamp** Mark Smith	32698	$1.75
☐	**The Surface of Earth** Reynolds Price	29306	$1.95
☐	**The Monkey Wrench Gang** Edward Abbey	30114	$1.95
☐	**Beyond the Bedroom Wall** Larry Woiwode	29454	$1.95
☐	**Jonathan Livingston Seagull** Richard Bach	34777	$1.75
☐	**Working** Studs Terkel	34660	$2.50
☐	**Shardik** Richard Adams	27359	$1.95
☐	**Anya** Susan Fromberg Schaeffer	25262	$1.95
☐	**Watership Down** Richard Adams	19810	$2.25

Available at better bookstores everywhere, or order direct from the publisher.

The New Novel by
MARGARET ATWOOD

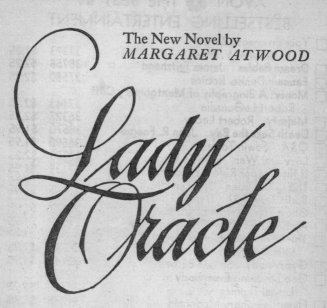

Lady
Oracle

"BRILLIANT AND FUNNY. I CAN'T TELL YOU
HOW EXHILARATING IT WAS TO READ IT—
EVERYTHING WORKS. AN EXTRAORDINARY
BOOK."

Joan Didion

"GLORIOUS, HILARIOUS, TOUCHING . . . FASTER
THAN A SPEEDING BULLET."

Cosmopolitan

"A RICH, SUBTLE, DEEP, DELICATE, NOURISHING
BOOK."

Philadelphia Inquirer

 Avon 35444 $1.95

AVON ◆ THE BEST IN
BESTSELLING ENTERTAINMENT

☐	Your Erroneous Zones Dr. Wayne W. Dyer	33373	$2.25
☐	Dream Babies James Fritzhand	35758	$2.25
☐	Fauna Denise Robins	37580	$2.25
☐	Monty: A Biography of Montgomery Clift Robert LaGuardia	37143	$2.25
☐	Majesty Robert Lacey	36327	$2.25
☐	Death Sails the Bay John R. Feegel	38570	$1.95
☐	Q&A Edwin Torres	36590	$1.95
☐	Love and War Patricia Hagan	37960	$2.25
☐	If the Reaper Ride Elizabeth Norman	37135	$1.95
☐	This Other Eden Marilyn Harris	36301	$2.25
☐	Berlin Tunnel 21 Donald Lindquist	36335	$2.25
☐	Ghost Fox James Houston	35733	$1.95
☐	Ambassador Stephen Longstreet	31997	$1.95
☐	The Boomerang Conspiracy Michael Stanley	35535	$1.95
☐	Gypsy Lady Shirlee Busbee	36145	$1.95
☐	Good Evening Everybody Lowell Thomas	35105	$2.25
☐	Flynn Gregory Mcdonald	34975	$1.95
☐	Lovefire Julia Grice	34538	$1.95
☐	The Search for Joseph Tully William H. Hallahan	33712	$1.95
☐	Delta Blood Barbara Ferry Johnson	32664	$1.95
☐	Wicked Loving Lies Rosemary Rogers	40378	$2.25
☐	Moonstruck Madness Laurie McBain	31385	$1.95
☐	ALIVE: The Story of the Andes Survivors Piers Paul Read	39164	$2.25
☐	Sweet Savage Love Rosemary Rogers	38869	$2.25
☐	The Flame and the Flower Kathleen E. Woodiwiss	35485	$2.25
☐	I'm OK—You're OK Thomas A. Harris, M.D.	28282	$2.25

Available at better bookstores everywhere, or order direct from the publisher.